F   Palmer,Catherine
Palm   Hide & Seek

Heart Quest Series

Praise

Find

"

"

"

"I
it

"
de
ar
w

"
B

"
o

"
st

"
P
K
You are one of my favorite authors."
—Doris Morrison; Wheaton, Illinois

A Kiss of Adventure

"Each of the Treasures of the Heart books is a delightful read. The energy, adventure, and romance kept me intrigued to the end. I will definitely recommend this series to my friends."
—Francine Rivers, best-selling author

"This entertaining book is hard to put down."
—*CBA Marketplace*

"Elements of *The African Queen* and *Romancing the Stone* blend in this action-filled romance. Light, romantic fun." —*Library Journal*

A Whisper of Danger

"Delightful reading."
—Stephanie Wallace; San Diego, California

"At last, a Christian romance with real emotions. The only negative side to your books is that I can't get enough of them!" —Liz Hunt; Glasgow, Scotland

"It is sometimes hard to find books that are both spiritually uplifting and entertaining. Your books are both!" —Angela Martin; Fredericktown, Missouri

Prairie Rose

"In Rosie, Palmer has created an entertaining and humorous character. Highly recommended."
—*Library Journal*

"Begins with a bang and doesn't let up till the end. The author expertly presents the tragedy and triumph of the human experience."
—*A Closer Look*

HEART
QUEST

HeartQuest brings you romantic fiction
with a foundation of biblical truth.
Adventure, mystery, intrigue, and suspense
mingle in these heartwarming stories of
men and women of faith striving to build
a love that will last a lifetime.

May HeartQuest books sweep you
into the arms of God, who longs for you
and pursues you always.

Hide & Seek

CATHERINE PALMER

Romance fiction from
Tyndale House Publishers, Inc.
WHEATON, ILLINOIS

Visit Tyndale's exciting Web site at www.tyndale.com

Check out the latest about HeartQuest Books at www.heartquest.com

Copyright © 2001 by Catherine Palmer. All rights reserved.
Cover illustration copyright © 2000 by Toni Kurresch. All rights reserved.
Author's photo copyright © 2000 by Childress Studio. All rights reserved.
Interior map copyright © 1999 by Jerry Dadds. All rights reserved.

HeartQuest is a registered trademark of Tyndale House Publishers, Inc.

Edited by Kathryn S. Olson

Designed by Melinda Schumacher

Scripture quotations in Ruby's memory are taken from the *Holy Bible,* King James Version.

The epigraph and portions of Scripture read from the Bible are taken from the *Holy Bible,* New Living Translation, copyright © 1996. Used by permission of Tyndale House Publishers, Inc., Wheaton, Illinois 60189. All rights reserved.

Library of Congress Cataloging-in-Publication Data

Palmer, Catherine
   Hide and seek / Catherine Palmer.
      p. cm. — (HeartQuest)
   ISBN 0-8423-1165-3 (sc)
      1. Fathers and daughers—Fiction. 2. Widowers—Fiction. 3. Missouri—Fiction.
   I. Title. II. Series.

   PS3566.A495 H5 2001
   813'.54—dc21   00-066639

Printed in the United States of America

07   06   05   04   03   02   01
 9   8   7   6   5   4   3   2   1

For Kristie McGonegal—
friend, teacher, encourager,
and prayer partner.
Thank you!

The Chalmers House

Dandy Donuts & Bake Shop

the Public Library

Amb

PARK

Walnut Street

Mansion Street

DAILY HERALD

TASTEE HUT

DANDY DONUTS & BAKE SHOP

DONUTS & BAKE

DANDY

LIBRARY

side

Finders Keepers Antiques Shop

The Corner Market

The Nifty Cafe

Hide me in the shadow of your wings.
PSALM 17:8

Acknowledgments

Without the devoted help of so many people, this book would not exist. I want to thank my beloved husband, Tim, for his faithfulness in reading and editing each of my manuscripts before it goes out. Kathy Olson's professional, loving, and judicious in-house editing is invaluable. I praise God for allowing me to work with this wonderful woman. My deepest appreciation also goes to the HeartQuest team, whose dedication to our mission can be seen in every novel. Becky Nesbitt, Kathy Olson, Anne Goldsmith, Diane Eble, Danielle Crilly, and Jan Pigott—I love you, fellow gardeners! The vision and encouragement of Ron Beers and Ken Petersen have paved the path for everything I do. May God bless you both. I thank Dr. Kenneth Taylor and Mark Taylor for supporting my ministry and for being such beacons in the world of Christian publishing. And Travis Thrasher, of course, you are my rock. Thanks for making Tyndale so much fun to write for!

ONE

Darcy Damyon knew she had found her hiding place. As the air-conditioned Greyhound bus pulled into the sleepy town of Ambleside, she scanned the deserted sidewalks, empty cafe, and shuttered stores. A glance at a sign told her this was Main Street, yet even the local ice cream stand had been locked tightly against the doldrums of a hot Missouri afternoon.

The stillness was odd for a Saturday, Darcy thought. Yet a quiet, dull sort of town was just what she had prayed for— a place where she could fade away, evaporate, blend in as easily as a leaf on one of the oak trees that sheltered the town square. A place where she could be free.

The Greyhound lumbered around a corner onto Mansion Street just as the doors of a small stone chapel burst open. Women poured down the steps in a flood of blue, pink, and yellow dresses and flowered hats; men in suits, ties, and shiny shoes. Darcy craned her neck back over the cracked vinyl seat as a puff of rose petals blossomed in the air over the crowd. A bride, gowned in billowing white silk and wearing a veil of drifting tulle, fairly danced through the pink cascade with her handsome groom striding proudly beside her.

A wedding. Darcy covered her mouth with her hand and shrank down into her seat. So, the whole town had shut down for a wedding. She closed her eyes and tried to block the image of her own hasty marriage before a justice of the peace. She'd pulled on her only dress, a shapeless blue-

and-brown plaid. Bill had worn denim jeans and boots. She had been seventeen and far too innocent to suspect what lay ahead.

Take this away, God, Darcy cried silently as she huddled in the bus. *I'm not that naive, reckless girl anymore. I'm a new woman . . . new in you. Oh, Christ, hide me from my past!*

Forcing back tears that sprang from both fear and remorse, Darcy rehearsed the facts she had invented to begin her new life of freedom. She was no longer going to be known as Darcy Damyon. She was Jo Callaway, hastily named for a county she had crossed on her long bus ride from Vandalia. She was twenty-five now—that much was true. Though she had grown up on a hog farm in southern Missouri, she had decided to say she hailed from Arkansas. And that she had never been married.

The Greyhound passed a small brick library decked out in honeycomb-pleated crepe paper wedding bells. The donut shop beside it displayed a three-tiered white cake festooned with pink roses. Next door at the men's clothing shop, a formal tuxedo stood proudly in the window. Darcy shook her head, wondering whose marriage had caused such universal celebration.

"Ambleside," the bus driver intoned through his micro-phone as the Greyhound pulled to a stop. Darcy stood and tucked her paper bag under her arm. Making her way down the aisle past three dozing passengers, she felt a small chill slide down her spine. With a single step out of the bus and onto the sidewalk, she would sever herself forever from the last link with the past six years of her life.

She would be free.

Lifting her chin, Darcy descended into a quiet, hot world of green trees, buzzing cicadas, the scent of diesel fumes, and utter anonymity. As the doors whooshed shut behind her and the bus pulled away, she drank down a deep breath. In Ambleside, Missouri, no one knew her. No one knew what she had done, or where she had been, or how she had lived. She was Jo Callaway, and her life was starting over.

"I hate you!" The library door down the street burst open and a golden-haired child flew down the steps. "I hate you, Montgomery Easton, and I think your friend is stupid, dumb, and retarded!"

"You take that back, Heather!" A whirlwind of red braids blew through the door and barreled down the street in hot pursuit of the blonde tormentor. "Take it back!"

The blonde, a look of triumph on her face, raced toward Darcy. Laughing, the child paused a moment and swung around. "You're stupid, too, Montgomery, even if your mommy did die!"

At that, the redhead came to a halt, her little chest heaving. Blue eyes wide with dismay, she stared as her enemy danced around the corner of the bus station and vanished. Then her lips pulled back into a snarl and she exploded into a full-tilt run.

"I'm gonna kill you, Heather!" the child shouted. "I'm gonna kill you."

The words rocketed through Darcy as the red-haired Montgomery bore down, tears of rage streaming down her cheeks. *I'm gonna kill you. . . . I'm gonna kill you.*

"No," Darcy cried, throwing her arms around the little girl. "Don't say that. Never say that." At the impact, woman and child tumbled to the sidewalk. Darcy's paper sack slid across the concrete.

"Lemme go!" The child punched Darcy on the arm. "I hate Heather. I'm gonna beat her up."

"No!" Darcy held on tight. "You can't do that. Listen to me, Little-bit; you don't want to do that."

The child bent over suddenly, clapped her small hands over her eyes, and began to sob. The anguish and heartache that poured through the small, heated body in her arms shocked Darcy. How long since she had allowed another human this close? How long since she had seen such raw emotion? How long since she had touched a child?

Uncertain, Darcy reached out toward Montgomery. The tiny pearls of the little girl's spine formed a narrow line beneath her cotton T-shirt. Her fragile ribs heaved in sorrow. Slowly, Darcy stroked her fingers up to the child's neck, where downy red hair met soft pink skin.

"It'll be all right," Darcy whispered in a tender voice she hadn't heard in years. "You'll be okay, Little-bit."

"I'm not Little-bit. I'm Montgomery Easton." Sitting up, the girl drew back and stared at the woman. Her nose wrinkled. "Who're you?"

"I'm . . ." At the sight of the defiant, tear-filled blue eyes, the lie Darcy had prepared so carefully stuck in her throat. *Always tell the truth,* the leader of her Bible study group had taught her. *God loves the truth, and he hates lies.*

No. Darcy knew that if she told the truth, she couldn't hide. *God, forgive my sin.* "I'm Jo," she said. "Jo Callaway."

Montgomery gave a sniff. "You stink."

"I do?"

"Yeah. You smell like when Daddy forgets to take the clothes out of the washer for a week, and they get all yucky-stinko."

"Oh." Darcy swallowed and released the girl. The shield she had momentarily dropped rose again. "Well, some people stink," she said, her voice defiant. "So what?"

The girl stuck out her chin. "So, you shouldn't have stopped me, Stink-lady. It won't do any good either, because I'm still gonna beat up Heather."

Darcy stood. "If you beat her up, you know who'll be in trouble? You. And that'll mean Heather is right—you *are* stupid."

"I'm not stupid. I'm in the gifted program at school, so there." The child brushed her hand over her wet cheek and gave a loud sniffle. "Anyway, why aren't you at the wedding?"

"Why aren't you?"

"Because my dad and me are too sad to go to weddings." Montgomery crossed her arms and gazed down the street at the crowd milling around the stone chapel. "My mom and dad got married in that church. But that was before I was born and before she died."

"How did your mom die?"

"A brain tumor." She flipped a long red braid over her shoulder. "It was a long time ago. Last summer."

"So who got married today?"

"Zachary Chalmers and Elizabeth Hayes. They own that house." Montgomery pointed in the opposite direction at an imposing mansion. The large brick building with its climbing ivy and tiers of scaffolding was obviously under restoration. "They're the parents of my best friend, Nick. Heather thinks Nick's an idiot, but he's not. He's just different."

Darcy picked up her paper bag. "You're smart to see that."

"Like I told you, I'm gifted."

"Well, Miss Smarty, maybe you can tell me where to find the nearest hotel."

"There aren't any hotels in Ambleside. You'll have to go to Jefferson City. They've got plenty over there."

Darcy tried to breathe. "I'm not going to Jefferson City. I came here. There has to be a hotel."

"Nope." As she shook her head, the red braids swung. "No hotels. You're out of luck, lady."

"Montgomery!" The shout spun the little girl around on her toes. A tall, muscular man with thick brown hair had emerged from the library. "What are you doing at the bus stop, Monkey?"

"I almost caught Heather, Dad," Montgomery called. "I'd have given her a black eye if this lady hadn't knocked me down."

At those words, the man started down the sidewalk, looking for all the world like an angry bull. "Hey, there," he called, lowering his head. "Did you hit my daughter?"

"Don't worry, Daddy, I'm not hurt," Montgomery assured her father, dismissing Darcy with a backward wave of her hand. "She came to town looking for a hotel. She doesn't believe me that we don't have hotels in Ambleside."

The man reached out and took his daughter's hand. His blue eyes flicked across Darcy, assessing and then dismissing. "No hotels," he said.

"But wait!" Darcy moved after them as they started back toward the library. "What about a rooming house or a hostel or something?"

"Nope."

"Where do people stay when they come to town?"

"With friends."

"Don't strangers ever come to Ambleside?"

The man stopped and turned at the library door. Those blue eyes studied the intruder more carefully this time. A spark of interest seemed to flicker for a moment, but it was quickly veiled by glazed indifference. Perhaps even hostility.

Darcy took a step back, concerned that the odor from her musty clothes had reached the man's nose. Or maybe she was standing too close to the daughter of whom he was so protective. Or perhaps he recognized her from the pictures that had been plastered across the newspapers so many years before.

"I . . . uh . . . I just got into town," Darcy said, pushing wisps of her blonde hair into the braid that ran down her back. "On the bus, you know. I'm looking for work."

The blue eyes snapped up to her face. "We don't get many strangers in Ambleside. What's your name?"

"I'm . . ." The lie again. "I'm Jo Callaway."

"Like the county up north?"

She nodded, suddenly fearful. Callaway County. The surname was a dead giveaway. Clearly fake. Couldn't she have been more creative?

"Well, there aren't many jobs in Ambleside, Mrs. Callaway," the man told her.

"Miss Callaway. I'm not married. I've never been married. And I'm from Arkansas."

"Arkansas, huh? How come you came in on the Chicago bus?"

"Oh." She twisted the top of her paper bag. "Well, I was up north . . . temporarily . . . visiting. But I was born and raised in Arkansas. Northern Arkansas."

"Anyhow, if you want a hotel, you'll have to try Jefferson City."

"I can't," she said quickly. "I mean, I . . . I came here."

"Sorry." He gave a shrug. "No hotels and no jobs."

"Tough darts," Montgomery added.

As father and daughter started back into the library, the man gave the child's pigtail a tug. "That wasn't nice, Monkey."

"Well, she grabbed me when I was just about to catch Heather."

Darcy stood outside in the baking heat and stared at the library door as it eased shut. In the large pane of glass, she could see her reflection. Dismal. Jeans that had hung on the boyish hips of a nineteen-year-old now curved far too tightly over her womanly form. The old blue T-shirt, stretched out of shape around the hem, was the mildew culprit. And hair that used to be clipped into a pixie cut had grown over the past six years into a mane of so many different lengths it was impossible to style. The thick braid

Darcy had attempted that morning had the appearance of a frayed rope, while tendrils hung around her chin like hay escaping from a bale.

She turned from her reflection and studied the little town. By now the wedding crowd had dispersed from the church grounds. Around the square, sidewalks began to fill as stores reopened for business. A group of teens gathered at the Tastee Hut. Lights came on in the donut shop and the cafe across the square.

Rolling her paper bag more tightly in her hands, Darcy tried to pray. Surely someone in this town needed help. God wouldn't have led her this far only to abandon her. When she'd started out this morning, she'd had just enough money to buy a bus ticket that would take her a hundred miles in any direction and leave enough cash for two or three nights in a cheap hotel. That was all.

As she'd purchased her ticket, Darcy had asked God to guide her. *Take me to freedom, Lord,* she'd prayed. *Please give me a job so I can prove I'm responsible. Give me a chance to make it as a worthy, responsible Christian woman. Just one chance. That's all I need.*

Words of rejection echoing in her head, Darcy again forced a prayer to her lips. She knew she had lied to the man and his daughter about her name and her past, but surely that sin was nothing compared to the sins of her earlier life. Would God punish her for this very small lie, even though she was trying her best to live for him?

"It certainly was a hot day for a wedding," a high-pitched voice said. Darcy broke from her trance as a stooped woman with cottony white hair and strands of pearls from her collarbone to her chin approached the library. "I cannot imagine why they waited so many months to hold the ceremony," the woman continued. "In my day, the wedding usually followed quite closely on the heels of the betrothal announcement. Why, Mr. McCann, God rest his soul,

insisted on marrying me a mere six weeks from the date
of our engagement."

Darcy reached out and opened the door for the older
woman.

"Thank you, my dear. Do come inside where it's cool."
The woman tottered in on thick-heeled white patent leather
shoes, her violet dress swishing at her ankles.

Darcy followed, more grateful than she realized she'd be
for the breath of cool air in the small, dark library. As her
eyes adjusted, she made out the figures of several young
children seated at a long oak table, where they were
engrossed in listening to Montgomery read a Dr. Seuss
book.

The little redhead and her father neither knew nor cared
about strangers in town. But maybe this older lady would
be different. Darcy approached the waist-high desk on
which the woman had set her purse. Ruby McCann, the
sign before her read. Librarian.

"Now then, what sort of books might I help you locate,
my dear?" Mrs. McCann placed a pair of half-moon spectacles on her nose and peered through them at Darcy. "We
have a very full fiction section. . . ." Pausing, she sniffed.
"Young lady, you must learn to dry your clothes completely
before you put them into your armoire. One can never
escape the unfortunate malodor of mildew."

"Sorry." Darcy stepped back. "I was . . . uh . . . I was just
wondering if you knew of a hotel nearby."

"I told her we don't have any hotels in Ambleside." Montgomery's father emerged from a back room as he spoke.
"And no jobs either."

The old lady jerked upright, and her spectacles slid from
her nose to the desk. "Good heavens! Is that Luke Easton?
You gave me quite a start, young man. What on earth were
you doing in my audiovisual room? You know the general
public is not permitted there."

Darcy was pleased to see the Easton fellow squirm under the scrutiny of the tiny librar[...]. "I was just hanging out until you got back from the wedding, Mrs. McCann," he said.

"Hanging out?" Her narrow lips pinched together in disapproval.

"Well, you had asked me to put those books on the cart into alphabetical order, ma'am. I thought I'd work on the job while Montgomery was reading to the other kids."

"Alphabetical order, Mr. Easton?"

The man glanced at Darcy as if she might clarify things. *"A, B, C,"* he began, *"D, E—"*

"I *know* alphabetical order," Mrs. McCann snapped. "I have worked in this library for more than forty years, young man."

"Yes, ma'am. And you asked me to help out here today, remember? You wanted me to watch the kids and file your books so you and everybody else in town could go to the Chalmers wedding."

The librarian's shoulders sank. "Did I ask you to do that?" she said softly. "How odd. The memory does slip now and again, doesn't it?"

"Yes, Mrs. McCann. It does."

"Well, well, back to your alphabetizing, Mr. Easton." The librarian picked up her glasses and set them on her nose again. "And how may I help you, young lady?"

"Um . . . I was looking for a hotel," Darcy repeated, noting that Luke Easton didn't budge. "And a place to work."

"Oh, Ambleside has not had a hotel since 1943. The River Street Hotel used to stand right on the corner where Bud's Hardware is now located. The owner's son went off to fight in the war and was tragically killed. Bataan, you know. A terrible place. His father never recovered from the loss. The hotel shut down, and the building remained empty until the civil rights movement of the sixties. That's when the only

African-American family in Ambleside purchased the property. It has been in the hands of the Huffs since 1968." She completed her recitation and beamed.

"I believe you have a very fine memory, Mrs. McCann," Darcy said.

"Bless you. And now, how may I serve you? Were you looking for something in fiction? I can recommend several excellent novels."

This time it was Darcy who glanced at the blue-eyed Luke Easton for assistance. He gave a shrug and shook his head. "Mrs. McCann," he said, "there's no place in Ambleside that takes in visitors, is there?"

"Visitors? Of course we welcome visitors to our town. Hospitality is a hallmark of the Ambleside community. In fact, many prominent visitors have taken their rest in the comfortable guesthouse that Mr. McCann and I have always maintained on our property. May I ask who has arrived in Ambleside, Mr. Easton?"

Darcy shifted from one foot to the other. "I came to town on the bus a few minutes ago."

"You are the guest?" Small brown eyes peered at Darcy through the half-moon spectacles. "Why, certainly, you must stay with us. One moment, please, and I shall fetch the guesthouse key."

Darcy stared in silent amazement as the elderly woman searched through her large white purse. What sort of trusting soul would give a key to a total stranger? For all Mrs. McCann knew, Darcy might strip the guesthouse bare and take off with the loot. With a false identity to protect her, she might just make it to Kansas.

And then what?

"Here you are, my dear," the librarian said, handing Darcy a collection of keys on a large metal ring. "I'm so befuddled this afternoon that I can't sort out which key belongs to what. Just take them all, why don't you? I believe this one is the guesthouse key, but it might be this. Now, here's my house key, ⌀ that I'm sure. And I feel certain this is the key to my car. It's a DeSoto, you know, and I keep it in tip-top shape. Now, these open the library doors. I must have them back before nightfall. Can you manage that?"

Darcy tried to breathe as she grasped the ring of metal keys. "Yes, I'll return them."

She would. She really would—no matter how tempting it might be to take advantage of her benefactor.

"Now look here, Mrs. McCann," Luke Easton said, lifting the keys from Darcy's palm before she could react. "You don't need to turn your guesthouse over to this woman. She's looking for a hotel."

"I beg your pardon!" The librarian snatched the keys from Easton's hand and returned them to Darcy. "I shall share my guesthouse with whomever I please, thank you very much. And you, sir, are standing behind the circulation desk, which is an area off-limits to the general public."

Easton stepped around the desk, the look of an admonished schoolboy on his face. "But, Mrs. McCann, you told me to—"

"Now then, Mr. Easton, I believe I have had quite enough of your insubordination today. I shall expect you to escort our lovely guest to my property and show her to her quarters."

"But I'm supposed to—"

"Mr. Easton!" The old woman leaned over the desk and peered up at him through her spectacles. "Honestly, the manners of the younger generation leave me in utter despair. And now look. My public is descending upon me *en masse!*"

The door had opened to a stream of parents arriving to pick up their children after the wedding reception. The library erupted in a chorus of squeals and greetings. Tiny feet leaped up and down on the wooden floor, creating a thunderous rumble through the silent halls. Mrs. McCann clapped her hands over her ears and rushed around the circulation desk in a futile attempt to restore order.

Darcy clutched the ring of keys. "I'm out of here."

"Hold on." Easton's huge, callused hand clamped around her wrist. "Where are you going with those keys?"

"To the guesthouse." *And don't try to stop me,* she added to herself.

Luke glanced across the room at the old woman whose white hair glowed in the dim light as she tottered around trying to hush the children. Then he returned his focus to the newcomer in town. "We don't know anything about you," he said as his own little red-haired daughter joined him. "You're a stranger."

"I told you, I'm Jo Callaway, I came in on the bus, and I'm from—"

"Arkansas. Yeah, I remember."

"So, what's the problem?"

"You can't move into Mrs. McCann's place."

"Why not? She invited me." Jerking her arm free, Darcy gave her head a toss. "Look, I just need a place to stay until I can find a job."

"You're not going to find a job. There's nothing in Ambleside."

"There'll be something."

"What kind of work can you do?"

Now it was Darcy's turn for discomfort. She didn't exactly qualify for a wide range of employment options. "I can do anything," she said. "You name it; I can do it."

"Give me an example."

"Hey, buster, what is this? I'm not on trial here, you know. I've earned my GED and two whole years of college credits. More than you ever did, I'll bet. I've worked in a laundry, and I've kept files in order, and I know how to cook."

"That's it?"

She frowned. "No, that's not it. I can take care of live-stock, too. Hogs." Searching the recesses of her mind, she poured out the last of her skills. "I helped my dad build a barn once, and I can hang wallpaper and paint just about anything, and I know how to shingle. And besides that, I can split firewood."

"We don't need any firewood splitters in Ambleside."

"Tough darts." Darcy tucked her paper bag under her arm and marched out of the library. Easton and his daughter were a couple of snooty firebrands, the kind of people who could drive a woman nuts.

"Hey, you," he called out behind her. "Miss Callaway."

She paused on the sidewalk and let out a growl of frus-tration under her breath. "What now?" she muttered, her hands gripping the key ring.

"How can you get to Mrs. McCann's house if you don't know the way?" Montgomery, her red braids swinging, skipped up to Darcy's side. "Me and Daddy are going to show you the right way."

Darcy studied the little redhead. "Thanks, Little-bit."

"I think Daddy ought to give you a job, because he's been griping about all the painting and wallpapering that needs to be done in the mansion. My dad is a carpenter, and he got hired by Mr. Chalmers to rebuild the mansion. It was falling down with termites and rotten wood and every-thing. Daddy hates to paint and wallpaper, but you said you could do that. I heard you."

Darcy lifted her head as Montgomery's father came to a stop beside them. "*You* need somebody?" she asked.

"No," he said firmly. "I don't. I don't need anybody."

Two

Grateful the McCann house stood only a block from the town square, Luke Easton took his daughter's hand and crossed the street. Beside them, the newcomer marched forward as though nothing and nobody could stop her. Luke gave the woman a quick glance to confirm again that she wasn't the least bit attractive. For some reason, he found her hard to categorize, and he'd been compelled to keep studying her out of the corner of his eye.

With her shaggy blonde hair and too-tight jeans, she gave an initial impression of ragged poverty. She smelled sour, her T-shirt bagged around her hips, and the work boots on her feet clomped along as if to announce she wasn't wearing socks.

And what was the deal with that rolled-up paper bag under her arm? Was that all the luggage she owned? He couldn't imagine traveling from Arkansas to northern Missouri to visit friends and taking along only a half-empty paper sack.

"I'm a good cook," Jo announced, swinging her head to give Luke a defiant stare. Long-lashed gray eyes regarded him coolly. "And I've counted a cafe, a donut shop, and a hamburger stand right on this very square. I'll bet at least one of them could use an extra hand. I'd work for minimum wage."

"Al Huff barbecues ribs at his service station," Montgomery chimed in. "His sign says Eat, Get Gas. Everybody laughs, but he makes really good baked beans. I bet you could help him."

"Sure I could. One year my baked beans won a blue ribbon at the county fair, and the judge wrote that mine were the tastiest beans he ever ate. You want to know my secret?"

"Yeah," Montgomery said.

"It's honey. How about that?"

The smile that lit up the woman's face dashed every negative opinion of her Luke had managed to form. Radiant, glowing, Jo Callaway transformed suddenly into a youthful, carefree beauty. As she lifted her golden braid to cool the back of her neck, she gave the impression of royalty—a fine chin, straight shoulders, and a long, pale neck. Not only was she pretty, Luke decided, but Jo had a streak of stubbornness that rivaled his own.

Unlike Ellie, who had been serenely faith-filled and compliant even in the slow-motion weeks of her painful death, this woman had a prickly kind of spunk. For some reason he couldn't explain, Luke felt an urge to goad her. Maybe it was because arguing made him feel alive, and he hadn't felt alive for a very long time.

"Al Huff doesn't need anyone to help him bake his beans," he said. "Nobody bakes beans better than Al. Besides that, the Tastee Hut only hires teenagers. And Ez and Alma have managed the Nifty Cafe for years without any employees. So it looks like you're out of luck, Miss Callaway."

"Luck?" Her chin jutted forward. "I don't believe in luck."

"You'd better start. You're going to need a lot of it if you hope to find work in Ambleside."

"Look, buster." She stopped and set one hand on her hip. "When I want your advice, I'll ask for it. And luck or no luck, I'm here to stay."

"Everybody I know believes in luck," Montgomery said as

the three began walking again. "People always say, 'good luck,' and 'that was a lucky break,' and stuff like that. How can you not believe in luck?"

"Because I believe in God. You can't put your faith in both."

The blunt statement startled Luke. Jo Callaway didn't look anything like the typical Christians he'd known all his life. He couldn't imagine her sitting demurely in church, legs crossed and hands folded in her lap. The image of this woman marching headfirst into the chapel in Ambleside gave Luke some amusement. Would the members of the close-knit congregation welcome her? Would they even allow her into the building?

"Daddy and I used to believe in God," Montgomery was telling Jo. "When my mommy was alive, we went to church every Sunday, and Daddy was a deacon."

"We still believe in God, Monkey," Luke said, surprised at his daughter's words. It hadn't occurred to him how she must have interpreted his actions following Ellie's death. "Mom would want you to keep believing in God."

"But you said God doesn't listen to us, and he doesn't answer our prayers. I heard you tell Elizabeth Hayes that you had trusted God and served him all your life, but he let Mommy die anyway. After that, we stopped praying at meals and bedtime. We don't read the Bible anymore. And we never go to church."

"That's just great," Jo said, giving Luke a look of reproach. "Listen, Little-bit, God hears us, and he answers our prayers—even if we don't always like the answer."

"And if you believe that . . ." Luke's voice trailed off.

"I learned the truth the hard way," Jo said, pinning those huge gray eyes on him. "You think you had it rough? Trust me, there's people who've had it a lot worse than you ever did."

"Yeah? When was the last time you watched someone you loved die right before your eyes?"

"Six years ago," she said.

Her answer startled him. Maybe there was more to her than met the eye. But before he could respond, she went on. "Now where's that librarian's house? I'm tired of talking to you."

To the melody of Montgomery's giggles, Luke led the group up to the massive iron gate that surrounded the old McCann estate. Wilmer McCann had made his money in railroading, and his death had left his wife one of the richest widows in the county. For as long as Luke could remember, Ruby McCann had worked in the library, mingling with the townsfolk as though she were no better off than any of them.

As they walked along a boxwood-lined path, Luke considered the fact that Mrs. McCann owned many of the buildings surrounding the square. Half the town paid their rent into an account in the McCann-established First City Bank of Ambleside. And the new subdivision going up just outside the city limits had been developed from McCann property—a section of land on which Luke planned to establish his own future.

Though his father was president of the local bank, Luke had been both disinherited and banned from the family for refusing to submit to Frank Easton's iron will for his son. Instead of becoming a banker, Luke had learned carpentry. Using his hard-earned skills, he had made a successful living until his wife's medical bills had wiped out their savings and left the underinsured family deeply in debt. Now Luke staked his hopes on the houses that soon would be under construction in the McCann subdivision. He counted on his carpentry talents to earn a living for himself and his daughter.

"There's the guesthouse," Montgomery said, pointing out

the steep-roofed cottage that stood down a small lane from the larger, nineteenth-century home. "It looks like a doll's house, doesn't it? Can we go inside, Daddy?"

"That depends on whether Miss Callaway is too tired of us to let us in."

Jo shrugged as she began trying the keys on the large ring. "You can come inside if you want. Maybe this is your lucky day."

"But you don't believe in luck!" Montgomery protested.

"It was a little joke." Jo turned the knob, and the round-topped wooden door swung open. "Luck didn't bring me to Ambleside. I wouldn't be walking into this guesthouse now if God weren't watching over me, Montgomery. He brought me here, and he's going to help me find a job—no matter what your dad thinks."

"Wow!" As they walked into the cottage, Montgomery gave a twirl of delight that sent her red braids flying. "It *is* a doll's house. Wait till Nick sees this place. He'll have a cow! Can I bring my friend over here to play after church tomorrow, Miss Callaway? His mom and dad are leaving for Hawaii on their honeymoon, and Nick's staying with us for two whole weeks. Did you see the kitchen? It has pots and pans. And there's a little cuckoo clock with a chain that has pinecones on it."

Luke folded his arms, leaned against the arched portal between the living room and dining room, and appraised the rooms and furnishings. Ruby McCann's guesthouse had that musty smell of an old building closed up tight for decades. Ancient lace curtains hung limp against crumbling wallpaper. The fireplace contained an old gas heater that Luke suspected would fill the place with carbon monoxide. Though the electricity was on and an old black rotary-dial telephone stood on a table near the door, Luke had a feeling the wiring could go up in flames with just a spark. And the furniture was that overstuffed, round-armed variety

featured in old black-and-white movies. All the same, the
two females raced from room to room exclaiming with hap-
piness, as though they had just discovered a theme park
with a thousand different rides.

"A bathtub!" Jo cried. "A whole, entire bathtub."

"It's got a plug on a chain," Montgomery said, joining the
chorus of glee. "And the sink is wearing a skirt!"

"Did you see the table and chairs, Little-bit? Each chair
has a heart cut out of the back."

"Like the Seven Dwarfs' chairs! Oh, I want to sit in these
chairs and have lunch. Can me and Nick come over and eat
with you tomorrow, Miss Callaway? You wouldn't mind,
would you? We could bring the sandwiches."

"Well, I—" Pausing in her whirlwind tour, the young
woman looked across the room at Luke. "I might be busy
tomorrow. I need to look for a job."

"You can't do that on Sunday," Montgomery said.
"Nobody will be open except the new gas mart out on the
highway. You can't start looking for jobs until Monday.
Tomorrow you could go to church, and then we could all
come over here and eat lunch."

"Now, hold on a minute, Monkey," Luke said. "We've just
met Miss Callaway, and she may have other plans for her
day."

"No, I don't," Jo offered. "I'm going to church, and then
I'll eat lunch. I don't care if Little-bit and her friend come
over here, as long as they bring their own food. I'm not in
a position to run a soup kitchen."

"What's a soup kitchen?" Montgomery asked.

"Don't worry," Luke said. "You won't ever need to
know."

"Oh, yeah?" Jo gave a bitter laugh. "You can't be sure
about that, Mr. Easton. Listen to me, Little-bit. A soup
kitchen's a place where you can get a meal when you're
busted flat. They serve up good hot food, and sometimes

they'll give you a coat or a blanket to keep you warm at night."

"But can't you just get into your own bed at night?"

"Not everybody in this world has a bed."

The redhead pondered this for a moment. "Then they're not lucky, and I don't care what you say about luck. My dad's right. If there was a God who cared about us, everyone would have a warm bed with lots of blankets. So you wouldn't need soup kitchens. I'm lucky. My dad made my bed himself, because he's a carpenter."

The woman peered down into the child's eyes. "If God didn't care about you, Little-bit, why did he give you such a good daddy?"

At the compliment, Luke felt a strange warmth spread through his chest. Though he couldn't figure out why the words of this aggravating woman would matter, somehow they did. Before Ellie's illness, Luke's wife had been the main influence on their daughter. Now, her father was all Montgomery had. It had been rough, adjusting to the role of full-time, single parent to the precocious little girl. Luke wasn't at all sure he was doing a good job of it.

Jo Callaway's praise had given him an unexpected lift. He knew the woman was blunt and outspoken. If she said Luke was a good dad, that's what she thought.

"If we believe in God," Montgomery said, turning her focus on her father, "then why don't we go to church anymore?"

Luke frowned. "You don't have to go to church to believe in God."

Jo let out a hissing breath and rolled her eyes as she turned away. "Yeah, right. Do your religion in solitary. That makes sense. I've got news for you, buster. If you ever want to learn anything, or grow stronger, or meet people you can count on when trouble comes down the pike, you have to get out of the hole."

"What hole?" Montgomery asked.

Jo's face stiffened. "It's just an expression. What I'm trying to say is that your dad ought to take you to church. Now, if you two wouldn't mind giving me some space, I'd like to settle in here and unpack."

"That could take a while." Luke glanced at the wadded paper bag on the table by the door. "Come on, Monkey."

He took his daughter's hand, barely getting her out the door before Jo shut it firmly behind them. As they started down the path, Luke turned the conversation over in his mind. Did he believe in God anymore? Ellie's death had been such a blow that he wondered if he'd ever get over it. Even now, almost a year later, he sometimes was overwhelmed by loss and grief. Anger, too. And all those emotions were directed at God.

"I guess you can't be mad at somebody if you don't think they exist," Montgomery said, giving the boxwood hedge a kick with the toe of her sneaker. "So, maybe we do believe in God, Daddy."

"I guess we do."

"Jo Callaway sure does. She's weird. I bet Mrs. McCann will drop over dead when Jo shows up at church tomorrow in that stinky T-shirt."

Luke chuckled, wondering how the mildew odor had faded from his thoughts so completely—and how those big gray eyes had taken its place in his conscious mind. That tangle of a blonde braid, too. And that radiant smile.

"I wouldn't mind going to church tomorrow," Montgomery said. "Nick won't understand why we don't take him while his parents are in Hawaii. He's not mad at God. He believes God got him out of that Romanian orphanage and gave him a new mom. And he's sure God brought Mr. Chalmers to town to become his daddy. Nick even thinks God will give me a new mom."

Luke paused on the path. "Do you want a new mom, Montgomery?"

"No." She shrugged. "I wish we could have my real mommy back."

"Me, too, Monkey."

"But I wouldn't mind if we had another person who was sort of like a mom. You know, somebody who could braid my hair the right way and cook us some good meals and grow tomatoes in the garden. Stuff like that. Like maybe take me shopping. Or paint my fingernails. You know."

"Sure." Luke's vision of himself as an adequate father suddenly deflated like a punctured balloon.

"So, are we going to take Nick to church tomorrow? We could sit beside Jo Callaway, and maybe that way she wouldn't feel so lonely."

Luke looked over his shoulder at the cottage guesthouse. At that moment, Jo's slender arm pushed open the leaded, diamond-paned window beside the front door. In less than a breath, the window on the opposite wall creaked open. And then, as though she were a bird seeking freedom, the woman flew from window to window in the small house. Wooden sashes lifted, lace curtains fluttered out into the breeze, glass panes sparkled in the sunshine.

"You'd better go tell Jo we'll sit beside her in church tomorrow morning," Montgomery said, giving her father's hand a tug. "And then we'll bring sandwiches over to her house for lunch."

Luke wasn't quite sure how he found himself walking back along the path to the small cottage. The facts were clear: he didn't know or have any reason to trust Jo Callaway. She looked like a refugee from somebody's rag pile. She was pricklier than any cactus. And besides all that, he didn't want to go to church tomorrow. Yet here he was, pausing on her half-moon doorstep, preparing to invite the

woman to sit with him in Sunday worship service the following morning.

"Hey, Mom, it's Darcy," a voice said through the open
window. "No, I can't tell you where I am."

Luke's hand halted on its way to the knocker. *Darcy?*

"Because I just can't," the woman he knew as Jo Callaway
continued. "Look, Mom, I can't talk long. I'm going to have
to pay for this call, and I don't have a job yet. . . . Well, I
just got here, that's why. I wanted to tell you I'm okay, and
I hope you'll go see Mr. Abel for me. Tell him I'll be sending money to pay on my bill as soon as I find work. Yeah,
it's more than three thousand dollars. . . . No, I'm not coming home. . . . You know why."

Luke lowered his hand and started to turn away. He
shouldn't be listening.

"What?" A note of terror rang through the woman's voice,
halting Luke in his tracks. "When did he come to the house?
Does he know? No, don't tell him I called you! I don't want
him to come looking for me, that's why."

When she spoke again, the fear had been replaced by
desperation. "Because I know how he feels about me. I
know what he'll do. . . . I have to—to make it through this
on my own. Don't tell him anything about me. Just let me
try to be free, okay?"

The click of the receiver was followed by a soft sobbing.
Luke wavered for a moment, debating whether or not to
knock. An unexpected urge to open the door and comfort
the woman was replaced by cold reality. Luke's list of facts
about the town's newcomer had just grown longer—Jo
Callaway was really named Darcy, she owed a large debt to
a man named Abel, and she was hiding out in Ambleside.

Those facts outweighed the sparkle in her gray eyes and
the sunshine in her smile. Shoving his hands deeply into his
pockets, Luke set off down the path to tell his daughter
they'd be unable to meet with Miss "Jo Callaway" tomorrow.

Monday morning, Darcy ran her fingers through her tangled hair and decided her first purchase would have to be a brush—if she were ever able to get a job and start earning a paycheck. Staring at herself in the mirror, she sighed. Who would hire a woman who looked like she had just straggled out of someone's laundry hamper? Though she had handwashed her T-shirt Saturday night, she had no iron to press out the wrinkles. And she didn't dare spend her tiny amount of cash on anything but food. Her first priority was to stay fed and sheltered. She'd worry about her appearance later.

Noticing the paper sack that contained a few folded bills, a change of underwear, her identification papers, and a couple of important addresses, Darcy grabbed it and stuffed it under a couch cushion. The phone call to her mother two days earlier had reawakened every fear inside her. If the Damyon family discovered where she was living, then one or more of them would come after her. And if they found her . . . she pushed the paper bag farther under the cushion. Hide herself. Hide her past. Hide everything.

Still down on her knees, Darcy folded her hands and rested her forehead on them. A few quiet moments in prayer would help to fortify her for the day ahead. Maybe Luke Easton had been right about the value of practicing your faith in private. In church the day before, everyone had turned to stare at the denim-clad stranger who seated herself on the last pew. A few people greeted the newcomer, but no one welcomed her as warmly as she had hoped. Luke and his daughter were nowhere in sight, and they hadn't shown up for lunch either. Though Darcy wanted anonymity, she couldn't deny her loneliness.

Help me not to need people, Father, she lifted up in prayer. *I can't let anyone get too close, so help me not to mind if they push me away. And if you see fit, please open somebody's heart to give me a job today, so I can—*

"Knock, knock!" Ruby McCann opened the front door and walked right into the living room. "There you are, my dear. I thought I'd stop by on my way to the library this morning to wish you well in your search for employment."

The elderly woman stood beaming as Darcy scrambled to her feet. "Thank you. I . . . uh . . . I'm hoping I can find something full time."

"That might be difficult, I'm afraid." The librarian set her purse and matching tote bag on the floor; then she seated herself in one of the overstuffed armchairs as though she had all the time in the world. "Ambleside is proud of its healthy economy. Not even the Great Depression was able to defeat the stalwart citizens of our community. We have a virtually even ratio of jobs to laborers. Now tell me what sort of work you do, my dear."

Darcy sat down on the edge of the sofa. "I have two years of college under my belt," she said. Then she recited the list of job skills she had memorized following her encounter with Luke Easton. "I can do laundry, cook, clean, file, tend hogs, hang wallpaper, paint walls, and shingle roofs."

"My goodness." Mrs. McCann fingered the string of pearls at her neck. "What an accomplished young lady you are, although I can't imagine you'll find your laundry, cooking, and hog aptitudes useful in Ambleside. You might see if Mr. Sawyer, the town lawyer, could use someone to help him file papers. Otherwise, I think your best option is to seek work from Mr. Luke Easton, who is restoring Chalmers House as a place of business on the town square. I under-stand his skills with paint and wallpaper leave something to be desired. And he might be able to use your assistance in the matter of shingling. Shall I make an introduction?"

Darcy frowned in confusion. "But I already met Luke Easton. On Saturday. In the library."

"Saturday, very good. Then you are aware of his fine qualities. I'm told that Luke Easton is a fair employer and a steady man of good character."

"Yes, but he already told me he doesn't need anybody. And to tell you the truth, Mrs. McCann, I don't really care for the man. He argues too much."

"Luke Easton? Heavens, I can't imagine that. I don't believe I've heard him speak more than five words together since I've known him—and that is a great many years." She chuckled. "Now before I leave for my day at the library, I've brought something for you."

"For me?" Darcy hadn't been given a gift in years. She felt a strange, childlike delight spread through her as the librarian began going through the contents of her tote bag.

"Seeing you in church reminded me that I wanted to do this."

"In church?"

"Yes, my dear, I'm quite certain I saw you there. You sat three rows behind me."

Darcy blinked. What was the woman getting at? Of course she had seen her in church. The two had walked home together. "Yes, I did," she said carefully.

"And?" Mrs. McCann shook her head. "Come, come, my dear. I know you're going to begin your job search, and I suspect that your wardrobe is limited. So . . ."

Lifting the tote bag into her lap, the librarian began to pull out an array of colorful clothing. Peacock blue silk was followed by shimmery floral satin. Skirts gathered at the waist, slim skirts, ankle-length skirts. Short-sleeved blouses, ruffle-collared blouses, button-up blouses. A pair of sandals, a hairbrush, even a string of pearls. Pearls!

As she draped the garments over the arm of her chair, Mrs. McCann reminisced. "I purchased this blouse in Hawaii

on the occasion of our twenty-fifth wedding anniversary.
. . . This dress is from a very exclusive boutique in Boston,
. . . and this peach velvet is the most divine shade, don't
you think?"

Darcy couldn't disguise her shock. "But I can't wear your
clothes and jewelry, Mrs. McCann! I'm just a guest. And . . .
you don't even know me."

"Nonsense, my dear. You mustn't go out into society in
those rags. I'm sorry to be blunt, but there's the truth of the
matter. If you wish to find respectable employment, you
must look respectable. Otherwise, you will indeed find
yourself slopping hogs."

With that, the woman rose from her chair and walked out
of the guest cottage. "Go and see Luke Easton," she called
over her shoulder. "He'll give you a job. I'm sure of it."

Darcy stared after her benefactor as she tottered down
the path between the boxwoods. *What a strange woman!*
Mrs. McCann clearly was well educated and well-off, but
Darcy felt sure the librarian had lost a few of her marbles.

As she ran her fingers over the expensive fabrics piled on
the armchair, Darcy tried to imagine what God had in store
for her. Why had he sent her this eccentric fairy godmother?
Why had he provided these clothes and this house? What
work would he give her to do here in Ambleside?

And why, when all reason told her to stay hidden and
aloof, had God thrown Luke Easton and his little red-haired
daughter into her path?

"A job?" Nathan Zimmerman shook his head. "I'm sure
sorry, ma'am, but I've got all the help I need. I hire high
school kids to work for me in the afternoon. That's my busi-
est time. But you know who might could use some help?
Luke Easton, over at the mansion. I hear he's not such a
good hand with wallpaper and paint."

Darcy tried to smile as she left Zimmerman's Sundries. She had applied for work at four businesses so far, and the message had been the same at each. The *Daily Herald* only published a newspaper once a week these days, and it had more employees than it needed. The Tastee Hut hired only teenagers. Darcy had given the police station a wide berth, but at Kaye's Kut-n-Kurl next door, she learned that the perky owner was running at full staff. "You ought to try Luke Easton," each person suggested helpfully. "Luke's a fine carpenter, but folks say he can't paint worth a flip."

As she crossed Main Street, Darcy tried to think positively. Wearing one of Ruby McCann's soft pink skirts and a white blouse, she felt a little like Cinderella at the ball. So where was Prince Charming? Darcy had to shake her head at her own thoughts. She'd been down the fairy-tale road once before—so certain she had found the love of her life, a man who would protect her and care for her always. The night she had gone to the hospital with three ribs broken at the hand of her husband, her fairy tale had shattered.

Never again, she vowed as she bypassed the office of John Sawyer, attorney-at-law. She'd spent enough time in a lawyer's office already. Darcy pushed open the door of Redee-Quick Drugs and drank in the scent of caramel popcorn, vanilla-scented candles, and cough syrup. Rows of faded greeting cards lined one wall. Behind the counter, a man of about sixty lifted his head and regarded her from behind a pair of round tortoiseshell-rimmed glasses. "Be with you in a minute."

Darcy wandered between aisles stacked with boxes of diapers, multiple vitamins, inexpensive giftware, and ladies' hosiery. When the pharmacist beckoned, she hurried to his counter. "My name is Jo Callaway," she said. "I'm looking for work."

"Cleo Mueller, mayor of Ambleside." He gave her a nod.

"I heard you'd come to town. Saw you at church yesterday, in fact. We don't get many newcomers."

"I can see why. I'm having a hard time finding a job."

"Most folks who move to town come here because they've already got one. We don't have many open up."

"How about you, Mr. Mueller? Do you need help? I could sweep, dust the cards, stock your shelves—"

"No, ma'am, I'm doing just fine. But I'll tell you where you ought to go. Luke Easton is refurbishing the old Chalmers House over on Walnut Street. He probably could use a hired hand. The man can build anything, but the word is he's clueless when it comes to painting and hanging wallpaper."

Darcy nodded. "I'll keep looking."

But it was the same at the Nifty Cafe, Bud's Hardware, and the Corner Market. "You know who you ought to ask for a job?" the market owner, who called himself Boompah, asked in a thick European accent. "Go over there to Chalmers House. That Luke Easton is a very fine carpenter, but I have heard he is not good with painting."

"Or wallpapering."

"He's very bad with wallpapering." The old man beamed. "Why don't you ask him? He could give you a job, I'm sure of it."

The ladies' clothing store owner was outside sweeping her sidewalk. Pearlene Fox was her name, but she didn't need any help, thank you very much. The antiques shop was closed because its proprietress was away on her honeymoon. The bus depot didn't do much business these days. The haberdashery hired only men. Dandy Donuts had just taken on a new employee for the early shift, but why not try Luke Easton over at the old mansion? He was terrible with painting and wallpapering, or so the rumor went.

Darcy stepped out onto the sidewalk and studied the large brick house that faced the square. Luke Easton had already told her that he didn't need any employees. More significant, Darcy didn't want to work for the man. Something about him intrigued her, made her wish for companionship and communion, laughter and disagreement, and all the things that made a person feel human. It was clear Luke enjoyed baiting her, and their arguments had somehow prodded her to life. But she couldn't afford any personal relationships here in Ambleside. She didn't have the luxury to really live—not the way others lived. Not with friendships and community and family.

This was the town where she would hide until she had paid back every debt she owed. Until then, she had no choice but to exist in the hard shell of her own making and move silently past those who were free of the consequences she must bear.

But how could she pay back her debts without a job? Darcy let out a breath of frustration. The banana she'd eaten for lunch wasn't going to hold her much longer. She had to find work—and it had to be near the town square. Without a car, she would have to walk to work. *Father God, there has to be something here for me! What is it? Where am I supposed to go?*

Darcy glanced at the old brick library, where two days earlier she had met her wacky fairy godmother. So, she was back where she'd begun. Thus far, the only one who had helped her at all was Ruby McCann. And Ruby had told her to ask Luke Easton for a job. So had everyone else, for that matter. This entire day, Darcy had been asking God for direction and guidance, and she'd been sure she was getting no answer. Had she been mistaken?

Squaring her shoulders, Darcy turned again to Chalmers House. *Okay, Lord, here I go.*

THREE

"Someone's here to see you, boss!"

At the interruption, Luke Easton's hand jerked, and his carpenter's level slid down the wall at a forty-five degree angle. "Floyd, I thought you were working on that wiring in the study."

"Yeah, boss, but look who's here." The electrician took off his cap and scratched his bald head. "It's a lady." He leaned over to whisper in Luke's ear. "I seen her comin' a long way off. She's been circlin' the town all day, goin' from store to store, till I had just about figured out we was gonna get a visit from her too. And then, sure enough, here she come."

"If you were wiring the study, Floyd, how come you know all about the comings and goings of some lady doing her shopping?" Luke set his level on the floor and regarded the small retired electrician he had hired to rewire the old mansion. "Am I going to have to fire you again?"

Floyd grinned, his three good teeth gleaming in his pink gums. "'Fore you get all mad at me, boss, you ought to take a gander at this gal. She's somethin' else, lemme tell you."

"Floyd, you'd think a Muscovy duck was pretty."

"Them Muscovys are good eatin', boss," Floyd said, following him toward the foyer. "You smoke 'em up just right, and you can't beat a Muscovy."

"The point is, they're ugly."

"But they're delicious."

"What I'm trying to tell you is—" Luke paused and stared

at the entrancing woman who sto●● just inside the doorway. Tall, slender, her blonde hair caught up high on her
head in a loose bun, she took on the glow of the late afternoon sun. She wore a white blouse and a pink skirt, and
she seemed to float as she moved toward the two men.

"Hi," she said softly, her gray eyes fastening on Luke's
face.

He sucked down a breath of air that lodged just behind
one of his ribs. "Uh . . ."

"I know you said you didn't need anybody, but I hear
you're a lousy painter."

The bluntness of the words snapped Luke back into
focus. He'd seen this woman before. It was Jo—Darcy—
whoever. The woman who had come to town on the bus,
moved into Ruby McCann's guesthouse, and was looking
for a job. The gray eyes and long lashes searched his face
as he put together the memory of a pair of ill-fitting jeans,
a ragged T-shirt, and a pair of old work boots.

"Who told you I can't paint?" Luke asked her. He could
hear Floyd snickering beside him.

"Folks around town. Everywhere I went asking for work,
people told me you needed a painter and a paperhanger
here at the mansion. And that's what I do."

Now Luke had the woman fully in mind again—that firm
little chin, those unwavering eyes, that sharp tongue.
"What's that name you gave yourself again?" he asked and
noted a flicker of dismay in her eyes.

"I'm Jo Callaway," she said.

"Like the county up north," Floyd put in. "The Kingdom
of Callaway. Long history. I think they made a movie about
it with somebody famous for the star. John Wayne, maybe.
You belong to them Callaways, ma'am?"

"No," she said. "I'm just me, and I paint like a pro."

"You could use a painter, boss," Floyd said. "Your

paintin' is flat lousy, and that's about all I have to say on the matter."

"Then how about you getting back to wiring the library?"

"I reckon I could." Floyd stuck his hands into the pockets of his overalls and grinned at his employer. "So, you gonna hire the lady?"

Luke faced the young woman. "I told you before, Miss Callaway, I don't need anybody."

"That ain't so, boss," Floyd said. "You need a painter."

Luke felt his blood pressure rise. The realization that the attractive young woman was witnessing all of this disconcerted him. He vaguely wondered why it mattered what she thought of him. But it did. "I was hoping you'd get that chandelier back up on the ceiling before next year, Floyd."

"All the same, if we's gonna have us a new hired hand, I'd like to meet her."

"You've met her."

"Then you're gonna hire her?"

"I didn't say that."

"I can wallpaper, too," Jo Callaway said. "I'm quite good."

"Boy howdy, now there's a stroke of luck," Floyd said. "We got in a whole shipment of wallpaper to start coverin' the downstairs rooms. Reproduction historical archive paper, y'know? Anyhow, it didn't come prepasted or nothin'. You can't just soak it in the bathtub. You've got to use glue and all. Me and the boss was about to throw in the towel the other day when we seen what we was up against with that wallpaper. But now, here you are, just like an answer to prayer."

Luke glared at the little electrician, aware that Jo's big gray eyes were observing him intently. "Floyd, if you don't mind, I'll handle this myself."

"Sure you will, boss. I just think she's a godsend, if y'know what I mean."

"Hey, boss, were we planning to put some more

insulation up in the—" a muscular young man with a shock
of bright red hair leaped down the final six steps of the oak
staircase and landed with a thud on the foyer's marble
floor—"attic? Oops, excuse me, ma'am. I didn't realize anyone was down here."

Gabriel Zimmerman whipped off his baseball cap and
flushed a brilliant crimson at the sight of the tall blonde in
their midst. Luke groaned inwardly over the behavior of his
two employees. At twenty, Gabe hovered between respect-
ability and hooliganism. He'd been caught spray-painting
his girlfriend's name on the park fountain the previous summer, and he was known at the Corner Market as a regular
gumball thief. If it weren't for the job Luke had given him,
Gabe would be spending his days loitering around the
square. As it was, no one could be sure what the young
man might pull next.

"Yeah, we're going to insulate the attic," Luke told his
employee, "but my order hasn't come in yet. Aren't you
supposed to be stripping that woodwork in the upstairs
bathroom?"

"Who's this, boss?" Gabe positively gawked at Jo
Callaway. "She a friend of yours?"

"I'm Jo Callaway."

"Like the county up north?"

"That's what I ast her," Floyd said. "But she ain't related
to them movie Callaways. She's gonna hang up that fancy
wallpaper we got."

"The stuff that didn't have any glue on it?"

"Yep, and she paints, too. You know the boss is a lousy
painter."

"Now, hold on a minute here." Luke put up his hand. He
had worked hard to establish himself as a skilled builder,
and it bothered him to have his work disparaged in front of
this intriguing stranger. "I'm not a lousy painter, and I'll be
the one deciding who I hire and who I don't. Maybe I

ought to let one of your fellows go, so I'll have the money
to pay the lady, huh? Is that what you want?"

Gabe gave his boss a wounded look and started back up
the stairs. "The floorboards up there in the bathroom are
wet. I reckon the first time anybody sits on that pot, the
whole thing's going to crash right through the floor."

"I'll check on it in a minute." Luke made a mental note.
If it wasn't one thing, it was another with this old house.
Restoring a historical structure that hadn't been cared for in
fifty years was proving to be a real challenge. But the overwhelming debt after Ellie's hospitalization and treatment
meant Luke had little choice in which construction jobs he
accepted. And Zachary Chalmers, the mansion's owner, had
been more than a friend during his dark months of
mourning.

"You oughta show Miz Callaway the wallpaper, boss,"
Floyd spoke up. "I bet she never saw wallpaper that didn't
come with glue on the back."

"You can't just put it in the bathtub," Gabe called from
somewhere upstairs. "It ain't vinyl. It'll turn to mush. You
have to buy wallpaper glue and brush it on."

Luke looked at Jo and shrugged. "I guess you can see I've
already got more help than I need around this place."

"I know how to put up wallpaper that hasn't been
prepasted." Jo fiddled with a piece of hair that had slipped
out of her bun as Floyd wandered back to his job rewiring
the study. "My mom used to take on jobs all around, and I
went with her to help out. It's the expensive papers and the
ones from England that don't have glue on the back. But
we always brushed on glue no matter what, so the paper
wouldn't come down even if the roof blew off and the wall
got rained on. I know how to put it up without any
trouble."

He stared at her, trying to reconcile the image of this
stunning golden-haired angel in the pink skirt with his

memory of the ragged, tough-talking woman who'd gotten
off the bus two days ago. She crossed her arms, regarded
him with those big gray eyes, and then cleared her throat.

"The secret is in how you prepare the wall," she continued. "You have to prime it just right. If you don't, the paper
won't stick well when you hang it. And when you're ready
to take it down after a few years, you'll wind up pulling it
off in little one-inch strips."

Luke tried to think what to say to this woman. He could
barely afford to pay another worker. As it was, he was
doing well to keep Gabe and Floyd on at minimum wage.
Neither of them depended on Luke for survival the way Jo
Callaway would. Floyd had his pension, and Gabe still lived
at home with his parents. But Jo had nowhere to go, no
place to live, nothing but that paper sack and her made-up
name.

"I can paint cabinets and do any kind of trim work," she
said, as though she sensed his hesitation. "I found out that
if you buy the right brush and you learn how to use it, you
can work without splashing the paint all over creation. I got
to where I never even used a drop cloth. Mom used to say
it was a miracle how well I painted."

Luke felt himself waver. He had to admit it would be a
relief to turn the paint and wallpaper work over to someone
else. He really was lousy at it. But he didn't trust this
woman. "So you did all that painting when you lived in
Arkansas, huh?"

She sucked down a breath. "Um . . . yes. Arkansas."

"And your mom was a paperhanger. What did your dad
do?"

"Is this part of the job application?" That hardness
returned to her voice.

"I'm just curious."

"He's a hog farmer." She tilted her chin. "What does your
father do? I'm just curious, you know."

Luke looked away. *Touché*. "He's a bank president."

"Here in town?"

"Does it matter?"

"It seems to matter to *you* where *I* grew up." She shrugged. "Well, with a banker for a father, you must be a rich boy. Surely you can hire someone to hang your wallpaper."

"My father has nothing to do with the way I choose to earn my living." Luke thought of the man who had cut him off because he was infuriated by his son's choice of career. The two hadn't spoken in more than ten years, and Luke would never stoop to ask for money from such a man.

As he prepared to tell Jo Callaway that she wouldn't be getting a job from him, Luke spotted his daughter and her best friend greeting the mailman on the sidewalk outside Chalmers House. "School's out for the afternoon," he said. "I've got to keep an eye on the kids."

"I could watch them for you," she said, following him toward the door.

"I don't need—"

"Yes, you do. I can help you. I can do anything. Please, Mr. Easton, you're my last hope. Don't turn me away."

"Montgomery!" Luke called, unwilling to let the woman's plea enter his heart. He stepped out onto the wide front porch. "Nick! You kids come on up here."

"Hey, Mr. Easton," the postman called, handing the children a stack of mail. "Thought I'd go ahead and bring these over here, rather than drop them at your house. 'Fraid it looks like more bills."

"Hey, Pop." Luke gave the man a wave. "So what else is new?"

Pop Creighton laughed as he strode across the grass toward the antiques shop next door to the mansion. Hands full of envelopes, Montgomery and Nick bounded onto the porch and threw their arms around Luke. Within a minute,

they had stuffed the mail into Luke's hands, shrugged off
their backpacks, dropped them onto the porch, greeted
Floyd, asked for cookies and milk, and begun to tell the
news of the day.

"Magunnery punched Herod," Nick said, "but Magunnery
didn't get into trouble, because everybody saw that Herod
was trying to push me off the swing."

"That's right," Montgomery piped up. "And I kept telling
Herod—I mean Heather—to leave Nick alone, and she
wouldn't."

"And then I fell off the swing, right onto my bottom.
That's when my jeans ripped, and I was scared it would
show my private parts, because Mommy told me you
should never show them to anybody. But then I remembered I had on my underpants."

"And Heather just stood there laughing at Nick, and
before I could even think about it, I punched her in the
chin."

"Then the principal came and took everybody to her
office, but Magunnery and me didn't get into very much
trouble. We just had to miss the rest of recess, and it was
almost over anyway. Mrs. Wrinkles sewed up my jeans. But
the principal called Herod's mommy. So, she's not very
lucky, but we are."

"There's no such thing as luck, Nick," Montgomery said,
laying a hand on Nick's shoulder. "Not if you believe in
God."

"If you believe in God, Little-bit, you shouldn't go around
punching people in the chin." Jo Callaway's voice silenced
both children.

Luke watched his daughter's blue eyes go wide. "Hey,
you're that lady. Nick, she's the one who moved into Mrs.
McCann's house. And this is my best friend, Nick."

Jo stuck out her hand. "Nick, pleased to meet you."

"I don't think you stink," he said, his green eyes solemn.

"I told Magunnery it isn't nice to say someone stinks, even if they do. My mom teaches me about manners all the time. Why did you stink?"

Luke cleared his throat. "Hey, you kids go back to the kitchen and look in that cooler I brought over from the house this morning. I put a carton of milk inside, and there are some Oreos on the counter."

"Oreos!" Montgomery's red braids swung outward as she grabbed Nick's hand.

"Oreos are the cookies that leave the little black crumbs between your teeth," Nick told Jo. "If you eat those cookies in Sunday school, and then somebody takes your picture after you say 'cheese,' your mom might get very embarrassed. Especially if they put the picture on the bulletin board."

"I'll remember that," Jo said as the two children made a dash through the house, their sneakers pounding on the raw wood floor. She covered her mouth with her hand, barely hiding her smile as she faced Luke.

"Nick's mom adopted him from Romania," he explained, hardly looking up as he leafed through the bills in his hands. "You get used to him after a while."

Luke had grown accustomed to the letterhead from the cancer hospital in Houston where Ellie's brain surgery had been performed, from the home-health-care service, the pharmacy, and the local physicians who regularly sent their bills. As a self-employed carpenter, he had never been able to afford much health insurance. But then, he had never expected such a tragedy to strike his healthy, young wife.

Since before Ellie's death, Luke had been chipping away at the monumental sum of money he now owed in medical bills—more than any human could reasonably pay off in a lifetime. Though he wondered if there would ever be a day when he could call himself debt-free, Luke wasn't about to throw up his hands in despair. With hard work and the continuing demand for his skills, he was determined to whittle down the obligations until they were manageable.

It was the letter at the bottom of the pile that shook him. The name of a collection agency had been printed in large red letters across the top. After stuffing the other letters into his back pocket, he ripped open the envelope and shook out the letter into his hand.

"So, what do you think?" Jo Callaway was asking. "I can watch the kids in the afternoons. I can paint and wallpaper. I can even fix snacks and suppers for you."

Ignoring her, Luke scanned the curt message. His house payment had been late three months in a row, the letter informed him, and a small business loan was in arrears. The local bank had turned the matter over to a collection agency. Luke jammed the notice into his pocket with the rest of the mail.

"I can't hire you," he snapped at the woman on the porch. "I don't have the money."

"I'll work for minimum wage." She started after him as he headed for the foyer. "I'll work for less than minimum wage. You're my last hope. If I don't get a job in this town, I'm sunk."

"Yeah, well, I'm already sunk," he said, swinging around.

"Then let me drown with you."

Luke looked into the woman's pleading eyes, aware of a softness and a sorrow he'd never seen there before. The hard edge was gone. Desperation tore through her, a despair he recognized all too well.

"Why?" he asked. "Why me?"

She twisted her hands together as she had when she'd been carrying the brown paper bag. "Because I think . . . I think God sent me to you."

"God?" He leaned a shoulder against the door frame that led into the front parlor. With a laugh, he shook his head. "I think you got that part wrong, Jo Callaway. If God was going to send you help, he'd have sent you to somebody besides me."

"Maybe he was sending *you* help."

"I don't need your help. I told you that already."

"Yes, you do." She jerked the bills from his back jeans pocket. "How are you going to get these paid off if you don't have somebody who can hang wallpaper? You think the owner of this building will pay you for a lousy paint job? The sooner you get this project finished, the sooner you'll get paid. Without my help, you and those two employees of yours will be rambling around in this mansion till the cows come home."

"I can't pay you." He grabbed the bills. "I can't pay for your labor."

"I've got a place to stay. Just give me enough money to buy food."

"I'm not even sure I can afford that."

"Then I'll eat with you and Little-bit."

"Eat with me and Montgomery?"

"You got any better ideas, buster?" She brushed past him and surveyed the parlor. "Now, where's that wallpaper? I need to know what I'm up against."

"Ride with me!" Ruby McCann rolled down the window of her big DeSoto and waved at Darcy. "I'm just going over to the Corner Market to pick up my morning milk, and then I'll drop you at the mansion. You won't be late!"

Contemplating the layout of the town and the distance from Ruby's driveway to the market, Darcy knew she would indeed be late for her first day of work. Not that anyone was really expecting her to show up. Following their conversation the previous afternoon, Luke Easton had wandered off to help the children with their snack. When he didn't return, Darcy went and found Floyd in the study. The old man gave her a toothless smile. "I don't have no idee if you got the job," he told her. "With the boss, you just never do know. He ain't much of a people person, not since his wife died. You got to kindy guess what he's a'thinkin'."

Darcy never had been good at guessing people's thoughts. But she knew her own. She was going to paint and wallpaper that mansion until somebody threw her out. And when the job was done, she'd claim her part of the pay.

"All right, I'll go with you," she told Ruby, and she climbed into the huge old car. "Look, Mrs. McCann, if I take your groceries back to the house for you, would that be worth a dollar or two?"

The librarian gunned the engine, and the DeSoto lurched down the driveway. "I always keep my milk at the library until I'm ready to go home for the day. I have a small refrigerator in the workroom. But thank you for offering. I assume you have no money."

"To put it bluntly."

"I am always blunt." Ruby pulled to a stop halfway into the intersection of Main and River Streets and craned to look both ways for oncoming traffic. "It never pays to be coy, my dear."

Darcy caught her breath as the DeSoto shot forward again, narrowly missing a gray sports car. Ruby gave its gasping driver her little wave. "That's John Sawyer," she told Darcy. "He's our local attorney. Sawyer-the-lawyer, people call him. I find that a bit demeaning, don't you? Oh, there's our dear mayor opening the Redee-Quick. Cleo Mueller is a fine pharmacist, but I don't know what we'll do when he decides to retire from public office."

This time Ruby's little wave inadvertently turned the steering wheel to the right. The DeSoto's front tire rolled up onto the curb and back down to the street. Ruby drove on unaware.

"I have always found it disconcerting," she said, "to consider the things that we suppose give us freedom. You, for example, are in need of money. Without it, you feel you cannot be a truly liberated woman."

"I just don't want to go hungry."

"This car gives me the same false sense of freedom." Ruby pulled to a stop less than an inch from a parking meter that stood in front of the market. "Money, cars, jobs—all these things really have nothing to do with freedom. Do you know, I once based my sense of liberty on my spouse? Oh, yes, I was convinced that Mr. McCann and I, in our happy marriage and loving home, were truly the freest of people. When he died, I felt that I was suddenly bound in chains from which I could never escape—chains of loneliness, despair, hopelessness. I was a prisoner to my unhappiness. And yet, how wrong, wrong, wrong I was to believe that skim is as flavorful as whole milk. Oh, it might be healthier in terms of fat, but the taste is appalling."

Ruby frowned for a moment before unlatching her door and stepping out onto the sidewalk. Darcy stared as the determined woman gave the grocer her little wave and entered the store. What was the deal with Ruby McCann? It had been six years since Darcy had been forced to think very far outside herself and her own survival. Just getting through each day had required concentration and stamina. Now that she was starting over, she had expected her focus to remain narrow. After all, she didn't want to know anyone here in Ambleside, and she sure didn't want them to know her. She just wanted to get by.

All the same, Darcy felt an unexpected concern for the woman who had become her fairy godmother. Climbing from the car, she nodded to the elderly grocer and followed Ruby into the store. As her eyes adjusted to the dim light, Darcy scanned the empty aisles until she located the woman standing alone in front of a display of bananas.

"Mrs. McCann?" She realized right away that Ruby was sobbing, hands cupping her face and shoulders heaving. Alarm shot through Darcy. "Mrs. McCann, is something the matter?"

"Oh, dear. Oh, dear."

Darcy tentatively reached out and laid her hand on the librarian's soft arm. Instantly, Ruby rested her cheek on the younger woman's shoulder. "I'm lost," Ruby whispered between sobs, "quite, quite lost."

"It's okay," Darcy said, holding her close. "I'm here."

"I'm so frightened. Terribly frightened."

"There's nothing to be afraid of. This is just the grocery store."

"But I can't . . . I can't remember why I came in. What am I doing here? And what are those things?"

"They're bananas," Darcy said gently, "but you came for milk. Whole milk, because it tastes better than skim."

"Oh, yes." The white head nodded. "Whole milk. Thank you, my dear. Bless you."

"I got your milk up here at the counter already, Mrs. McCann," the grocer called from the front of the store. "What you doing back there by the bananas, eh? You can't change your habits on me now, not after all these years. You never buy your fruit until after work, remember?"

Ruby looked up at Darcy, a smile forming on her trembling lips. As the older woman started for the counter, Darcy caught her arm to stop her. Using her fingertips, Darcy brushed away the tears that streaked Ruby's weathered cheeks.

"Milk," Darcy reminded her softly.

"And fruit after work."

As she left the store, Darcy focused on the mansion down the street. If freedom didn't come from having money or a solid job or a good marriage, where did it come from? She

had been counting on this town and her work here to set
her free from the debts and fears that bound her to the past.

Slowly crossing the street, she wondered how Ruby
would have finished her little sermon on freedom. Was it
ritual and routine that set a person free? Buying milk every
morning, or sweeping the sidewalk three times a day, the
way the clothing store owner did? Or was it having people
you could rely on, like the kindly grocer or a young
stranger in town who could help you remember your
purpose?

Or did possessing health truly set you free? Physical
health. Mental health. The ability to recall who you were
and what you intended to do with your life.

Darcy passed the antiques shop and started up the sidewalk that led to Chalmers House. This wasn't the first time
she wished she could sit down for a heart-to-heart talk with
her Bible study leader. Surely the women in the worship
group would know the definition of true freedom. Why had
Darcy waited so many years before setting foot in the small
chapel that had become her sanctuary?

There was still so much to learn, so many unanswered
questions.

"You came!" Floyd stuck his head out of an upper-story
window and waved a pair of pliers at Darcy. "We didn't
think you was a'comin', missy. You're late, don't y'know,
and the boss don't like his workers showin' up late."

"Luke is expecting me?"

"He's a'countin' on you, missy. He's a lousy painter. And
that wallpaper didn't come with no glue on it. Sure the boss
is expectin' you." He gave her a grin. "He needs you."

FOUR

"You just can't beat these Chee-tos," Floyd said, giving his orange-stained fingers a lick. "They're made with real cheese, y'know."

Darcy sat on the floor in a corner of the cavernous kitchen and silently thanked God for the peanut butter and jelly sandwich, apple, and pile of Chee-tos in her lap. She'd come to work on an empty stomach, with no hope for lunch. But right at noon, everyone working in the mansion headed for the kitchen and began to assemble their meal from the ingredients spread across the counter. She had to assume that Luke Easton was the provider.

"Chee-tos come in little balls or puffs," Floyd continued, "but myself, I prefer these here fried ones. They've got just the right crunch, y'know? Why, I recall the first time I ever et Chee-tos. Mamie packed me some in my lunch when I was a'workin' down to the dock. That was in the days when Ambleside had us a good bit of river traffic, and I was a'wirin' up some signals for the boats. Anyways, I opened up that lunch box and seen them Chee-tos, and you coulda knocked me over with a feather."

"Is that so?" Gabe asked. He was well into his second sandwich. Darcy had noticed, wondering if she dared to eat another one herself. "You know something, Floyd? You're always making a big deal out of nothing. Chee-tos. Good grief."

"Well, if you're used to potato chips and you come acrosst Chee-tos for the first time, it's a mighty big deal."

"That's sad, is what it is." Gabe gave a snort. "Pitiful."

"Gabe." Luke gave the younger man a scowl. "Shut up."

Darcy shifted in her corner. She was accustomed to rough talk and hostility. In fact, she had gotten to where she hardly noticed it. Certainly she never got involved.

But just as her concerns about Ruby McCann had nagged at Darcy all morning, now she felt an unexpected tug of sympathy for Floyd. She couldn't imagine why Gabe was belittling him over the Chee-tos.

Luke eyed her across the room. "Did you get that wallpaper sorted out?" he asked, his first words to her all morning. "The rolls are coded. Elizabeth Chalmers picked it out, and there are certain patterns for certain rooms."

"I've got it labeled. Where do you want me to start?"

"I think Floyd's nearly finished wiring the study. But you'll have to paint the woodwork first."

"Paint the wood in the study," Gabe muttered. "Strip the wood in the bathroom. How come that crazy Chalmers lady can't make up her mind?"

"Elizabeth Chalmers is not crazy," Floyd said. "She's one smart gal, if you ask me."

"Nobody asked you," Gabe retorted.

"Hey, Gabe." Luke gave the boy's shoulder a shove. "Lay off Floyd. What's your problem?"

"I don't have a problem. You got a problem?"

Darcy could feel the tension building in the room. *Time to exit,* she thought. She wanted no part of the relationships among these men. Getting to her feet, she gave a last glance at the open bread bag and the peanut butter jar. So much for a second sandwich.

"The only problem I got," Gabe was saying, "is you guys. Floyd's been trying to wire that chandelier for nearly a week. And you can't figure out where the termites got in. And now we've got *her.*" He stuck his chin at Darcy. "A woman trying to work construction."

"She's gonna hang wallpaper," Floyd said. "That ain't construction."

"I may put her to stripping woodwork in the bathroom," Luke said. "You'd better adjust your attitude, Gabe, or I'll adjust your backside right out the front door."

Darcy leaned against the wall, assessing the situation. She felt like she'd stepped onto another planet. What was the deal here? What would make a young man so angry that he would shoot off his mouth to the point of getting fired?

"You can't tell me how to live my life!" Gabe snarled. "What do *you* know anyhow? You hide in your little house like some kind of monk. Well, that ain't me. I'm a free man, you know? I'm stepping out. Gonna do *my* thing."

"Free, huh?" Darcy spoke up. "Did your girlfriend break up with you, Gabe?"

The young man swung around, his eyes wide. "What'd you say?"

Darcy shrugged. "Just wondering."

"As a matter of fact, I broke up with her. And you want to know why? Because she's just like the rest of you people around here. Do this, do that. Well, I don't have to do anything I don't want. I'm my own man."

He was on his feet now, his face flushed with anger. Darcy had seen such anguish before, such desperation. Gabe unbuckled his tool belt and tossed it onto a counter.

"I don't even have to work at this stupid job if I don't want to," he spat. "I quit."

"Gabe, what are you doing?" Luke asked. "You can't quit."

"Oh yeah? I just did."

The young man strode through the kitchen and out the back door. The screen slammed shut behind him. Darcy winced at the sound.

Luke was shaking his head. "He'll be back," he said.

"Yep, I reckon so." Floyd crunched on a Chee-to for a

moment. "Bein' old ain't so hot, you know. I lost most of
my teeth, and my hair's all gone, and I got to head for the
bathroom near about ever' ten minutes. But I wouldn't want
to be young again, no sir. I wouldn't trade my seventy-two
years for Gabe's twenty. Not for nothin' in this ol' world.
And that's a fact."

Darcy smiled. Despite her intention to stay aloof and distant from the people in town, she couldn't deny that Floyd
had already earned a tender spot in her heart. If she had
the money, she'd keep him in Chee-tos for the rest of his
life.

"Well," Floyd said, grunting as he stood, "I reckon it's
about time to test that chandelier. If I got them wires right,
we're gonna have us one shimmerin' light fixture. I never
saw so much crystal in all my life. How 'bout you, Miss
Callaway?"

"You can call me Jo." She shook her head. "I don't
believe I've ever seen such a piece."

"Then you haven't looked in the dining room," Luke said.
"That one has about twice as many lights."

"Don't tell me that, boss. I might get plumb discouraged."
Floyd whistled as he ambled toward the study.

Darcy glanced at Luke to find him grinning. "How much
you want to bet it won't work? He's thought he had it three
times already."

"I think he's done it this time," Darcy said. "You can buy
my dinner if I'm right."

"And you can cook mine if *I'm* right."

Unable to squelch the bubble of pleasure that rose inside
her chest, Darcy turned quickly to the kitchen sink. "I'd
better make sure these paintbrushes are clean," she said. "I
guess I'll be using that hunter green on the wainscoting."

"The paint cans are out in the truck," Luke told her as he
headed back to work.

Darcy glanced over her shoulder at him, only to find

Luke casting a quick backward look at the same moment. Their eyes met for an instant; then he pulled away and stepped out of the kitchen. Shaken, Darcy dipped her head and grabbed a handful of wet brushes. Oh, why had she ever run into such a man in the first place?

Luke was handsome and hardworking, a loving father and a lonely widower. But he was completely out of bounds! Darcy had lied to him about her name and her past—and she knew she could never let him know the truth. If he knew her secret, he wouldn't want her working for him, spending time with his precious daughter. He certainly wouldn't entertain any romantic thoughts about her.

Darcy scrubbed the brushes with warm water and soap, rinsing out every vestige of the ivory paint embedded in the bristles. She had come to this town to pay off her debts and hide from her enemies. She would build a new life here, but it must be an isolated, indifferent life. She couldn't care about dear Floyd. She couldn't care for sad little Montgomery. She couldn't worry about confused Ruby McCann. And she couldn't feel anything—anything at all—for Luke Easton.

As she lifted her focus from the sink, Darcy noticed a movement outside the window just beyond a large lilac bush in the yard. It was Gabe Zimmerman. He was hunched down in the grass, and if she wasn't mistaken, the young man was sobbing his eyes out.

Oh, Lord! Darcy lifted up. *I'm trying not to get involved with these people. But Gabe's hurting, and I feel so bad for him. Should I go out there, Father?*

She studied the dripping brushes in her hand. She would need to shake them dry, of course. So she would have to go outside. And . . .

Before she could change her mind, Darcy headed out the back door and down the porch steps. She crossed the yard toward the lilac bush and began snapping the brushes one at a time to flick off the remaining water. Her heart pounding, she tilted her head slightly in the direction of the young man.

"I'm with you on the painting," she said. "I think it ought to all be stripped or all be painted. Personally, I prefer bare wood."

Gabe said nothing.

Darcy continued to shake the brushes. "If you paint a bathroom, you've got to do it the right way." She smoothed the bristles into a neat point. "All that steam can peel the paint right off the wood."

"It's cracked up like an alligator's skin," Gabe said.

"Easier to scrape off that way, I guess."

"Needs stripper, too, though."

"Ever tried paint thinner? That can do the job about as well as anything." She looked across at Gabe. His eyes were red. "I took the varnish off an old fireplace mantel one time. It was rough—all kinds of curlicues and shelves and little doodads. That paint thinner dissolved the black varnish and took the mantel right down to the wood. Golden oak. Turned out beautiful."

"If you're so good at stripping paint and hanging wallpaper and all that, how come you came to this Podunk town looking for a job?"

The belligerence was back in his voice. Darcy stacked the brushes together. "If you're so upset about losing your girlfriend, why'd you break up with her in the first place?"

"I told you. She bosses me around."

"You don't strike me as the type to get bossed around, Gabe."

He hung his head. "She wants me to marry her."

"How far along is she?"

He lifted his head, surprise written in his eyes. Then he let out a long breath. "Maybe a couple of months."

"How old is she?" Darcy kept her voice even. "Finished high school yet?"

"Sixteen." He gave a harsh laugh. "I'm twenty. I could get sent to prison for statutory rape."

"Been in trouble before?"

"Small things. Stealing gumballs. Vandalism."

"Vandalism? Whoa." She knelt down on the grass beside him.

"I spray-painted her name on the fountain in the park."

Darcy shook her head. "Bad idea."

"The cops knew it was me right away."

"You won't go to prison for getting your girlfriend pregnant. But you'll have to pay child support."

"I wish she'd just get an abortion and be done with it."

"Really?" Darcy could feel the wet paintbrushes soaking the knee of her jeans. "I think God created life, and I don't believe he's given us the right to destroy it. How about adoption?"

"Forget it. She wants to keep the baby. She's all goo-goo about it. Wait till her parents find out. They'll disown her."

"Maybe not."

"They'll probably want us to get married too. Man, that's all she can think about. She's sixteen, and she's reading bride magazines and dreaming of a big wedding and a white dress. Well, guess what? I'm not getting married. No way."

"Married or not, if she has that baby, you're going to be responsible for it."

"I know. Why'd she have to go and get pregnant anyhow?"

"I suspect you know why she got pregnant."

"Stupid, stupid, stupid." He tore a leaf off the lilac bush and shredded it into tiny bits.

Darcy reached out and laid her hand on his arm. "Gabe, you've got yourself in a tight spot. The worst thing you can do right now is give up your job. No matter what happens, you're going to need money. Why don't you come back in the house, and we'll give that thinner a try? I bet the paint just rolls right off those bathroom walls."

He sat for a moment, staring at a spot of lawn between his feet. Then he slowly got to his feet and started back toward the mansion. Darcy followed, grabbing a can of paint and another of thinner from the back of Luke's pickup. By the time she got through the door, she could hear Gabe climbing the steps. She carried the paint thinner up to the little bathroom where he'd been working and set it just outside the door.

Darcy had never believed she was the only person in the world with troubles. As she headed back down to the study, she recalled the mixed-up, crazy family she'd grown up in. Her father was a fall-down drunk from Friday night to Sunday afternoon every single weekend of her life. Her mother, soft and loving, kept everything inside until she had ulcers eating through her stomach. Their house and yard reeked of hog waste from the pens nearby. None of Darcy's three brothers and two sisters ever had any friends outside the family. They were all poor and underfed, and the pig smell just wouldn't wash off. Both of Darcy's sisters got pregnant by the same man, who refused to marry either of them. By the time Darcy ran off to get married, there were three toddlers running around the house, and two of her brothers had dropped out of school to join their father in his alcoholic pastimes. Only one brother was stable, and while he had offered Darcy a place to stay, she knew that being anywhere near her family would make it that much easier for the Damyons to find her.

She knew a thing or two about troubles, Darcy thought as she began wiping the woodwork clean. And she knew about consequences. What she hadn't learned about until recently was love. God's love.

"All right," Floyd announced, breaking into her memories, "I'm gonna give this ol' chandelier another try. We're gonna trip the lights fantastic. You ready, Miss Jo?"

"I'm ready, Mr. Floyd." She straightened from her dusting as he walked across the room to the wall switch.

"Here she goes."

He flipped the switch. Fifty tiny lightbulbs flickered to life. The crystal teardrops twinkled. And then smoke began to drift out of the top of the fixture. A tiny line of sparks ran across the ceiling, knocking chips of plaster to the floor. The bulbs started bursting like popcorn.

"Jumpin' jeepers!" Floyd cried out.

"Turn it off!" Darcy started across the room. "Hit the switch, Floyd! It's going to catch fire!"

She had almost reached him when the floor beneath her feet gave way. Wood planks splintered and cracked as Darcy slid straight down into a black hole. In the moments of disbelief, Alice in Wonderland, with her golden hair, blue headband, and floating skirt, flashed through Darcy's mind as she fell endlessly down and down she landed feetfirst in the basement of the old house. Her heels and ankles jolted with the shock as she crumpled to her knees in pain. Overhead, she could hear shouting, cries of alarm.

"I'm down here!" she called. "In the basement!" When no one came to her aid, she realized the focus upstairs was on a small fire that had indeed broken out.

"Somebody get a bucket of water!" Floyd was hollering.

"Grab the extinguisher!" Luke yelled. "Jo, it's in the kitchen. By the counter!"

"Hey, I'm in the basement!"

"What's going on in here?" It was Gabe. "You caught the place on fire, Floyd, you old coot!"

"I'm going for the extinguisher," she heard Luke say. It sounded like he was leaving the room.

"Yoo-hoo! I'm in the basement. Anybody up there?"

"I knew you couldn't wire that chandelier." Gabe's voice again.

"You try it sometime, boy. It ain't no piece of cake, and that's a fact."

"Stand back!" Luke was back, and she assumed he had the fire extinguisher now.

From her position on a pile of broken boards, Darcy soon heard the hiss of foam. She touched her ankles, wondering if she'd broken both of them. That would be great, wouldn't it? Her first—and last—day on the job. Her knees didn't feel so wonderful either, come to think of it. Fortunately, she had landed on a bunch of blankets or something. In the darkness, it was hard to tell.

"Fire's out," Luke announced overhead. "Floyd, get that chandelier down from there. I'm taking both of them over to Bud's Hardware this afternoon."

"He's going to get a professional to do the job right," Gabe added.

Floyd snorted. "Listen here, kid, I'm a boney-fide electrician. I wired railroad ____ for thirty years, and I can just about do it blind. But I never laid no claim to chandeliers. What're you doin' here anyhow, Gabe? I thought you quit."

"Hey!" Darcy shouted. "I could use some help down here."

There was a moment of surprised silence before the sound of running feet echoed across the study floor. Three heads appeared in the jagged circle of light over Darcy's head.

She attempted a smile. "I found where the termites got in."

"Well, if that don't beat a pig a-pecking," Floyd said. "You went plumb through the floor, Miss Jo."

"Duh," Gabe said. "I think she's got that figured out, Floyd."

Darcy was about to say something when the basement

lights came on, and Luke ran to her side. He knelt on the floor and pushed away the splintered planks. "Are you hurt?" he demanded. "Anything broken?"

"I don't think so." In the light, she saw she'd landed on an old mattress, mildewed and damp, but it had cushioned her fall. "How's the fire?"

"Out." Luke glanced up at the hole and the two faces peering down. "Move away from those rotten boards, you goobers. And get back to work, how about it?"

Darcy lifted one leg and moved her foot back and forth, testing the ankle. "Hurts. I'm thanking God for this old mattress, bad as it smells. I hit both knees, too."

She rubbed them as she tested her other ankle.

"I'll take you over to the clinic," Luke said. "You probably ought to have X rays."

"No, it's okay—"

"Look, I've got insurance. You need—"

"I don't want to talk to a doctor."

"In spite of all those bills you saw, I'm not broke. I take care of my employees."

"Luke." She put her hand on his arm. How could she make him understand her reluctance had nothing to do with his financial status? She didn't dare set foot in a doctor's office. She had no identification as Jo Callaway.

"I'm not going to a clinic, Luke," she said. "I'm all right."

"You fell a good twelve feet straight down."

"Just help me stand, that's all. If I'm going to cook supper for you and Montgomery, I'll need to be on my feet." She gave him a wink and held out her hands.

He stared at her. "No cooking for you."

"You can't deny that fire, buster. I lost the bet. You and Little-bit are having fried chicken, hot biscuits, and my blue-ribbon baked beans tonight for dinner—whether you want to or not."

Luke let out a breath, bent down, and slipped his arm around her waist. "You're driving me crazy, you know that?"

"I got Gabe back to work for you, didn't I?" She grimaced as she got to her feet. Her legs were smarting, but she wasn't about to let Luke know how bad they hurt.

"My juvenile delinquent came back just in time to help put out Floyd's fire. I ought to can all three of you, abandon this project, and go to work pumping gas for Al Huff."

Darcy chuckled. "We're not that bad, are we? The ceiling needed to be replastered anyway, and now you know where the termites have been working."

They started across the floor, and Darcy tried to make herself focus on her sore legs. It wasn't easy. A long time had passed since she'd been this close to a man, she realized. Years since she'd felt the strength of a male arm around her waist, male fingers woven through hers. It was just the length of time, she told herself, and not Luke Easton himself, that made her feel so powerfully aware, so suddenly lonely and aching. Darcy had promised herself she would never go near a man again. Never trust the tenderness that could grow violent so quickly. Never count on the love that was only a thin line from hatred.

As she hobbled through the cluttered basement toward the steps, Darcy pulled herself away from Luke. She could stand on her own two feet, no matter how tender they felt. She had brought herself through five years of torment. Then this past year, she had found God—true freedom, true hope, true love.

She reached for the metal handrail. God was all she needed, and he hadn't brought her to Ambleside to get all weak-kneed over Luke Easton or anyone else. "I've got it now," she said, putting her full weight on her feet as she started up the steps.

But Luke kept his arm around her all the same. He said nothing, and she could hear him beside her, smell that vague scent of masculine soap and shampoo, feel the pressure of his fingers against her waist. It was dark in the stairwell, and all she could do was just pray, pray, pray. *God, you know what a sinner I am. I don't deserve your love. I don't deserve any special consideration. But please, help me not to mess up. Just help me not to want the human things I can't have. Things I shouldn't even be thinking about.*

"Thanks," she managed, as they got to the top of the steps and moved out into the kitchen. She pulled away from him just as Gabe and Floyd came crashing through the back door.

"Got that study chandelier in the truck, boss," Floyd said, letting the screen slam behind him. His focus darted from Luke to Darcy. Then a slow smile crept across his lips. "Hey, you two—"

"How about the one in the dining room?" Luke cut in. "It's not going to come down from the ceiling all by itself, you know."

"Not unless Floyd tries to wire it," Gabe said.

Laughing, he and the older man headed for the dining room. Darcy forced her aching ankles in the direction of the study. She had painting to do, and she certainly wasn't going to make the mistake of looking back over her shoulder at Luke Easton. Not this time.

FIVE

At first, Luke hoped Jo wouldn't come. Then, he decided to hope that if she did show up, she would be wearing those ratty old jeans. And the mildewed T-shirt. And the clompy work boots.

Then the doorbell rang.

Montgomery and Nick raced to let Jo inside. Luke could hear them giggling with delight at having company for dinner.

That's when she walked into the kitchen. "Hey," she said. "Here I am."

He turned from the table where he'd been wiping up a week's worth of crumbs, and there she stood in a pale blue sleeveless dress with tiny bows on the shoulders, a pair of pretty sandals, and her hair piled up on her head like a golden crown. His mouth went dry, and for a second, Luke thought he wasn't going to be able to utter a word.

"Got any chicken?" she said, coming toward him. "And I'll need an apron."

"Uh," he managed, as Montgomery skipped across the room and grabbed Ellie's old white apron.

"You can wear this," she said.

No, Luke wanted to protest. *Not that one. That's Ellie's. That's my wife's apron. Nobody touches her things.* But Jo Callaway was already slipping it over her head, and Montgomery began tying the sash into a bow.

"We bought a chicken from the Corner Market," Nick announced, throwing open the refrigerator. "It's a dead one.

Mr. Easton said he didn't think you would come, but we bought the chicken anyway. This is the kind without the feathers."

Jo laughed and took the packet of meat from the little boy. "That's my favorite kind."

"You don't eat the feathers or the feet," Nick said. "My mommy told me that. I miss her. She and my new daddy went to Wowie."

"Maui," Montgomery corrected. "It's part of Hawaii."

Luke stared as if a trio of fairies had just flown into his kitchen. Jo opened the canister of flour, poured some into a bowl, and began adding spices to it from the rack beside the cabinet. Ellie had bought that rack. She never put spices into the flour.

"Hawaii is a group of islands," Jo explained. "But it's a state, too. I'm going to visit there someday."

"Are you going to go on a honeymoon too?" Nick asked.

"Nope. I'm not."

"Don't you want to get married? You could have children. You could get them from Romania."

"Not everybody gets their children from Romania," Montgomery said. "I didn't come from an orphanage. I came right out of my mommy."

"Out of her?" Nick stared at Montgomery.

Luke decided it was time to speak up. "We keep the frying pans on the—"

"Got it." Jo lifted Ellie's favorite skillet from the overhead rack. "Oil. Better heat that up. And I'll need beans. I hope you've got some honey."

"For the honeymoon?" Nick asked.

"For the beans," Montgomery said. "It's Jo's secret recipe. She won the blue ribbon at the county fair."

"And my brother's hog went for the highest dollar at the auction. The bank bought it." Jo began dredging chicken in the spicy flour.

Luke returned to wiping crumbs off the table. It had been more than a year since Ellie's death, and no one but he, Montgomery, and Nick had set foot in the kitchen in all that time. Now this stranger was wearing Ellie's apron and using Ellie's spices and skillets and jabbering away about hogs. In spite of himself, Luke admitted that the presence of a woman in the kitchen—*this* woman—threatened to fill an emptiness inside him. An emptiness he was beginning to realize needed to be filled.

"We were a 4-H family," Jo was saying. "The county extension agent came over one day and signed us up. My daddy gave my little brother a hog to raise, and I went to work baking and cross-stitching. We were the only two of us kids that ever went to the 4-H meetings."

"What's 4-H?" Nick asked.

"It's a kind of club. Helps you learn practical things."

"One time in our Sunday school play, I was the practical son."

"Prodigal son," Montgomery corrected. "The school says Nick has a language disorder, but I think it comes from starting out in Romania. That's why he calls me Magunnery."

"What do I call you?" Nick asked.

"Magunnery. You've always called me that."

Luke watched his daughter kneading the biscuit dough Jo had mixed up in one of Ellie's crockery bowls. Flour dusted the front of the child's polka-dot T-shirt, and she was grinning from pigtail to pigtail. Luke couldn't remember the last time he'd seen his daughter so happy.

Well, there hadn't been a whole lot to giggle about since Ellie's death. Luke spent his days working hard to pay off the mountain of medical bills and his nights staring at the TV. The whole house seemed heavy and quiet. Empty.

Much of the time until the Chalmers wedding, Montgomery had stayed at the apartment where Nick and his mom lived. Now that Zachary and Elizabeth were away, the two children played out in the Easton yard until bedtime. Luke couldn't blame them for wanting to escape his house. He hadn't even done much cleaning until this afternoon, when the prospect of company had propelled him to the broom closet. Again, he wondered why he felt the need to make a good impression on this woman.

As Jo placed the chicken into the crackling-hot oil, a rich aroma filled the little kitchen. Luke settled into a chair and watched as she showed the children how to stir honey into a saucepan of beans, add ketchup and brown sugar, and then throw in a dollop of mustard. Montgomery stirred the beans on the stove while Nick helped Jo cut out round biscuits with a jar lid. Luke thought about telling her that Ellie had a drawer full of cookie cutters, but he decided he'd just wait and see what else this woman had up her sleeve.

Though he didn't want to trust her and the memory of her strange phone call continued to bother him, Luke couldn't deny the appeal of the optimistic determination with which Jo embraced life. When something didn't work out quite the way she'd planned, she tried a different avenue. A town without a hotel led her to Ruby McCann's guesthouse. A futile day of job hunting pushed her right into the Chalmers Mansion. Jar lids became cookie cutters, a pair of forks took the place of tongs, tea towels turned into place mats. What drove this woman? And what secret was she hiding?

"Done!" she announced, ripping a length of paper towels from the roll to absorb the oil. Her triumphant smile sent an unfamiliar tingle through him. "Hold the plate, Little-bit. Both hands now—this chicken is heavy. Would you look at the size of that leg? Nick, I think it has your name on it."

"It does?" The boy craned to see as Jo loaded the plate with fried chicken. "I don't see my name at all."

"You don't? Well, I can just about hear that thigh calling to me."

"Really?"

"Those are just expressions, Nick," Montgomery explained. "They're words people use, but expressions don't really mean what they say."

"Set that on the table, Little-bit," Jo said, "and we'll take these biscuits out of the oven. Nick, can you find the butter in the refrigerator?"

"I can get it. I know where it is. It's in the glass box with the lid."

"Here's a bowl for the beans," Montgomery said. "Oh, Miss Callaway, this is going to be the best dinner I ever ate."

At that, Luke stiffened. Had Montgomery already forgotten her mother's wonderful cooking? The chocolate pies and the cheeseburgers she had loved so much? A pain wrenched through him at the thought that Ellie was fading from her daughter's memory already. He didn't like that, didn't want it, and yet he knew in many ways it was best for the child. He had mourned so much, and for so long, that he wondered if he would ever heal from the loss of his wife. He didn't want Montgomery to live with that kind of pain. But he didn't want her to forget Ellie either.

"Your mother was a great cook," he spoke up. "She used to make us chocolate pie, remember?"

Montgomery turned and stared at him for an instant, her eyes wide. "Chocolate pie," she said.

"I don't like the kind of pie with the white stuff on top," Nick declared. "It doesn't taste good. It tastes like clouds."

"How do you know what clouds taste like?" And Montgomery was lost to him again, racing to set the table and chatter with her little friend. "Clouds taste like water, because they're made out of moisture," she said wisely.

"Clouds don't taste like anything," Nick objected. "The airplanes can fly straight through them. Even birds."

"Sit down, everybody," Jo said as she placed the platter of chicken on the table. "Let's eat."

"We ought to pray first." Montgomery held out her hands. "When my mommy was alive, we always prayed at the table."

"That's a new one on me." Jo said, looking startled. Her focus darted to Luke, as though expecting him to explain the practice.

"Montgomery, you want to pray?" he asked. He took Jo's hand in his and reached for his daughter's small fingers. "Why don't you say grace?"

"You pray, Daddy," she said. "Please?"

Luke studied his plate, wondering if he could bring himself to speak words he no longer could believe. How long had it been since he'd lifted up a blessing? How long since he'd even tried to pray? Anger had choked away his faith. Now he would have to lie in front of his daughter.

"Dear God," he began. *Why did you take my wife? Why did you let Montgomery's mother die? Why . . . ?*

He cleared his throat and tried again. "Dear God, thank you for this meal. Bless it to the nourishment of our bodies. Lead, guide, and direct us. Amen."

When Luke finished, he reached for the chicken and hoped someone would start the chatter again. There was a moment of silence as the plates and bowls were passed around the table.

Then Nick piped up. "I think *lead, guide,* and *direct* mean the same thing," he said. "In my class at school, we call them cinnamons."

"Synonyms," Montgomery corrected.

"That's right. Why do the deacons in church always ask God to lead, guide, and direct us, Mr. Easton? My teacher told me if you say the same thing three times, people will

get bored. They will want to change the topic. So why do
we say *lead, guide, and direct?"*

"I never heard it before," Jo said.

"You didn't?" Montgomery asked. "What church did you
go to before you moved to Ambleside?"

"Just a church." Her cheeks flushed. "A chapel really. But
I've only been a Christian about a year. Maybe they said
lead, guide, and direct, and I just wasn't paying attention."

"It doesn't matter," Luke said. "It's just an expression."

"You didn't mean what you said in your prayer, Mr.
Easton?" Nick asked. "Magunnery told me expressions don't
really mean what they say, like 'the chicken leg has your
name on it.' So, you don't really want God to lead, guide,
and direct you?"

"Nick," Luke said, "eat your dinner."

The group around the table fell silent at that. Luke wondered if he'd been too harsh. But what could he tell the
child? *No, I don't believe God will lead me. I don't want him
to lead me. I don't intend to follow a God who allows brain
tumors to grow in the head of an innocent, loving mother.
I don't want his guidance, I don't want his direction, and
I don't want anything to do with him.*

"Everything is delicious," Nick pronounced. "Especially
the beans."

With that, conversation resumed with the children insist-
ing that Jo describe in detail her fall through the mansion
floor. Finally, Luke gave a satisfied sigh and pushed his
plate away.

"How about if you kids go water the plants on the porch
over at Finders Keepers?" he asked as Jo stood and began
to clear away the dishes. "You can hook that hose up to the
faucet on the wall. And try not to get water on the
windows."

Rising, he helped Jo load the plates and glasses into the
dishwasher. The youngsters bounded out the door, eager to

play in the water for a few minutes. He knew they'd come
back soaking wet, but it would give them something to do
until bedtime. Jo had started to fill the sink with suds to
wash the frying pan, but Luke reached over and turned off
the faucet.

"I can take care of that later," he said. "Thanks for dinner.
It was good."

"Did you like the beans?" She crossed her arms and
looked across at him. "Or did we put in too much mustard?"

"The beans were fine."

"Fine?"

"They were tasty." He nodded. "So, do you want me to
drive you home, or can you walk?"

"I can walk." She shrugged and started for the door.

Luke watched her go, and he fought himself to keep from
calling her back. Maybe she would want to take a stroll
around the town square with him. Or help the kids water
the plants. Or sit and watch a TV show.

She was so pretty in that blue dress. And he was so
lonely.

No, he couldn't do that. He didn't really know her. And
how would Ellie feel if he allowed himself to spend time
with another woman? She wouldn't feel anything, of course.
Still, just looking at another woman felt like betrayal.

"Oops, I remembered there's something I need to tell
you," Jo said, turning in the doorway. "Mind if I stay a
minute?"

"I guess—"

"Thanks." She sat right down in Ellie's favorite chair. Luke
had left things just as they had always been there, with his
wife's Bible open on the table and her pill bottles lined up
in a row. No one had sat in that chair for a year, as though
it were somehow on reserve, expecting Ellie to come back,
waiting for her to take her place in their family again.

"Or I could drive you home," he tried, wanting Jo to get out of the chair. "Or we could take a walk."

"It's Mrs. McCann." Jo crossed her legs and picked up Ellie's highlighter pen. She took the cap off and studied the yellow nib. "I'm worried about her."

"Oh?" Luke sat in his own chair across the living room. "Is she sick?"

"I'm not sure." She picked up Ellie's Bible and began thumbing through the thin pages. "She's kind of forgetful, you know. It seems like she's talking about one thing, and then right in the middle of it, she starts in on something else. In the Corner Market, she walked over to the bananas and started crying."

"Why?"

"She told me she couldn't remember what they were called. So I told her, and she said she feels so lost sometimes. I'm wondering if she might be having trouble with her mind." She set the opened Bible down in her lap. "Your wife really loved this book, didn't she? She marked all through it. It must have helped her when she was sick."

"No," he said. "It didn't help at all."

"Not you, maybe, but it helped her. See how she copied down these verses in the back so she could find them easier? *'God is our refuge and strength, always ready to help in times of trouble.'* A person wouldn't write that if she didn't believe it."

"You shouldn't be looking in there. It's private."

"It's God's Word. It's not private."

"Look, would you put the Bible back on the table? And I don't know what you want me to do about Mrs. McCann. She's getting old. She's probably a little forgetful."

"She didn't remember bananas." Jo set the Bible down and stood. *"Bananas."*

"What do you think we ought to do?"

"I think she needs to see a doctor. Have some tests."

"There are a lot of good doctors in Jefferson City. You could call and set something up for her."

"She'll need you to drive her to the city."

He sighed, thinking of the huge house on the square and the monumental amount of work it was requiring. "Mrs. McCann drives, you know," he said. "She has a car."

"She nearly drove it through the window of the Corner Market the other day, Luke. Mrs. McCann will not make it all the way to Jefferson City in one piece. She needs your help." Jo got up and walked toward the door again. "Look, I realize your wife died and things have been hard for you and Montgomery. I know about tough times. But you don't curl up in solitary forever. You get out of the hole. You go on. Little-bit needs you. So does Mrs. McCann."

Luke got up and followed her as she opened the door and started across the porch. When she got to the steps, she turned. "I'll make the appointment. And I'll tell Mrs. McCann you'll drive her to the city."

"You're coming, too," he called back. "I'm not doing this on my own."

"Fine then. We'll do it together."

As she headed down the sidewalk, the skirt of her blue dress danced in the breeze that drifted across the town from the Missouri River. Luke watched her go. Then he stepped over to the table and picked up Ellie's Bible.

Darcy smoothed the last length of wallpaper with her brush and began rolling the seam. In half an hour, she and Luke would pick up Mrs. McCann at the library and drive her to Jefferson City.

Though Darcy felt reluctant to be among so many people, she couldn't deny her excitement over the trip. For the first time in six years she'd be in a city. She'd see a shopping mall, a supermarket, tall buildings, subdivisions.

After straightening up her tools, she hurried to the second-floor bathroom and changed into one of Ruby's skirts, a soft blouse, and the sandals she'd borrowed. As she brushed her hair, she lifted up a quick prayer for the older woman's safety and health. In the days since she had made the doctor's appointment, Darcy and Ruby had spent most of their evenings together in the big yard that surrounded the McCann house. They pulled weeds from flower beds and clipped roses for Ruby's bouquets. Then they sat in wicker chairs on the porch and watched the sun go down.

Ruby was confused about the doctor, Darcy reminded herself as she headed down the stairs again to find Luke. It would be important for Darcy to stay close at hand, to help explain things, and to make sure Ruby wasn't frightened by the experience in Jefferson City. Hearing voices in the study, Darcy headed in that direction. But as the first words reached her, she paused outside the door.

"I got to tell you that folks are talkin' about Miss Jo," Floyd was saying. "Nobody knows where she come from, and nobody knows what she's a'doin' here in town."

"She's working for me," Luke said. "That ought to be obvious."

"But how come, is the question. I was over to the Nifty Cafe for breakfast the other day, you know, and I heard everybody talkin'. Pearlene Fox says Miss Jo is a'wearin' Ruby McCann's clothes. She seen Miss Jo at the Corner Market, and lo and behold, she was in this green dress from Liz Craigborn, or some such, and it was the very dress Ruby McCann had boughten at Très Chic this spring. Now, boss, Pearlene Fox knows dresses. You can't argue with that."

"Who's arguing? Jo came to town with nothing but a paper bag under her arm. I'm sure Ruby let her borrow some clothes. What's the big deal?"

"Ruby McCann is known as the biggest skinflint this side

of the Mississippi. Ain't no way she'd go lending out her dresses. Pearlene Fox says—"

"Pearlene Fox is the biggest busybody this side of the Mississippi. And if you keep spreading her gossip, that makes you one, too, Floyd."

"Pearlene thinks Miss Jo might've stole that dress."

"Pearlene ought to zip her lip."

Darcy leaned against the wall, her heart filled with gratitude at Luke's defense. She looked down at her gathered yellow skirt with its pattern of violets and trailing ivy, and she felt her cheeks go hot. The skirt was so pretty, and she had been so grateful to Ruby. Of course, it was embarrassing to wear borrowed clothing. But what choice did she have?

"There's folks that think she's tryin' to get in good with Mrs. McCann," Floyd said. "I told 'em she's just a real nice young lady that come to town a-lookin' for work. But Ez said she hooked up with Ruby right away. He said the two of 'em come into the Nifty one day and bought theirselves a couple of great big dinners. And then what do you know but Miss Jo reached right into Ruby's purse and went to countin' out the money to pay for it."

"Floyd, I don't know why you gossipy old hens can't find anything better to do on a Saturday morning than speculate about Jo Callaway."

"I just thought you ought to know, boss. People's talkin', that's all."

"People in this town always talk."

"Well, you want to know the worst of it?"

"Not really."

"Boompah Jungemeyer said Miss Jo come into the Corner Market one afternoon and she was a'totin' Ruby McCann's purse herself! She marched right in and went to throwin' groceries in the cart like nobody's business. And not just groceries, let me tell you. She bought some . . ."

At the muffled word, Darcy leaned almost into the room. Her heart was beating so hard, she could almost hear it.

"Some what?" Luke asked.

"Some panty hose. There, I done said it. Now, when was the last time you ever seen Ruby McCann a'wearin' panty hose?"

"To tell you the truth, Floyd, I never got around to looking at Ruby McCann's legs."

"Well, me neither, but—"

"But nothing. You and Boompah Jungemeyer and Pearlene Fox had better find something else to do with your time. Jo hasn't done anything wrong where Mrs. McCann is concerned. As a matter of fact, she's the one who made that doctor's appointment for her in Jeff City."

"But that's what I'm tryin' to tell you, boss. People's sayin' that Mrs. McCann was just fine until Miss Jo come to town and started livin' over to the guesthouse. Now the books is all ever-which-aways in the liberry. You can't find your *A*'s from your *Z*'s. Everytime she's out drivin', Ruby's been goin' on the red lights and stoppin' on the green. And she's quit buying her milk of a mornin'. It ain't right, is what folks is sayin'."

"What are you trying to tell me, Floyd?"

"I'm tellin' you that folks think Ruby McCann's gone crazy as a betsy bug. And they's speculatin' it might be Miss Jo's doin'."

Outside the study door, Darcy squeezed her fists tight and tried to make herself breathe. Unable to face the two men, she turned and paced outside onto the porch. As she looked around the town square, she felt as though a hundred eyes were peering at her, accusing her. And she knew she could never defend herself. What could she say to reassure people of her honesty and worth? Everything about her was a lie!

"There you are," Luke said, his voice startling her. "I

thought you were going to come find me. We'd better
hurry. Ruby's probably waiting for us."

He walked past Darcy and headed for his pickup parked
near the curb. Darcy followed, anger and frustration jug-
gling for room inside her chest. How dare these people talk
about her behind her back? She'd done nothing wrong! Oh,
but she had. She'd done everything in her life wrong. Just
one chance to make a fresh start was all she wanted. And
now it looked as though she'd moved to the wrong town,
taken the wrong job, and chosen to live next door to the
wrong woman.

"There she is," Luke said.

Ruby was sweeping redbud blossoms from the library
steps as Darcy left the pickup and hurried to her side.
"Ready to go, Mrs. McCann?" she said.

"Go? But I've only begun sweeping." Ruby's blouse had
been buttoned exactly one button off, so the collar lay
askew on her neck. "It's not five already, is it?"

Darcy touched her arm. "We're going to the doctor,
remember? We have a three-thirty appointment in Jefferson
City."

"The doctor? I don't need to go to a doctor." Her eyes
squinted as she looked Darcy up and down. "What's the
matter? Do you think something's wrong with me?"

"We made you an appointment with a neurologist,
remember? He's going to try to help us figure out why you
couldn't remember bananas."

Ruby swelled to her full height and glared at Darcy.
"Young lady, I remember bananas very well. I have eaten
them all my life due to their high potassium content."

"But you agreed to go to the doctor, Mrs. McCann." Darcy
wished she could shrink into the sidewalk. She felt like
everyone in town must be watching Ruby argue with her.

"I agreed to nothing of the sort! I am sweeping the sidewalk, as I do every day at three o'clock, and I will thank

you to mind your own business from now on." She reached down and grabbed a fistful of the yellow skirt Darcy was wearing. "And what are you doing in my clothes? I bought this skirt at the finest ladies' boutique in Jefferson City three years ago. You have no right to—"

"Mrs. McCann, hey there." Luke appeared on the steps and slipped his arm around the old lady. "You ready to go to the doctor in Jefferson City?"

"That woman is a thief!" Ruby whispered as Luke led her down the library steps. "She's wearing my skirt!"

Darcy hurried to the pickup and was shutting the door behind her when she spotted Pearlene Fox standing on the sidewalk near Dandy Donuts. One eyebrow raised, she stared at Darcy.

"I have to tend the library!" Ruby cried as Luke put the pickup in gear. "I can't take time off to go to the park!"

"To the doctor, Mrs. McCann," Luke said. He glanced across the agitated woman at Darcy. "Ellie got angry, too, toward the end. She didn't mean what she said, though. It was part of the problem in her brain."

Darcy nodded. "Luke, I'm sorry about your wife. The other night when I told you to get over it, that wasn't right of me."

He swallowed before he could speak. "It's okay. I needed to hear it. Sometimes things are just tough, you know."

"I know." Darcy folded her hands over her borrowed skirt and stared out the window. "Things can be very hard."

"You're both a pair of stinking polecats!" Ruby shouted. "That's what you are! I could just beat the bejeebers out of you. Stinking polecats!"

Darcy cast a quick look across at Luke. His mouth twitched. Then he began to chuckle. In a moment, Darcy shook her head and started laughing right along with him. Ruby glanced from one to the other. Then she took each of their free hands in hers and held them tightly.

"Praise the Lord and pass the mustard," she said, settling back into the seat and letting out a huge sigh. "Isn't this a fine day for an outing?"

Six

"I'd like to buy a money order, please." Darcy stood at a teller's window in a large downtown bank in Jefferson City. "Take a hundred dollars out of this check." She slid her first paycheck from Luke's construction company across the marble counter.

Although she had been willing to work for food, Luke had insisted on paying her minimum wage, just like his other employees. She knew he couldn't afford it, but she sure was glad to have the money.

The teller smiled as she took the check. Behind Darcy on a leather upholstered sofa, Luke and Ruby sat together reading magazines. The appointment with the neurologist had gone much better than Darcy had anticipated. Ruby was cooperative and perky, back to her usual imperious demeanor. She took several written and oral tests, and she chatted with the physician for nearly half an hour. Afterward, Luke stopped for ice cream at the Zesto stand on the road back to the highway, and he agreed to make a second stop at the bank so Darcy could buy a money order.

"I'm sorry, but I'm not familiar with this company," the teller said after examining the paycheck. "Since it's not a local business, I'll need to see some identification, please."

"Identification. But I . . ." Darcy tried to breathe. "Just to cash that check?"

"Do you have an account with us?"

"No, ma'am."

"It's our policy to see identification before we cash checks over fifty dollars, Miss Callaway."

"But I . . ." Darcy glanced over her shoulder at Luke and Ruby. "I don't have any ID."

"A driver's license?"

"No," she whispered.

"Any credit cards? Even voter registration would do."

Darcy shook her head. "Please, ma'am. I really do need the money order."

"I'll have to check with my supervisor. One moment, please."

Leaning her elbows on the cool marble, Darcy tried to pray. She desperately needed to cash this check. She was completely out of money for living expenses, and besides that, she had to start paying off her debts.

A tall man in a gray business suit appeared behind the counter and peered down at the check. "Good afternoon, Miss Callaway."

As he spoke her false name, she wished she could just fade away forever. "Hi," she said.

"So you work for the Easton Construction Company down the road in Ambleside?"

"Yes, sir." Her voice sounded wispy and far away. "Painting and wallpapering."

"But you have no identification?"

"What's the problem here?" Luke nudged Darcy as he stepped up to the counter. "I'm Luke Easton, this woman's employer. That's my business check."

"Are you aware that your employee has no identification?"

Luke studied Darcy for a minute. He seemed to be debating something, and she had the awful sense that he could see right through her.

He turned back to the banker. "I have identification." He pulled out his wallet and located his driver's license and three credit cards. The check is good. You can sell her a money order."

"Aha." The man scanned Luke's information and nodded at the teller, who wrote down the pertinent data. "That's fine then. We'll have this right out for you, Miss Callaway."

"I'd like the rest in cash," she said.

"Would you be interested in opening an account with us, Miss Callaway?" the teller asked. "We have both checking and savings plans."

"Not today."

Darcy took the printed money order and the small stack of bills, and she left the counter without another word. As she hurried out the door of the bank with the other two behind her, she could hear Luke explaining the situation to Ruby. The librarian expressed astonishment that anyone in this day and age could fail to have a driver's license.

On the ride back to Ambleside, Darcy couldn't bring herself to look at either of her traveling companions. Instead, she studied the passing landscape of rolling hills covered with oak and maple trees, white-fenced pastures dotted with cattle, and fields green with emerging corn and wheat. She had hoped to feel successful at this moment, satisfied with helping Ruby and grateful for the chance to start paying off her debts. Instead, she felt like a stinking polecat.

"Are you going to be all right now, Mrs. McCann?" Luke asked as he pulled the pickup to the front of her mansion and got out.

"Well, I don't exactly know what the doctor told me to do, Mr. Easton. I can't recall his words."

"You don't need to do a thing." Luke reached across the seat to help the tiny woman climb down. "The neurologist said he wouldn't have your test results right away. We'll be hearing from him in a few days."

"A few days," she repeated.

"That's right." He led her toward the front door. "Mrs. McCann, do you have anything to eat for dinner?"

"Oh, yes. Jo keeps me well supplied with groceries. She's such a dear girl."

Luke was smiling as he walked back to the pickup. Darcy had taken advantage of his absence to hop down from the cab and head toward the guesthouse.

"Thanks, Luke," she said, giving a quick wave. "I appreciate everything you did today. Really."

"Jo," he called after her, "I'd like to talk to you for a minute."

"Sorry, but I really don't have time right now." She inserted her key in the lock. "I need to get some supper going. And I have to fold a load of Ruby's laundry."

"Jo, hold on."

He put a hand on her wrist as the door swung open. "Montgomery and Nick will be okay with Boompah for a few more minutes. And Ruby's laundry can wait. I need to ask you about something. Can we sit?"

"Really, Luke, I ought to—"

"This will be fine." He walked into her house and settled into one of the overstuffed chairs beside the fireplace. "So, how about telling me your real name?"

Darcy let out a moan as she sank into the chair opposite his. "I can't talk about it, Luke. I'm sorry, but I just can't."

"Well, maybe I can't keep you on my payroll either."

She glanced up at him, heat flashing through her. "I haven't done anything wrong on the job. I've worked hard, and I've gotten along with Gabe and Floyd. I painted and papered the whole study, and you won't find a single streak—"

"Who are you?"

"It doesn't matter. I came to Ambleside, and I got a job, and I'm helping Ruby. I didn't steal anything from her, either."

"I didn't say you did."

"Floyd and some others think I'm trying to use her. I overheard him talking to you in the study this afternoon. Well, I'll have you know I never asked Ruby for a single thing. She brought over a sack of clothes for me to borrow, and she gives me her purse to take to the Corner Market and do her shopping. I keep her refrigerator stocked, her clothes washed and ironed, and her floors swept. You should have seen that place before I started looking after her—"

"I never said a thing about you and Ruby," Luke cut in. "I know you've been good for her."

"Then what's your problem? Why can't I just do my work? Why does everybody in this town have to speculate about me and accuse me of things I haven't done?"

"I'm not accusing you of anything. But I am your employer, and I deserve to know who you are."

Darcy knotted her fingers together. "I'm a woman trying to make a new life for herself. That's all."

"And what's your real name?"

She cleared her throat. "What difference does it make?"

"Darcy."

"How did you know!" She leapt out of the chair. "You've been checking up on me, haven't you?"

"I overheard you on the phone the day we met."

"I knew it! People are always prying into things that are none of their business."

"Who you are is my business."

"It is not. Have I stuck my nose into your personal life? You live in that little shrine to your dead wife like your house is some kind of holy altar. But I never asked about that, did I? I let you live however you want. You can sit around and mope for the rest of your life if you want to, and I'm not going to butt into it."

"I don't mope."

"Yes, you do. You mope."

"Well, you don't know anything about what I've been through."

"That's right. And I don't want to know."

"You have no idea what it's like to lose a spouse."

"Oh yes I do. I was married once, too, and my husband died. So don't think I don't know what you're feeling. I understand suffering and pain and remorse. I know what it's like to wish you could just start again without the past hanging over you. That's all I'm trying to do, okay? Just start over."

"You were married?" He stared at her.

Darcy drank down a breath. "Yes, a long time ago."

"How did he die?"

She paused, weighing her words. Looking at the floor, she said quietly, "Someone killed him."

He was silent as she paced the little living room. She wished he would go away. Leave her alone. Let her handle things by herself.

"Look," she began, "I don't—"

"Why did you change your name?"

"I told you. I'm trying to start over. I want to build a new life from the ground up. I had prayed that I could just move here and do my work without causing any notice at all. Now I find out I'm the focus of the town gossip. Look, if you tell anyone I changed my name—"

"I won't tell." He ran his hand over the round arm of the chair. "I'm sorry about your husband."

From behind him, she studied Luke's thick brown hair and broad shoulders. Could she ever tell this man how awful her husband had been? How terrible and cruel and domineering? How very opposite from Luke's loving, beautiful wife? Yes, they each had lost a spouse. But other than that simple fact, their losses could not possibly be more different.

"I really need to fold laundry," she said. "Ruby's expecting me."

Luke stood and slipped his hands into the pockets of his jeans. "I won't tell your secret," he said, turning to face her, "but you don't have to hide from me. You can be Darcy Whoever, if you want."

"No. I need to be Jo Callaway. I really need that."

"So, did you grow up in Arkansas?"

"Joplin," she whispered.

"Is your father a hog farmer?"

"Yes, and my mother hung wallpaper for a living. And I won the blue ribbon in 4-H. Most of what I've told you is true." She wrung her hands. "I've been trying so hard. I want to live the way I learned in chapel, the Christian way. I want to be pure and holy and right in the eyes of God. But if everyone knows who I am . . . if everyone knows my past . . . they won't give me a chance to grow in my faith. They'll judge me."

"People are going to judge you just for breathing. It's human nature. Is your past so bad, Jo?"

She looked away. "Yes," she said softly. "Real bad."

"There are things I'd like to hide from, too, you know. It's not Ellie's death so much as her life. The way I took her for granted. I got used to her, the things she did for me. I stopped treating her with the love and attention she deserved. After a while, the magic died right out of our marriage, and I didn't do a thing to try to win her back. I was working hard, and she was taking care of Montgomery. We were so busy. And then it was too late for me to be the kind of husband to her that I should have been."

Darcy stood near the sofa and wished she could reach out to Luke. The pain in his eyes called to her. But what could she tell him? She hadn't been the kind of wife she ought to have been either. She'd made a complete mess of her marriage.

"I may not be doing the greatest job of living, Jo," Luke said, "but I'm not hiding."

"Are you sure?"

"Okay, I'll admit I don't exactly feel like painting the town red."

She smiled. "Neither do I. Mostly, I'd just like to live in a quiet way, minding my own business. I'd like to join the church and move into my own place. I want to help out where I can. Ruby's very sweet, and I'm worried about her. It's just hard when—"

"I think you're a good woman," he cut in. "Pure and holy and right in God's eyes. You remember that when Pearlene Fox and the others start their tongue-wagging."

"Thanks, Luke." For some reason, she felt suddenly shy. It was the first time in years that anyone had spoken well of her, and it was such an enormous gift that she hardly knew how to accept it. Luke knew that she had lied about her name, that she had experienced a painful past, that she was not at all pure. Yet he believed that somehow through God's grace, she had risen above all of it. A tide of grateful emotion welled up inside her.

"You've been so helpful to me," she said, searching his blue eyes. "I know I sort of forced you to hire me, and I made you take Ruby to the doctor. And I butted into your house for dinner—"

The shrill jangle of the old telephone cut off her words. A shiver ran through Darcy as she picked up the receiver. Who could be calling her? Who knew her number?

"Hello?" she said.

"Darcy, it's your mother." The voice was tense. "How are you getting along?"

"I'm fine." She looked across at Luke. He was staring at her. "How's Dad?"

"About the same. Listen, I can't talk long. Money's tight, you know. I wanted to tell you that Will Damyon came by the trailer a few minutes ago. He told me he's going to track you down."

"Did you tell him anything?" Darcy felt as though she were choking. "You didn't give him my phone number—"

"Of course not, honey. He's mean and threatening, but I won't let him buffalo me. Listen, I want you to go to the police and tell them about it. You're going to need protection from that man."

"I can't go to the police. I don't want anyone—" She glanced across at Luke again. His face was solemn, his eyes filled with concern. "Mom, I can't talk right now."

"Honey, that man is going to kill you if he can. He told me he didn't think you'd paid enough for what happened to his son. Now, you get yourself some protection, hear me?"

"Yes, Mom."

"Don't go anywhere without somebody watching your back. Will Damyon is determined to have his revenge, and I just can't stand to think about . . . after all you've been through, honey . . . and what if he . . ." She began to sob. "What if he shoots you or . . ."

"Don't cry, Mama. I'll be all right. I won't let Will hurt me."

"You promise me, now. Promise you'll get help?"

"I promise. Don't worry."

"I love you, sweetheart. I do."

"I know, Mama. I love you, too." Darcy said good-bye and set the receiver back in the cradle of the black telephone. For a moment, she stood staring at it, hugging herself in fear. Her husband's father intended to kill her.

"Jo?" Luke's voice drew her from her paralysis. "Are you all right?"

"I'll be fine."

"You sounded scared."

She squeezed her eyes shut. Scared? Yes, she was scared.

Her whole life, it seemed, had been colored with fear. Her father's drunken rages had terrified her as a child. And then she had married a man so quick to erupt with anger that she lived on the edge of panic. She'd had no idea what would set him off. For the brief years of their marriage, she had hardly dared to fall asleep at night, wondering if he would barge into their bedroom and begin to beat her because something had gone wrong at work, or he'd been drinking, or she'd irritated him in one small way or another. And now her dead husband's father was determined to sear the terror on her heart.

"I am afraid," she acknowledged, unable to look at Luke. "In my life, there have been some hard times. But I've learned that God doesn't want me to live in fear."

"He's not going to protect you from the hard times, though. I learned that about God."

She lifted her head. "Not all of them. You're right about that. But God is with me, Luke. He wants the best for me. Most of all, he loves me. I believe that."

His blue eyes went soft. "You do, don't you? I can see it in you."

"So do you."

"I'm not sure anymore. I used to think I knew where I stood. I had it all figured out, you know. God and religion."

"If you had God figured out, you're more amazing than I thought." She felt a smile creep across her mouth. "I don't understand him much at all. I don't know how he works or why he does what he does. I don't have any idea what he's planned for my life. I just know he loves me. That's enough."

"That's faith." He reached out and caught her fingers. "Jo, if you need help—"

"I can manage. But thanks."

He gave her a nod and released her hand. "See you tomorrow then."

"Tomorrow."

When the door shut behind him, she turned the dead bolt. As she moved to the window with its tiny diamond-shaped panes, she wrapped one hand around the fingers Luke had held. The warmth of his touch shivered through her, tingling to her elbow and up through her shoulder. How good his hand had felt, how strong and firm. But she had trusted in the strength of a man once before—only to find it turned on her. No, she would trust only in God now, in Jesus Christ, her Savior. Maybe God had allowed Luke Easton into her life, but Darcy knew she could never count on any human again. Luke was just a man, and experience had taught her to be wary. How could a woman ever know?

She thought of a Bible verse that had been part of a song the women sang in the Bible study she used to attend. As she moved to the kitchen to begin preparing her supper, she sang it softly. "The joy of the Lord is my strength." The words danced through the arched doorways and finally filled the tiny house. "The joy of the Lord is my strength . . . the joy of the Lord is my strength."

Standing on a ladder, Luke tightened the final screw that held the renegade chandelier to the study's ceiling. His crew stood below, staring up at the crystal contraption with its fifty tiny lightbulbs. Bud Huff, owner of the local hardware store, waited at the switch on the far wall. Working evenings, Bud had spent more than two weeks rewiring the fixture. Now the moment of truth had arrived again.

"Flip the switch, Bud," Luke called across the room.

"Wait—where's the fire extinguisher?" Gabe cried.

"Got 'er right here." Floyd held up the red metal canister. "Let 'er rip, Bud!"

With great ceremony, Bud reached out and flipped up

the switch. All fifty lightbulbs began to glow. The crystals shimmered with blue and red fire.

"Don't count on nothin' yet!" Floyd said. "Right here's where we lost 'er the last time."

Luke held his breath and stared at the chandelier. The lights stayed on. The ceiling medallion didn't smoke. The plaster didn't catch fire.

"I think you've done it, Bud," Luke said.

At that moment, the chandelier went dark. The box fan in the window fell silent. The lights in the grand foyer snuffed out. A groan rose from the crowd.

"It's the fuse," Jo said. "I bet it couldn't handle all the wattage."

Floyd shook his head as Luke began to descend the ladder. "I think it's that chandelier. There's somethin' plumb wrong with it."

"It's this whole stupid house," Gabe said. "Mr. Chalmers ought to just bulldoze the thing into the river."

"Well, well, well." Bud stared up at the fixture. "All that work right down the tubes. I could just about spit."

"Mail!" Pop Creighton called out from the foyer. "Anybody here? Luke? What happened to the lights?"

"In here," Floyd called. "We got this chandelier that flat won't light up. Now she's blown out every wire in these front rooms."

The mailman made his way into the room and handed Luke a stack of letters. Setting the rest of the pile on a worktable nearby, Luke opened a notice from the bank. Aware it would contain something unpleasant, he turned to his crew. "Gabe, you and Floyd better get back to work. And Jo, why don't you—"

"We can't see to work, boss," Floyd said. "It's just about pitch-black in this house, don't you know."

"Then go take a break outside." He walked over to an open window and turned his focus to the letter in his hand.

The bank stated a growing concern about the status of Luke's accounts—both his home mortgage and his small business loan. The officers felt they ought to take a look into the solvency of his company.

There wasn't much to tell. He held the contract for the Chalmers Mansion project, and that was it. The job was keeping him busy enough that he hadn't bid on any work for the future, though he did plan to pursue some contracts in the new McCann subdivision. He knew he'd be competing with companies in Jefferson City and Columbia, but he felt sure he could earn the right to build houses there. People in Ambleside respected his work.

But what would the bank think of Luke's employees? He hadn't done detailed background checks on them because, frankly, he had to take what he could get. But he believed in his workers. He took the pencil from behind his ear and picked up a scrap of wallpaper. "Floyd," he called through the window toward the group gathered in the front yard, "you worked for the railroads, right?"

"Naw," Floyd said, as Luke scribbled the information on the back of the wallpaper. "Department of Transportation is who I worked for. I handled railroad stuff most of the time, and when there was boat traffic, I helped out with that, too."

"Had you done much work on houses before this project?"

"Not on your Nellie. I was a signal man, myself. But I figured there couldn't be too much difference between doin' that and wirin' a house."

"Yeah, and that's how come we had a fire in here the last time you tried to wire that chandelier," Gabe said, snickering.

Luke studied the young man. Gabe had had no prior experience in construction. When he'd said he was willing to work, Luke had decided to take a chance on him. Though

Gabe was sometimes temperamental, Luke didn't regret his decision.

And then there was Luke's newest employee. The mysterious Miss Callaway. Would he list her home as Arkansas or Missouri? Currently, she lived as a transient in a guesthouse. And she certainly had no degree in interior design.

Luke let out a breath as he folded the letter and pushed it into his pocket. He was going to have to do something to rectify his financial situation. But what choices did he have?

"Luke?" Jo beckoned him from the doorway. "Can I interrupt you for a minute?"

Discouraged, he headed toward her. Surely the bank knew he would pay back his loans in time. He'd been paying all along, but Ellie's illness had complicated everything. The awful thought that he might lose the home in which he was raising his daughter reared up inside him.

"Luke, it's a letter from the neurologist," Jo said, handing him a sealed envelope. "I noticed it in the mail you left on the worktable, and I thought I'd take it to Ruby. But it's addressed to you."

Luke ripped open the envelope. Jo leaned against his shoulder, reading alongside of him. As they both reached the same paragraph, she let out a cry.

"Oh, no!" She covered her mouth with her hand. Her eyes filled with tears. "Luke, did you read it?"

"Yes," he said, shoving the letter back inside the envelope. "Will you go with me to talk to her?"

"Of course."

"Do you think she'll even understand what it means that she has Alzheimer's disease?"

"I do. And that's the worst part of it."

SEVEN

"Come in, come in! How lovely to see you both." Ruby held open the door. "How very, very kind of you to drop by."

As Darcy passed the small elderly woman, she spotted a bright pink curler in her hair. The silvery white strands were twisted around the foam, almost as though the curler had been intended as a decoration. On the temple opposite the curler, a bright rhinestone clip lay nestled among the soft waves.

"Let me help you with this," Darcy said gently, reaching up to slide the curler from Ruby's hair. "There you go."

"My goodness." Ruby giggled as she dropped the curler into her pocket. "I wonder if I had that in my hair all day at the library. The children were awfully twittery during the reading hour."

"What did you read?"

"I tried *Pride and Prejudice,* but they weren't following the plot at all. I was reaching for *Pippi Longstocking,* when all of a sudden there it was—*Pride and Prejudice.* A more wonderful book has never been written. But it was too much for the children. It's really meant for adults. I wonder how it ended up in the juvenile section. Oh well, things have been topsy-turvy lately. The library's patrons never have been careful when searching for books."

"Ruby, what's that smell?" Darcy asked, suddenly aware of an acrid tang to the air in the huge marble-floored foyer.

"Something's burning," Luke said. "I'll check the kitchen."

Darcy was right behind him as he rounded the corner

into the black-and-white tiled room. On the stove, a large saucepan billowed pungent black smoke. Luke grabbed a hot pad, jerked the pan off the burner, and carried it to the sink.

"I think it might have been soup," he said, as he ran cold water over the mess. Steam plumed forth. "Or maybe rice."

"Do you think it's been on the stove since lunch? Oh, Luke, I wonder if Ruby has eaten anything all day."

"Just be glad she didn't burn her whole house down."

"Goodness gracious." Ruby waved her hand in front of her face. "What have you two been doing in my kitchen? Is something burning? Really, I cannot allow you access to the kitchen if you can't do better than this."

Her heart aching, Darcy crossed the room and took Ruby's arm. "Come to the parlor. Luke and I need to talk with you."

"And what about the mess you've made? How I long for the days when I had house help. Those were blissful years indeed! But after a time, Mr. McCann grew uncomfortable with the presence of others in the home, so we dismissed the staff. He is such a private man, you know. He enjoys his solitude and silence, and I can't blame him."

Darcy seated Ruby on a gold-upholstered settee and sat down beside her. Luke took the red velvet chair opposite them. It seemed a little odd, the two of them in their dusty jeans and T-shirts, while Ruby was attired in a dress of pale gray silk. She fingered the pearls at her neck, as though she were a debutante at a party. Luke leaned forward, wrists on his knees, and linked his fingers together.

"How've you been feeling these days, Mrs. McCann?" he asked.

"Quite well, thank you. And you?"

"I'm fine." He smiled and glanced at Darcy. "Anyway, we wanted to talk to you about the doctor. The neurologist."

"Oh, yes. He was a very nice man, I thought. So genteel."

"Luke got a letter from the doctor this afternoon," Darcy said, laying her hand on Ruby's arm.

"Yes," Luke went on. "He wanted to let me know the results of your tests, so that I could come and talk to you in person."

"What did I tell you?" Ruby exclaimed. "That physician is all politeness! How very civil of him."

"Well, the thing is, the tests have turned up some cause for concern. The neurologist wants to see you again, Mrs. McCann. But he didn't want to wait until the appointment to alert us to the situation."

"Which situation is that?"

"The tests seem to show," Luke said, "that you have a disease. It's a degenerative brain disease, Mrs. McCann. It's called—"

"Alzheimer's!" she exclaimed, jumping up from the settee. "I knew it! I knew it too well! Am I wrong?"

"No, Mrs. McCann. You're not wrong."

"Well, that is just . . . that is just . . . just . . . just . . ."

"It's upsetting," Darcy said. "But it's not the end of the world."

"Oh, yes it is!" Ruby rounded on Darcy. "Don't sit there and tell me it's nothing, because I know better! I'm not stupid."

"Of course not—"

"I've read about Alzheimer's. I know how it is, forgetting this and that until you've forgotten your very own name! And not remembering bananas and how to make oatmeal . . . and how to use the toi . . . toilet . . ." She sank back onto the settee and began to sob.

Darcy slipped her arms around the old woman and held her close. "You'll always have your friends, Ruby."

"I won't remember their names!"

"But they'll remember yours, and that's the main thing. You'll be surrounded by love and concern."

"Where is Wilmer? I need my husband. I can't go on . . . go on . . ."

Luke crossed to the settee and sat down on the other side of Mrs. McCann. Reaching out, he lifted her from Darcy's embrace and wrapped his arms around the frail figure. He leaned his cheek against her wispy white hair.

"You *can* go on," he said. "At some point, everybody comes to a crossroad, a time when they realize their life is changing. Mrs. McCann, right this minute you can choose to surrender to this problem and go down in flames. Or you can choose to keep on doing the things you're able to do and live your life to the fullest."

"You're speaking of your wife, aren't you?" Ruby said. "You're talking of Ellie and the brain tumor. She didn't give up, did she?"

"No, she didn't. Not even when she knew she wasn't going to get better. She made the most of the time she had. And I think that's what you're going to do, too."

"But I have no one. No one to help me. Wilmer and I never had children, you know. It wasn't possible, and there's all this . . . this house and the grounds. And what about my work at the library!"

At the fresh round of weeping, Luke laid his hand on Ruby's head, as though she were a small, disconsolate child. Darcy gazed at the two of them, her spirit crying along with Ruby's. She could hardly believe the sight of Luke holding the little woman in his arms, the tenderness and concern with which he comforted her. Had anyone ever been so gentle with Darcy? She couldn't remember a time, and her heart longed to be touched in such a way.

"Now then," Luke said, easing Ruby up from his shoulder, "I want you to do some things, Mrs. McCann. I'm going to write a list for you to follow. You need to check each thing off as you do it, okay?"

"All right." She slipped a white handkerchief from her

pocket and dabbed her eyes. "In some odd way, you know, this diagnosis is a relief to me. I couldn't understand why I'd been having so much trouble lately. Trouble with the small things of life. Do you know, I can't find my hairbrush. I looked all over for it this morning. Where on earth could I have put it?"

Darcy stood, grateful that she could do something to help. "I'll find your brush," she said. "And if you want, I'll make sure you've got your curlers out of your hair and your buttons done up right every morning. How would that be?"

Ruby dabbed at her cheeks some more. "You are a lovely girl. So kind. Don't you think so, Mr. Easton?"

"Yes," he said. "She's kind . . . and lovely."

Darcy met his eyes, aware of the heat flushing into her cheeks. Did he really think she was lovely? *Lovely*—the kind of word used to describe elegant women, beautiful creatures with fine manners and perfect speech. No one had ever called her lovely, and she knew she wasn't. But was it possible that she might become lovely one day? For so long Darcy had pictured herself as a tornado of destruction, uneducated and tough. A part of her always would carry that past, those terrible scars. But if loveliness came from inside, if it had to do with attitude and spirit, maybe she really could be a lovely woman someday.

Her spirits lifting, Darcy wandered through the house, searching for Ruby's brush. She peeked into cupboards, and she was amazed to find years' worth of useless things stashed away—hundreds of rubber bands, old plastic bags, clothing that must have dated back to World War II. There were unopened bills and newspapers that had never been read. How long had Ruby been suffering through her dementia in silence, too overwhelmed by the minute details of daily life to manage them and too embarrassed to share her distress?

"Here it is," Darcy said, returning to the parlor with an ivory-handled hairbrush. "It was in the refrigerator."

"Good heavens!" Ruby clasped the chilly brush to her chest. "I must have put it in there when I took out the milk this morning. I wonder where I set the milk."

"I found it on a shelf in the pantry," Darcy said. "I'll run over to the Corner Market in the morning and get you a fresh bottle. Have you eaten anything today, Ruby?"

"My usual bowl of oatmeal this morning."

"Oatmeal?" Darcy looked at Luke. "I bet that's what was on the stove. I'd better stay here and make sure you get something to eat, Ruby. How about a sandwich?"

"Nonsense!" The old woman took Luke and Darcy by the arms and pushed them toward the front door. "Both of you worry about me far too much. I'm not gone yet. I can fix my own sandwich, you know."

"But I'll be happy to help you."

"Certainly not!" As she started to shut the door behind them, Ruby glanced down at her hairbrush. "Now why on earth am I carrying this thing around?"

As she and Luke walked away from the large house, Darcy ran her hand along the back of her neck. The heat of the Missouri summer was beginning to intensify, and her long hair had grown damp in the humidity. Few of the businesses and homes in Ambleside could boast of central air-conditioning. Most had one or more window units whirring away during the daylight hours. A few box fans in the windows cooled the Chalmers and McCann houses. Darcy's little guest cottage didn't even have that luxury.

"Thanks for being there with me," Luke said as they reached his pickup. "I think Mrs. McCann took the news pretty well."

"Today she did. But tomorrow she may not remember a single thing we told her. Luke, I'm worried about what's going to happen to her."

"I made a list of things for her to take care of. She needs to visit Sawyer-the-lawyer and make sure her will is in order. While she's there, she can assign someone power of attorney. I recommended Pastor Paul. There's no question he'd do what's right for her. After she sees the lawyer, I want her to visit the bank and get a current statement of her accounts. Then she needs to head over to Redee-Quick and ask Cleo Mueller to make a list of all her medications. Once Pastor Paul has all that information, he can help her begin to make decisions about long-term care."

"But, Luke, she left her oatmeal on the stove *today*. Her whole house could have burned down."

"I realize that."

"She had a curler in her hair, and she put her brush in the refrigerator, and I don't know when was the last time she had anything to eat. I'm afraid she can't take care of herself much longer. Somebody's got to step in and help her before she gets hurt."

"Are you thinking of quitting your job with me? Going to work for Ruby?"

Startled at the idea, Darcy looked up at the arching oak trees overhead. "I never thought about that. About getting paid for helping Ruby. I mean, I'm so grateful for the use of the guesthouse, I've been doing everything I can for her. I can't imagine charging her."

"She has money."

"But she's been so generous with me."

"Did it occur to you that she'll have to put her place up for sale? You won't be able to stay in the guesthouse forever." His blue eyes were deep. "I'd like you to stay on with my crew, Jo. I need your help. But if Ruby needs you more—"

"No, I can't do that, Luke. I'll help Ruby all I can, but I'm not a nurse. I need a steady job, and I like working for you. With the crew, I mean."

He was silent a moment. "My company's not in the greatest shape. I guess you have a right to know that. The bank is looking into its solvency. I'm not sure whether I can convince them I'm going to make good."

"I'd rather work for you than for anyone else in Ambleside." She slipped her hands into the back pockets of her jeans and squared her shoulders. "The sooner we get Chalmers House finished up, the better. You'll have that money to pay off some of your bills, and then you can bid on jobs in the McCann subdivision. I don't care what the bank thinks about your company. You've got an experienced crew, and we're doing a great job on the mansion. The exterminator took care of the termites, Floyd's going to rework the fuse box, and no one can criticize the work I've done on the wallpaper and paint. Gabe's even stripping wood like a pro now. Your company is going to make it just fine, Luke. If people would stop sticking their noses into other people's business—"

"The bank financed my company. Easton Construction *is* their business."

"No, it's not. All the bank cares about is getting its money back out of the deal—with plenty of interest. Easton Construction is *your* business. Building houses is your business. Bringing old buildings back to life is your business. And you'd better not let the moneylenders stand in your way."

"Moneylenders?" Luke grinned. "You're going to get out the whip and turn over the tellers' tables pretty soon?"

"I just don't appreciate folks messing where they shouldn't." She frowned. "Not with Floyd and Gabe and you. And me, too. We're good people, and we're doing the best we can. That's all anyone can expect."

"The bank expects more."

"Well, the bank can just—" She bit off the words that had come so quickly to her tongue. Where had this anger come from? From fear, perhaps. Darcy couldn't deny that the thought of losing her little guesthouse and her job with Easton Construction had shaken her. Her survival depended on a place to live and work to do. But it was more than that. All her life she'd watched the powerful try to squash the life out of those they considered beneath them.

"Don't worry about me, Jo," Luke said. "I've never buckled under to anyone who stood in my way. I may not be rich, and my company may be on shaky ground, but I won't give in. I'm no hero, but I'm not a coward either."

Darcy shook her head, thinking of the way he had held and comforted Ruby McCann. Lately he'd been looking an awful lot like a knight in shining armor.

She had started for the guesthouse when she remembered the appointment she had in Jefferson City. "One more thing," she said.

When she turned, she realized that Luke had been leaning against the hood of his pickup, watching her walk away. A warm glow of appreciation lighted his eyes. The idea that he might actually be attracted to her sent up red flags of warning. Though she liked Luke a lot, she knew there could never be any kind of attachment between them. She couldn't allow anything or anyone to interfere with her determination to live a life of solitude and stability. She could not afford to make any more mistakes in life. And people—men especially—had always brought trouble.

"I need to take Friday afternoon off," she said. "I have some business."

"What kind of business?"

"Personal." She crossed her arms protectively, forcing away any thought—any hope—that there might be something between them. "I can make up the hours on Saturday, if that's a problem."

"I thought you were planning to work on the foyer on Friday."

"I am. In the morning." She could feel his resistance, and it put her on the defense. "I'll get the work done."

"You just told me we needed to finish the Chalmers project as quickly as we could. Now you're heading off to who knows where."

"Jefferson City."

"How are you planning to get there?"

"On the bus."

He studied her. "Why?"

"It's none of your business, Luke. I have to go."

"Then I'll take you. I need to pick up some plumbing supplies anyway."

"I don't want you to take me. I'm going to ride the bus."

Looking too strong, too handsome, too welcome, he walked toward her. "Look, Jo, you know I heard that conversation you had with your mom on the phone the other day. I've done a lot of thinking about it. It's pretty obvious you're in some kind of trouble."

"I'm doing fine."

"I'm your boss, and I feel responsible for you."

"Well, you're not. I can take care of myself." She turned away and started down the sidewalk. "I don't need protection. I'm fine."

"And I'm taking you to Jefferson City, whether you like it or not."

"I'm riding the bus."

"We'll leave at noon."

"No, Luke!" She swung around. "You can't do this. I have to take care of some things on my own."

He walked toward her and put a hand on her arm. "Listen, Jo, I'm not the kind of man who stands aside when someone needs me. Gabe Zimmerman needed a job, and I took him on. Ruby McCann needs help, and I'm going to see that she gets it. You're in some kind of trouble. I'm not about to sit back and let you get hurt."

"Luke, I appreciate the offer. I really do. But . . ." She tugged her arm out of his grasp. "I don't need you. I don't need anybody, okay? I'm on my own, and I—"

She paused, remembering suddenly that she had surrendered her life to Christ. She was no longer on her own. The Holy Spirit lived inside her, and she had trusted him with her future. God had sent help in the form of quirky old Ruby. And for all she knew, he was putting Luke in her life for the same reason.

"We'll leave at noon," he repeated. "From Chalmers House."

She nodded. "All right."

"Everything's going to be okay," he said.

But as he walked back to his pickup and climbed in, Darcy had to admit that having Luke Easton in her life was more than okay. It was good.

"I'm coming in with you." Luke had made the decision on the drive from Ambleside. He waited to tell Jo until he pulled the pickup into a parking lot of the large state office building in Jefferson City. "We can stop at the plumbing place on the way out."

Jo looked across the cab at him, her face strained. She had pulled her blonde hair into a knot near the top of her head. The effect emphasized her long neck and slender figure. Ruby's blue dress—the one with the bows on the shoulders that Jo had worn to dinner—made her appear even more fragile. She had refused to tell him her destination, but he vividly recalled the fear in her voice when she had spoken with her mother. It had haunted him. Luke wasn't about to let anyone harm this woman.

Her voice was firm when she finally spoke. "You can't come in with me," she said. "I'm sorry."

She reached for the door handle and slipped out of the

pickup before he could stop her. He followed right on her heels. As they neared the door, she turned to him, her features pale.

"Please, Luke," she whispered. "I need to do this by myself."

"Why?"

"I want to be alone."

"But you're not alone, Jo. If I learned anything from Ellie's death, it's that. No one is completely alone. Zachary Chalmers stood by me during the worst of it, times when I didn't see how I could survive. And now I'm standing by you."

"Oh, Luke, there are things about me that I don't want anyone to know. I need my secrets."

"You can't hide forever. Your secrets will come out one way or another."

She clutched a manila file folder as though it were a life preserver. Though Luke couldn't imagine what kind of secrets such a vulnerable young woman could be hiding, he knew she was scared to death. He saw that her fear was based on something real and imminent.

"Let's go in," he said.

As though she were suddenly too exhausted to argue further, she turned away in silence and pushed open the door. Side by side they walked down the long, air-conditioned hallway to the elevator. After scanning the directory, Jo pressed the button that would take them to the third floor.

Luke read the sign: Probation and Parole.

As the elevator doors slid shut, he tried to prepare himself for what Jo must be facing. He knew her husband had been killed. Maybe the murderer was now out of prison and on parole. Luke could well imagine Jo's fear of a violent offender. If she were coming all this way to confront her husband's killer and to meet his parole officer, it would certainly explain the stress she was feeling. He had read how survivors of crimes often went to probation or parole meetings to make certain the perpetrator not only got his deserved punishment but also stayed away from the victim's family.

They left the elevator, and as they pushed open the door of the parole office, Luke knew his guess had been right. An elderly man stood to his feet the instant he spotted Jo, and she sucked in a deep gasp. Luke stepped to her side.

The man looked every bit a killer. His face was deeply tanned and scarred from ancient acne, and he wore a two-day growth of gray beard. Though he had on a shirt and tie, his collar was yellow with sweat and he had neglected to brush the dandruff from the shoulders of his worn navy suit jacket. He gave Jo a sneer.

"Well, if it isn't Darcy Damyon herself," he said. "And it looks like she's already got herself hooked up with a new man."

"Listen here," Luke said. "I'm just—"

"It's okay, Luke." Jo laid her hand on his arm. "This is Will Damyon. He was my husband's father."

"*Was* is right." The man looked at Luke, his eyes rheumy and red around the rims. "I guess she told you what she did to my son."

Luke turned to Jo in confusion. "What does he mean?"

She pulled her manila folder closer to her chest. "He means," she said, "that his son is dead. And I'm the one who killed him."

Eight

Luke felt off-kilter as he walked into the parole officer's small cubicle. It was as though he'd just stepped off a whirling ride at a carnival, yet the world continued to spin. He sat down in a chair near the door and focused on the woman he had been so ready to defend.

Jo—Darcy—had *murdered* her own *husband?* She was on parole? That meant a jury had found her guilty of the crime and a judge had sent her to prison. She was an ex-convict, a criminal, a violent offender. Not only that, but the woman had shown that she was a liar.

Luke felt sick to his stomach as he admitted to himself how little he really knew about her—not even her full name, until today. He reflected on the day she had gotten off the bus in Ambleside wearing her mildewed clothing and heavy boots. She had spoken like a street tough, and she'd practically tackled Montgomery on the sidewalk! How easily Luke had disregarded his initial impression of Darcy and had fallen under her spell. What a fool he was.

The parole officer, a short man with black hair and a little mustache, took down the names of everyone in the room. Then he began to question Darcy. She acknowledged that her full name was Darcy Damyon, and she said she was living in Ambleside.

"Have you found a job, Mrs. Damyon?" the man asked.

"I work for him." She pointed at Luke and then proceeded to pull her paycheck stub from the manila folder.

"It's construction work, sir. I'm hanging wallpaper and painting."

"Is this a full-time job?"

"Yes, sir. I work forty hours a week."

"You have a place to live?"

She explained about Ruby McCann and the guesthouse. Luke listened carefully to her words and wondered if he had been taken in by her apparent concern for the older woman. Maybe the townspeople had been right to suspect her. Maybe Darcy was taking advantage of Ruby after all.

"Let me check your file here a minute, Mrs. Damyon," the officer said. "I don't see that the parole board recommended any specific treatment programs for you. Mental health, sex offender, drug and alcohol, anger management—you don't qualify for any of those. You're not attending financial management workshops?"

"I had a good record in prison, sir. The board didn't think I needed further rehabilitation."

"I can see that. While incarcerated, you earned your GED and two years of college credit. You worked in the laundry and the kitchen. And you served six years of your twenty-year sentence—"

"She should have gotten the death penalty!" Will Damyon erupted. "She murdered my son. Shot him dead. Six years? Where's the justice in that, mister?"

"Apparently the parole board felt that Mrs. Damyon's conduct during her incarceration showed that she had been rehabilitated."

"Tell me how you rehabilitate somebody who would shoot a man in the head. Tell me that! Her own husband, and she pulled out a gun and murdered him."

"Sir, all of this was addressed during the trial."

"Mr. Damyon," Darcy said, "I'm sorry I killed Bill. I tried to—"

"Sorry? Sorry? I'm just sorry Bill didn't kill you first, that's what I'm sorry about. You took my son's life, and you should have paid with your own."

"Mr. Damyon," the officer said, "I'll have to ask you to keep your temper under control. The judicial system is aware of your concerns. Your letters to us are on file, and we've encouraged you to get in touch with the Victim Services division of the Department of Corrections."

"Victim Services? The victim is dead! My son is dead! What good can the government do him now?"

"Victim Services can provide support for you and your family. Here's the number to call." He scribbled something on a sheet of paper and passed it across the desk. "Mrs. Damyon, it looks like you're on track with your parole requirements. I'll be driving out to Ambleside to do a home visit sometime during this quarter. And, of course, you'll need to come to Jefferson City again next month to check in with me. Do you have any questions?"

"No, sir." Darcy stood.

"And, Mr. Damyon," the officer said, "I'd encourage you to allow this woman the time and space she needs to rebuild her life. And you really—"

"Don't tell me any more about your government programs. You people set a convicted killer free after six measly years. I don't like you. I don't trust you. And I don't think you've done right by my son!"

"I understand your feelings, sir." He held open the door and pointed Will Damyon out into the hall. "If I could have a word with you in private, Mrs. Damyon?"

"I have the right to hear what you tell her!" Mr. Damyon pushed his way back into the office. "You don't tell her a thing I don't hear."

"Very well. Then I'll make you both aware that if you threaten or harass Mrs. Damyon in any way, you will be subject to prosecution. A restraining order is one option."

"A restraining order against *me?*" Will Damyon turned to

Darcy, a sneer curling his lip. "Yeah, you see if the police can protect you from me, honey. If they do as good a job protecting you as they did my son, then you'll end up right where you belong."

"Sir, I must warn you—"

"Warn me all you want. It won't do you a bit of good." He turned and walked down the hall toward the elevator.

The parole officer looked at Darcy. "Mrs. Damyon, I would urge you to be alert and keep your distance from that man. You know he has the right to attend your parole meetings, but we want to do all we can to keep you safe. If you have any cause for concern, don't hesitate to contact my office."

"Thank you, sir."

Darcy shook his hand, clutched the manila folder tightly to her chest, and started down the hall. Luke walked by her side, confused and uncomfortable. He could understand Mr. Damyon's rage. If anyone ever harmed Montgomery, Luke felt he might do almost anything in revenge. But something in the way the parole officer had spoken to Darcy told Luke that she deserved a measure of respect.

They stepped into the elevator and started to the ground floor in silence. Darcy stared at her feet. Luke tried to figure out what he ought to do next. He certainly didn't want Darcy working for him any longer. But could he fire her? Did he have legal grounds? And what about her relationship with Ruby McCann? Somehow he had to put a stop to that. Ruby was in enough trouble without an ex-con for a houseguest.

"I was convicted of second degree murder," Darcy said, her voice low. She opened her manila folder and read from the top sheet of paper. "It's when someone—'with the purpose of causing serious physical injury to another person—causes the death of that person.' The murder was done without deliberation, and it's a Class A felony."

Luke glanced across at her. What was he supposed to say in response? *How nice. Thanks for sharing.*

"My husband had a history of domestic violence," Darcy continued in a low monotone, her focus on the floor. "It got to the point where the Joplin police knew the two of us by name. After I'd gone to bed, Bill would come home drunk and start in on me. I ended up in the hospital twice. With the help of an abuse crisis center, I filed for a separation. I took out a restraining order against him, but I was still scared of what he might do. I began sleeping with a pistol under my pillow. One night around midnight, he showed up at our trailer. When he broke through the bedroom door and started shouting at me, I woke up, pulled out the gun, and shot him. He died instantly."

She swallowed as the elevator doors slid open on the bottom floor. "It wasn't self-defense. Bill hadn't even touched me. I was given a twenty-year sentence."

Without looking at Luke, she stepped out of the elevator and started down the hall to the front door. He followed, considering her words. Though he couldn't be sure, he suspected she was telling the truth. And he knew she hadn't told him her story to defend herself. She hadn't tried to justify her behavior. Instead, the words were humble and matter-of-fact, as though she had decided Luke ought to be given the complete picture.

As they left the building, Luke spotted Will Damyon waiting on the sidewalk. The man's pain was understandable. At the same time, Mr. Damyon seemed to have a personality remarkably similar to the description of his son's. Luke could easily imagine the trauma Darcy must have suffered at her husband's hands, assuming the man had been anything at all like his disgusting father.

"Listen up here, girl," Will said when they were within earshot. "I have something to say to you, and I don't care if your pretty new boyfriend hears every word. You killed my son, and you're going to pay. You know what that means?"

"I've already paid," Darcy said. "I did six years in the state pen, Will. I'm trying to make a new life—"

"New life? Where's my son's new life, huh? You're the one who robbed him of his life. You don't deserve to breathe, let alone build yourself a new life!"

"I know that. I know I did the wrong thing. But if you'll just leave me alone, I promise I'll stay away from you and your family for the rest of my life. I'll never go near Joplin again. You won't even know I exist."

"I'll know you exist until the day you stop existing, girl." He jabbed a finger in her direction. "You're going back to prison, or you're going to die. One or the other. So get used to the idea."

"I'm calling the police," Luke said. "You can't—"

"I can do anything I want, buddy. She owes me. And if you know what's good for you, you'll stand back and let justice be done."

"Justice has been done. The parole board obviously decided—"

"Obviously, you've got the hootsie-tootsies for her just like my son did. Well, just get ready. One of these days you're going to wind up lying in a pool of your own blood."

Luke studied the pockmarked face red with anger. If anyone harmed his child, Luke knew he would feel exactly the same way Will Damyon felt. That fact could never be denied. Neither could the reality that the woman beside him had spent six years in a state penitentiary, had been given time off for her good behavior, and had moved to Ambleside to make a new start.

"Look, I don't know this woman very well," Luke told Will. "She's been working for me a couple of weeks, that's all."

"Well, now you know she's a complete fake. She's passing herself off as a fine, upstanding young lady when she's a cold-blooded murderer."

"Here's what I know about this woman. She can paint and hang wallpaper like a professional. She shows up for work on time, does her job, gets along with the crew, and doesn't cause me any trouble. And she's been kind to an old lady who's a friend of mine."

"Well, isn't that sweet? You also know she killed my son."

"Yes, sir, I do. And I've heard her apologize to you twice for it."

"I am sorry, Will," Darcy cut in. "I've regretted it every hour of every day since the moment I pulled that trigger."

"Your saying sorry doesn't mean a hill of beans to me!" Will grabbed Darcy's arm and yanked her toward him. "You're going to pay, you hear me!"

"No, you don't," Luke snapped, stepping between them. He knocked the man's hand away. "Don't touch her again."

Damyon responded by lunging toward Darcy. Luke put both hands on the older man's chest and shoved him into a waist-high hedge bordering the sidewalk. Damyon fell backward, caught by the branches of a box elder bush. His legs and torso twitched as he struggled to regain his footing.

"I don't have anything against you, Mr. Damyon. But this woman is my employee, and she's my friend. If you come near her again, I'll make sure the police know every word of what went on out here this afternoon. Come on, Jo—Darcy."

He nodded in the direction of his pickup. As they hurried across the drive toward the parking lot, Luke could hear Will Damyon shouting behind them.

"You got it, mister! Her name's Darcy—Darcy Damyon. That's who she is. She's a liar and a murderer. And I'm never going to rest until she's paid for what she did! I'll be coming for you, Darcy! You hear me, girl?"

Luke opened the pickup door and practically tossed Darcy inside. As he stepped to the driver's side, he could hear the older man continuing to rant.

"You better watch your back, you hear me, Darcy? I'm going to find out where you live, and then . . ."

Luke turned on the ignition, threw the pickup into gear, and peeled out of the parking lot. He was halfway back to Ambleside before he remembered the plumbing supplies.

Darcy licked her king-size vanilla ice cream cone as she handed change to the teenager behind the counter at the Tastee Hut. This was the first treat she had allowed herself since she'd started working for Easton Construction. So far, Darcy had sent the biggest part of her money to Joplin to pay off her lawyer. She mailed half of what was left to her mother to help the family. In the past six years, her folks had almost lost the hog farm due to her father's drinking. Now Darcy wanted to do her part to keep them all fed and clothed.

The remainder of her paycheck went to a new pair of work jeans, a few T-shirts, and a refrigerator full of food. But the late afternoon was sweltering, almost dripping with the high humidity, and Darcy had decided to treat herself to her first ice cream cone in six years.

She wanted to celebrate the fact that Luke had decided to keep her on in spite of everything he knew about her. But it was more than having a job that pleased her. Luke's confidence in her was uplifting, and she found herself constantly thinking of him—the way he had defended her, and the way his eyes had warmed when he asked her to stay. She knew he wanted to understand more about who she had been and who she was now—and that both pleased and frightened her.

As she walked out of the store, she recalled another sweltering day—a day when an ice cream cone had not been an option. She had been trying to hide from a woman she owed money to. She had spotted a line of inmates heading into the chapel, so she asked the guard for permission to join them.

Inside that hot little room, a woman from the Prison Fellowship organization stood up and declared that God loved every inmate there. Not only that, but the woman said she, too, loved each woman in the room. That was almost more than Darcy could comprehend, and her first reaction had been amusement. She actually snickered out loud, and the inmate beside her on the folding chairs jabbed her in the ribs. By the second meeting, Darcy had progressed to ridicule. At the third meeting, all she felt was anger. The fifth time she stepped into that chapel and heard the woman from Prison Fellowship say that God loved her, Darcy broke down sobbing. She hadn't been the same since. She was different—so very different inside. But the fear that someone might learn of her past still haunted her.

Moving down the street, she considered taking a shortcut to the McCann estate. The thought of strolling past the police station was almost more than she could endure right now. But she knew she couldn't be seen climbing over Ruby McCann's fence into her backyard. The town already thought of her as a stranger, a thief, a con artist.

Holding her chin as high as she could manage, Darcy passed City Hall and the police station and started down the sidewalk in front of Kaye's Kut-n-Kurl. The owner was sweeping the steps, a favorite pastime in Ambleside, and Darcy averted her eyes as she hurried by.

"Hey, there!" The voice was light, friendly. "You the new girl working over at Chalmers House? Miss Callaway?"

Darcy nodded and gave the woman a quick glance.

"I'm Kaye Zimmerman." The beautician had paused, leaning on her broom handle. She was small and pretty, with a head of glossy auburn hair piled up in a braided bun. Trailing down beside her ears, a matched pair of wispy ringlets danced in the breeze. "Gabe told me about you. He's my son."

"Oh, yes." Darcy wiped her sticky fingers on the thigh of her jeans. "Hi. Nice to meet you."

"I've seen you walking past here in the afternoons. You're staying with Ruby McCann, aren't you? I recognized you in that pink skirt of hers at church last Sunday. It's always been one of her favorites."

Darcy looked away. Not this again! How could she ever prove she hadn't stolen Ruby's clothes?

"Anyway, I just have to ask you a question," Kaye said. "I hope you don't mind."

Darcy tried to smile. She could hardly wait.

"Is that your real color?" Kaye gave an embarrassed giggle. "I mean, I know that's personal, but it's just so pretty and shiny. I'll bet I get ten women a week asking for that shade, but you know, you just can't get it out of a bottle."

"Oh, my hair color." Darcy let out her breath. "It's natural."

"I was afraid of that." Kaye walked over and lifted a strand that had fallen from Darcy's ponytail. "Pretty, pretty, pretty. I guess God's the only one who can get color that good. But how many layers have you got here, honey? What kind of style is this supposed to be?"

"Sort of a pixie cut. A long time ago."

"Must have been years since you had a trim!" Kaye shook her head. "I never saw so many layers in my life. It's a wonder you can get it all up into a ponytail. Why don't you come by sometime and let me straighten you out? I could shape you all up so elegant, maybe put in a little gel and style you just right. We could get you some fullness, I know for a fact. What do you say?"

"Well, it sounds nice." Darcy could feel herself flushing. "But right now, I really don't have the money for—"

"Forget about paying this first time. I'd do that hair just to get a better look at the color. What do you say?"

"Thank you, Mrs. Zimmerman."

"Kaye. That's what everybody calls me, honey."

"Kaye."

"And listen," she said, taking Darcy's elbow. "Don't pay a bit of attention to what folks around town are saying about you. I do Ruby's hair every Saturday morning, and she tells me how much help you are to her. Doing her laundry and running errands and all that. People are just jealous that she likes you so much, that's all. This town is full of gossips— and I'll tell you who's the worst. Pearlene Fox, that's who. She'll run anybody into the ground if she gets half a chance. She goes all the way to Jefferson City to get her hair done, you know, and I never saw a worse highlight job in my life. Heavy platinum streaks on top of her old brown roots, as if hair could ever look natural like that. Oh, listen to me running on. You just come on into the shop anytime, and I'll fix you right up."

"Thanks, Kaye."

"I'd call your color kind of an ash blonde, wouldn't you?" she said as she headed back to the steps with her broom. "But there's definitely some honey in it, and even a little gold. I sure do wish I could copy that color. I'd make a million bucks. 'Bye, now!"

Darcy practically ran around the corner and down the street to the entrance gates of the McCann estate. She had been so determined not to get involved in the lives of anyone in this town. But how could she avoid it? Even when she was minding her own business, people stopped her to insert themselves into her private world.

In chapel, Darcy's Prison Fellowship leader had explained how Christians were supposed to be servants, to reach out to others around them, to minister and to care. Inside the walls, this had been a very risky proposition. To stay out of trouble with the gangs, Darcy had always kept to herself. In six years she could claim few acquaintances, and not a single friend. But during her final months of incarceration, she'd begun to build some tentative relationships with others in the chapel group.

Now, the outside world seemed determined to grab Darcy and force her to get involved with everyone she met. Gabe and his girlfriend were in trouble, and Darcy knew that only God had the kind of answers that could help them. Kaye Zimmerman, as confident as she seemed, had no idea she was on her way to becoming a grandmother. Ruby McCann had been so loving and kind—how could Darcy ignore her needs? Little Montgomery clearly needed Christ's healing from her terrible loss. And then there was Luke, whose presence in her life stirred emotions she had hoped never to feel again.

Swallowing the last of her cone, she slipped through the tall iron entrance gates and started down the driveway to the house. She had developed a little ritual for each day. The routine had started after she and Luke learned Ruby had Alzheimer's disease.

Each morning, Darcy drove Ruby to the library, with a stop at the Corner Market to pick up a small carton of milk and some lunch items. Ruby drove herself home when the library closed at five. But every afternoon after work, Darcy paused at Ruby's house to take care of minor housekeeping tasks like checking the refrigerator for supplies and giving the kitchen a quick sweeping. Often, the two women had tea together on the front porch. Evening had become Darcy's favorite time of day.

As she knocked on the front door, she noticed that

Ruby's big DeSoto wasn't parked in its usual spot beside the lilac bush. Odd. By this time, Ruby usually had her teakettle going and was reading the Jefferson City newspaper in the front parlor. Darcy made her way along the side of the house to the multipaned bay window. The parlor was dark, the red velvet curtains drawn shut. Growing concerned, she returned to the front door and knocked again. When no one answered, she pushed open the door and stepped inside.

"Ruby? Are you here?" Her voice echoed along the marbled tiles. "I stopped by to throw in a load of laundry for you."

Checking both floors, Darcy quickly determined that the house was empty. Lights hadn't been turned on in the dining room or the kitchen. The bedrooms upstairs were dark. She hurried to the black rotary telephone near Ruby's bed and dialed the town library. No one answered.

Her heart throbbing, Darcy dialed Luke's house. Calling him was the last thing she wanted to do, but what choice did she have? As she listened to the ringing on the other end, a voice inside told her not to worry, that Ruby was probably doing a little grocery shopping or had gone to fill her gas tank. Darcy should just go on to the guesthouse and start her supper. She was tired, and she wasn't responsible for Ruby anyway—especially not in a town where everyone thought Darcy intended to con the old woman out of her wealth. She ought to just leave the situation alone, wait it out, see what would happen.

"Hello?"

Luke's voice dispelled every self-concerned thought from Darcy's head. "Ruby's missing," she told him. "Her car's gone, and the house is empty. She hasn't turned on any lights, so I don't even know if she's been home this afternoon. I called the library but—"

"I'll be right over. Stay there."

Darcy hung up the phone and went to the window. Where on earth could Ruby have gone at this hour? In the growing darkness, she spotted a small lump lying in the far distance beside the exit gates to the estate. *Oh, no!* Fear clenching her throat, Darcy raced down the stairs and out the front door. Out of the corner of her eye she could see Luke's pickup pulling through the entrance gates, but she knew she didn't dare stop.

"Ruby!" she shouted as she neared the fallen form. "Ruby, it's Jo."

But when she dropped to her knees, she realized that the shape on the gravel drive was nothing more than a pile of discarded clothing. A gray silk dress. A soft pink cashmere sweater. And Ruby's pearls.

"What's going on?" Luke pulled the pickup to a stop beside Darcy.

"It's her dress!" Darcy stood with the armful of clothing. "Ruby's pearl necklace. She never goes anywhere without her pearls. Oh, Luke, what's happened to Ruby?"

"Get into the pickup."

He reached across and threw open the door. As Darcy climbed in beside him, Luke was punching in a set of numbers on his cell phone. He spoke rapidly to the local police, informing them of the situation while he steered the pickup through the gates and out onto the street.

"Where are we going?" Darcy asked.

"Just driving around. Mick said he'd check with Boompah over at the Corner Market. And Ben's going to talk to Al Huff at the gas station. Then they'll come over to the house and take another look. Are you positive she's not there?"

"No sign of her anywhere." Darcy ran her hand across the gray silk. "This was the dress she had on this morning when I took her to work. And I'm pretty sure she was wearing this sweater, too. Luke, what if somebody kidnapped her?"

"Why would they do that?"

"Well, everyone says she's rich. Maybe someone thought he could get a ransom."

Luke glanced sideways at her. Darcy swallowed, remembering that he knew all about her and realizing he was probably aware of the speculation in town. What if people thought Darcy had done something to Ruby? If the dear elderly woman came to any kind of harm, Darcy might be blamed. She wondered what Luke had been thinking and if he regretted asking her to stay on. The thought that he might reject her, might find her repulsive, was more than she could bear.

Horrifying images suddenly filled her thoughts. "Oh, Luke! If the man took off Ruby's clothes, he wasn't planning to ransom her! Some pervert has her. Some psycho was probably waiting when she got home from the library. He stole her car, and he's taken her off to . . . to . . . oh, Luke, drive faster!"

"Faster to where?" He steered the pickup past the row of bungalows that lined River Street. "I don't have any idea where to start looking."

"What if he took her to the river?"

"That's the other way."

"Turn around! Pull in here."

He swerved onto a narrow gravel road. But as he started to back out onto the main street again, he leaned forward. "Do you see something? I thought I saw a glint through the trees."

"A glint?" Darcy squinted as the truck threaded through the thickly forested acreage. "I don't see—"

"This is the new McCann subdivision. It's being divided into lots and developed for . . . there's her car!"

"Do you have a gun? What if the man's armed? You need a weapon, Luke."

He stopped the pickup beside the DeSoto and jumped

out while it was still running. Darcy threw open the door
and peered through the windows of the old car.

"They're not here," she said. "He's taken her into the
forest."

"Ruby!"

"Don't call her! He'll know we're here. He might panic.
He might kill her."

"Ruby!" Luke ignored Darcy, walking down the side of
the paved road, shouting at the top of his lungs. "Ruby
McCann, where are you?"

"I'm right here. Is that you, dear?"

The small, tremulous voice came from deep within a
thicket of oak saplings. Darcy and Luke tore through the
brush, tripping over honeysuckle vines and jumping a narrow stream. Suddenly Darcy caught sight of a tiny figure on
a cluster of rocks down the creek bank. It was Ruby, wearing a white nylon petticoat, a pair of snagged stockings, and
her favorite pink high heels. She gave a little wave.

"Hello, hello!" She smiled as Darcy and Luke worked
their way down the bank toward her. "I'm so glad you
could join us. Welcome!"

Darcy paused beside the rocks, trying to catch her breath.
"Ruby, what on earth are you doing out here?"

"I'm waiting for my husband to come to tea, of course,"
she said. Her face softened as her blue eyes gazed off into
the distance. "Wilmer is such a dear man. I do not believe
I have loved anyone more tenderly in all my life."

Nine

"My husband owns all this land," Ruby explained, waving her hand to indicate the acres of thick forest surrounding the creek. She tugged on the hem of her lace-trimmed petticoat as Luke climbed the pile of rocks toward her perch. "McCann Estates is what we call the property. Nearly four hundred acres of prime Missouri forest. We have oak and maple and sycamore trees. And Wilmer says he's especially pleased at the fact that two streams run through the area, neither of them ever dry. Do you recognize this rivulet, Mr. Easton?"

Luke clambered onto the slab of limestone where Ruby was sitting. "Looks like Johnson Creek to me," he said, brushing a mosquito from her bare arm.

"Exactly right. The Johnsons were early settlers of this land, you know. But my husband's grandfather bought the property from them years ago." She glanced around. "Where is Wilmer? I expected him to turn up by now. But then, he's often late for tea."

Darcy had made it to the top of the stone pile, and she sat down beside Ruby. "How are you feeling, Mrs. McCann?" she asked, slipping her arm around the older woman's shoulders. "There's a little bit of chill in the breeze tonight."

"Do you think so?" Ruby squinted at her. "And what is your name, my dear? I don't believe we've met."

"I'm Jo. I'm staying in your guesthouse."

"Are you? How lovely to have it occupied. How do you find it? Are you comfortable?"

"It's wonderful." She pulled the pink sweater from the knot of clothing still in her arms. "Ruby, how about if you put this on?"

"Oh, I don't think so. I've been hot all day, my dear. So terribly, terribly hot."

"You know, I went over to the Tastee Hut and bought myself an ice cream cone after work. Maybe Luke would drive us all there, and we could get a hamburger. Would you like that?"

"Well, I'm waiting for . . ." She paused and fingered a piece of lace on her petticoat. "I'm waiting for . . . for someone. . . . Who am I waiting for? I can't seem to place the name."

Luke focused on Darcy's face, and in the waning sunlight, he saw a tear slide down her cheek. "For Wilmer," Darcy said softly. "But, Ruby, your husband won't come today. I'm sorry."

"We had such a nice funeral for Wilmer." Ruby took the sweater from Darcy's lap and slipped it around her shoulders. "Hundreds of mourners came, you know. My husband was a highly respected member of the Ambleside community."

Luke thought about his own wife, how it had been more than a year since her burial, and how sometimes it seemed like yesterday. Would there come a time when he was as confused as Ruby, thinking Ellie was still alive? Or would he find a way to build a new life, one in which Ellie was never forgotten but in which a hope, a love, a future would fill the lost and lonely spaces inside his heart?

He couldn't deny the occasional moment when he caught himself wishing for the sound of a woman's footsteps on the front porch. Or when he woke up in his big, lonely bed, longing for warm arms in the night. Or when

Montgomery cried out, and there was no one to cuddle her but a hard-muscled, whiskery daddy. Yet he knew he didn't want just any woman. In fact, he had tried to convince himself he was fine on his own. But recently, more often than he'd like to admit, he found himself wondering if Darcy could fill that void.

"I loved Wilmer very much," Ruby said. "Such a love cannot be easily forgotten. I considered our marriage a gift from God. Of course, it wasn't a perfect relationship. Some days Wilmer and I didn't see eye to eye. And we had illnesses, too. There was even a time when we had almost no money to speak of. Oh yes, it's true. We were young in the thirties and forties—those years of economic depression and war—and this forest certainly didn't put much food on the table. But our most poignant sorrow was our inability to have children. Yet, I can tell you with assurance that our marriage was God's blessing. Through every difficulty, I loved Wilmer and he loved me. Have you ever known such a love, Jo?"

Luke studied the younger woman's face, barely lit by the pale gold glow of sunset. She blotted another tear from her cheek. "No, Ruby," she said, "I've never known such a love."

"Then my heart aches for you, my dear," Ruby said. Luke realized his heart was aching for Darcy, too. "There is something inexplicably wonderful that occurs when I look into Wilmer's eyes and he looks into mine," Ruby went on. "The troubles and the disagreements vanish. And what is left is the bare truth of our love. It's more than love, really. It's a bond. A promise we made. A vow that cannot be broken."

Luke gently brushed another mosquito from Ruby's arm. She was going to itch the next day. But right now, lost in her memories, she didn't seem to notice anything. He wondered if he'd ever had such a bond with Ellie. Their love

had been strong and enduring. But had he stopped to treasure her, to look into her eyes, to vow that their promises
would never be broken?

"Odd isn't it, how bondage can set a person free," Ruby
said. "I was never so free as the day when I wedded my
earthly life to Wilmer's."

"That's like what they told us about God at the chapel,"
Darcy said. "They said giving away your heart to Christ sets
you free."

"Quite the same thing in many ways, my dear."

"And it happens with people, too? Committing yourself to
others sets you free?"

"Yes, indeed. How lonely, how confined, how desperate
one feels when there is no one . . ." Ruby paused, her voice
catching. "Loneliness is a terrible prison."

"But, Ruby, you have us," Luke said. "Jo and I came looking for you the minute we realized you weren't at your
house. Jo's got your dress and your pearls. And we're here
to take care of you."

"My pearls?" Ruby sat in silence for a moment. "Oh, dear.
I'm not at all certain where I am at the moment. I'm afraid
I've gotten myself lost, quite turned around."

"Then how about letting me carry you to my pickup so
I can take you back home? Would that be all right?"

"I would dearly love a hamburger from the Tastee Hut.
I am partial to their onion rings as well." She gave a little
laugh. "But you mustn't tell the library board. They wouldn't
like my eating onions, you know. When one is assisting
one's patrons, it's not polite to envelop them with onion
breath."

"I guess not." Luke lifted the tiny woman in his arms and
started down the pile of rocks. In the dim light, he could
just make out Ruby's pink high-heeled shoes and Darcy's
golden hair as she walked alongside.

Darcy managed to button Ruby's sweater as they drove

back into town. When they stopped at the Tastee Hut, Ruby seemed to have forgotten all about Wilmer and their imagined meeting in the forest. She dug into an order of onion rings as though she hadn't eaten in days. And her hamburger vanished almost before Darcy and Luke had theirs unwrapped.

When they arrived back at the McCann house, Ruby tottered inside as though it were perfectly normal to walk around eating onion rings while wearing a lace petticoat and pink high heels. Darcy started to follow her into the house, but Luke caught her hand.

"Listen, do you think she's safe here? Maybe we should do something about her," he said.

"I thought I'd sleep over here. To keep an eye on her."

"You'd better lock her into the bedroom."

Darcy looked away. "I don't want to do that."

"But she might wander away again. And what if she takes off her petticoat next time? What if she goes roaming all over town?"

"What if people hear that I've locked Ruby McCann into her own bedroom? They already think I'm stealing her clothes and trying to weasel my way into her good graces. They think I'm—"

"*You* know who you are. And *I* know who you are." He leaned one shoulder against a porch pillar. "I'll stand up for you, Darcy. I promise."

She looked down at her hands. "Ruby says promises set us free. But she's wrong. If you stand up for me, Luke, if people think you're on my side, you could get thrown into my own private little prison. It's not a great place to live, trust me."

He thought of his own lonely prison. His aching emptiness. His despair. Right now, the thought of sharing anything with another person seemed more than welcome.

"Look," he said. "I'll choose who I make promises to. I'll choose who I support. And I've said I'm with you."

She searched his face, her eyes large. "I don't know why," she whispered. "You know what I did."

"You went hunting for an old lady lost in the woods. That's what you did. That's who you are."

"But I—"

"Look, our past is a part of each of us, Darcy. Back in the forest when you were jabbering about perverts and yelling at me to get a gun, I saw a little bit of that past. And when Ruby was talking about Wilmer, I slipped back into my old life with Ellie. But my wife died, and you walked out of that prison. The way I see it, if either of us is going to move forward, we've got to stop looking back."

Darcy shook her head. "You act like we're both trying to overcome the same thing. But you loved your wife, Luke. I hated my husband. Ellie was taken from you by circumstances you couldn't control. I shot my husband to death with a handgun. You can't possibly understand how hard it is to put this behind me."

"How can I understand when you won't tell me what your life was like?"

"I told you about my husband, the things that happened between us."

"What about your life in prison? You haven't said anything about that."

"Prison was gray walls, locked doors, bolted cells. I had no friends. I learned right away that taking up another inmate's cause could lead to all kinds of trouble with the gangs inside the place. To stay out of the gangs, I kept myself away from everyone. If an inmate was being abused or harassed, I turned away. It was a matter of survival."

"But you're more than a survivor, Darcy," Luke said. "You're a victor. How did you come to be the way you are?

I believe you're a different woman now. What changed you?"

"Victory came through the words my Prison Fellowship leader spoke in chapel. She's the one who gave me the key that set me free from the walls I'd built around my own life. *'Those who become Christians become new persons.'* It's the only Bible verse I managed to memorize before they let me out. But it's the one I count on most. I want to be new and different."

"You are."

"When I look in the mirror, though, I see that same old person. I see a face with a broken jawbone. A swollen black eye. A hand holding a gun. A drab prison uniform. A number on my pocket. I was that woman for a long time, you know. Sometimes I'm afraid she's still around. Lurking. Waiting to jump out."

Luke couldn't resist reaching out to touch a wisp of hair that had fallen from her ponytail. At the contact of silk against his skin, his heart slammed against his chest.

"That's not who I see when I look at you," he said, aware of her eyes on his face. "I believe the woman you described existed a long time ago, Darcy. But the person standing here with me tonight is kind and thoughtful and good. She works hard, and she takes care of those who need her help. And she's very . . . very . . ."

He cupped her cheek, running his thumb under her eye and trying to imagine the man who would dare to strike out against such fragile beauty. Had Darcy's husband really broken her jaw? He moved his fingers beneath the delicate bone, aware of the softness of her skin.

"You're very beautiful," he said in a low voice.

She reached up and took his hand, lowering it from her face. "I can't, Luke. I can't be near you like this."

Her eyes were full and heavy lashed as she gazed up at him, and they were telling him the exact opposite of her spoken words. He struggled for breath, for clarity. Suddenly, he wanted nothing more than to take this woman in his arms and kiss her lips, know the warmth of her mouth, drink in the gentle curves of her body. It had been so long. And he was so lonely. And here they stood in the moonlight.

He leaned toward her, but she stepped back toward the door. "I have to check on Ruby," Darcy said softly, her focus never leaving his face. "And I need to . . . to not be alone with you. I need to be new and different, and I can't let myself feel . . . feel things."

"Is it so wrong?"

"Yes. Yes, it is. You're still in love with your wife's memory, and you need to take care of Montgomery. And I have to pay off my lawyer and build my new life. I can't get tangled up. It's already so complicated with Ruby and Gabe and now Kaye—"

"Who?"

"All these people. And you can't be one of them. You can't be in my life. Except that I work for you, but that's all. That's all, okay?"

"Okay." He understood what she was trying to say, even though he didn't want to hear it. Even though he didn't completely believe her.

"I have to check on Ruby."

"You said that."

She was standing at the edge of the doorway, her hand on the frame. She brushed back a tendril of hair, tucking it behind her ear, and then she drank down a deep breath.

"It's just that I made such a mess of things before," she told him. "I chose the wrong man for all the wrong reasons, and then it just got worse. It wasn't all Bill's fault, either. I was a wreck of a human being, confused and selfish and young. And just plain stupid part of the time. I made a lot of mistakes. I don't want to do that again. Any of it."

"I'm not Bill."

"I know."

"And you're not the woman you were."

"I know that, too. But, Luke, there's been only one thing really right in my life. And that's my faith in Christ. I need to keep my focus on him. His plan for me is to do my job. To help Ruby and pay off my lawyer and stay away from Will Damyon. That's all I can handle right now, okay?"

"Okay."

"So, I'm going to check on Ruby."

He nodded, stepped up to the doorway, and kissed her gently on the cheek. "Good night, Darcy," he said.

He could hear Ruby calling as he walked back toward his pickup. He knew he shouldn't have kissed Darcy. But he was glad he had.

Darcy stepped out of Kaye's Kut-n-Kurl feeling like a million bucks. Her hair brushed the tops of her shoulders in a bouncy, blunt cut that had evened out most of the layers. A sample bottle of styling gel weighted the pocket of her skirt, yet her feet fairly floated down the steps.

"Now don't forget to bend over and blow-dry that hair upside down," Kaye called. "We sure did get fullness, didn't we?"

"I'm so full, I could just about burst!" Darcy lifted her arms and did a little twirl that sent her skirt ballooning out into a pouf of green fabric. She could hear Kaye giggling behind her, and she gave the stylist a wave. "See you at the picnic this evening!" Though Kaye didn't know it—and Darcy herself was reluctant to admit it—much of Darcy's elation stemmed from the joy she felt in her growing relationship with Luke.

"Wear shorts! It's going to be hot," Kaye called after her.

Darcy looked up at the sky. She didn't own any shorts,

and she couldn't afford to buy a pair just for the Saturday church picnic. Ruby's cotton skirt would have to do. Besides, a line of dark clouds was gathering over the Missouri River, and the humidity was so high she could feel a trickle of perspiration running down her spine. Her short experience in central Missouri told her that the picnickers were going to be grateful that Chalmers Park had a large covered pavilion to protect them from the rain. The fact that she might be spending time with Luke away from work made her nervous and excited. She hoped he would show up.

Concerned about having left Ruby alone for two hours, Darcy hurried down the sidewalk and through the gates of the McCann home. Though nothing serious had happened in the days following the incident in the forest, Darcy felt that she needed to keep a constant watch on her friend. She had spent every night in the bedroom just down the hall from Ruby's, and she found herself needing to do almost everything for the elderly woman.

As Darcy stepped into the cool foyer of the house, she heard Ruby singing in the kitchen. Most of the time, things went along in perfect harmony. Ruby still spent her days at the library—though Darcy wondered what she did there—and her evenings sitting at home looking at the newspaper and sipping her tea.

But she never could manage her buttons or zippers. She left curlers in her hair. The milk regularly ended up in the pantry, while the garden spade and a bottle of expensive perfume had found their way into the refrigerator.

"Well, what do you think?" Darcy asked as she breezed into the kitchen and did a pirouette for Ruby.

"Stunning!" The older woman raised her hands in astonishment. "You are a vision, my dear! That Kaye Zimmerman is a miracle worker. She can really give a woman fullness.

I do believe Mr. Luke Easton will faint dead away when
he lays eyes on you."

Darcy's laugh caught in her throat as she spotted the vast
array of food on the counter. Ruby had opened every bag
of bread, sack of potatoes, can of vegetables, and jar of
peanut butter in the pantry. Utensils and plastic bags and
bowls were scattered everywhere. Pots bubbled on the
stove.

"What are you doing, Ruby?" Darcy asked.

"Preparing for the church picnic, of course. One ought to
take enough to share with one's neighbors. That has always
been my philosophy, and Wilmer agrees wholeheartedly."

"But, Ruby, you've opened three jars of spaghetti sauce.
And what about all these cans of soup?"

"I had in mind a casserole I used to make. Wilmer loves
it. But then the recipe escaped me entirely. It had a
tomato-sauce base, I recall. And I thought it called for
noodles."

"Oh, Ruby!" Darcy grabbed a pot from the burner as the
last of the liquid boiled away from a huge soggy lump of
macaroni. "There's no water left here. The noodles have all
turned to glue."

"Well, I've forgotten the recipe anyway, so what are you
being so testy about?" The aspect of Ruby's disease that
made her the most difficult to deal with suddenly emerged
full force as she began to shout in a shrill voice, "You interfere in everything I try to do, young lady! I don't know why
I hired you in the first place. Wilmer is quite right about
you employees. You're worthless!"

"Ruby—"

"My name is Mrs. McCann, and you're fired! There, how's
that? You can just take your things and go." She reached out
and slapped Darcy across the cheek. "Naughty girl! Get
away from me. Don't touch me!"

Cupping her stinging cheek, Darcy stepped backward as

a stream of foul language poured from Ruby's soft lips. Where had this genteel woman even heard such words? *Dear God,* Darcy lifted up, *help me know what to do!* Suddenly wishing for Luke's calming presence, she stepped away from the counter as Ruby moved toward her again.

"The whole world is a fleshpot of sin and destruction," Ruby cried, "and you're the . . . the . . ." Stopping in the middle of the kitchen, she burst into tears. "Oh, I don't know! I just don't know!"

"It's all right, Ruby," Darcy said.

"No, no. I'm falling to bits. Everything around me is just pickles and chairs . . . and the casserole was always Wilmer's favorite . . . but now I can't put on my pearls, you know . . . and I'm so . . . so . . ."

"Oh, Ruby, it's very confusing. I know it is." Darcy crossed the floor and took the old woman in her arms. "Why don't we pick up some hamburgers at the Tastee Hut and take them to the picnic? I have five dollars, and that should just about cover it. Here, let me fix the buttons on your blouse."

Darcy undid the row of mismatched buttons and fastened them in the right order. She turned off all the burners, put away some of the food, and decided to abandon the rest for later. Then she led Ruby over to the sink and washed a mixture of spaghetti sauce and chocolate syrup off her hands. The whole time, Ruby just kept on crying, while Darcy prayed as hard as she could for the wisdom to know what to do.

She had the sudden realization that prison life had been almost easy compared to this. In prison there were no variables! Mealtimes were always the same, the food was provided, the clothing never changed, and the people around her were tightly controlled. If anyone bothered her, she could always request protective custody.

That's what she wanted right now, Darcy realized.

Protective custody! She needed God to put her in a little room where nobody could need her. There wouldn't be any old ladies to slap her and then hug her. There wouldn't be hair that needed upside-down blow-drying. And there certainly wouldn't be a man kissing her on the cheek.

Steering the old DeSoto to the Tastee Hut's drive-through, Darcy placed an order and waited for it to arrive. As she pulled back onto the street, she saw Ruby dig into the onion rings. They were gone by the time Darcy parked in the large lot. The moment she stepped out of the car, she was joined by Elizabeth and Zachary Chalmers and their son, Nick. Darcy had crossed paths with the newlyweds only a couple of times, although Zachary regularly came to the mansion to confer with Luke.

"Looks like rain," Elizabeth said as she helped Ruby out of the DeSoto. "I'm glad we have the pavilion."

"It doesn't look like rain to me, Mom," Nick said. "It looks like plain air."

"I mean it looks like it's *going* to rain. Hey, there are Luke and Montgomery! Zachary, can you believe Luke actually came?" The young woman leaned toward Darcy. "Luke stopped attending church around the time Ellie died."

"He used to be a bacon," Nick announced.

"A deacon," his father clarified. "This is a good sign. Let's ask if he and Montgomery want to join us. And how about you, Mrs. McCann?"

"I have eaten all the onion rings," Ruby said, "and they were utterly delicious."

As the two groups neared each other, Darcy glanced around for an escape route. Though she had spoken with Luke since the kiss on the front porch, she had managed to keep the conversation short and focused only on the work in the old Chalmers Mansion. The incident had disturbed her more than she wanted to admit. Somehow Luke's words and his touch had transported her out of the small world she had been trying so desperately to control. His kiss had reminded her she was a woman. A human being.

The days following the moments on Ruby's porch had left Darcy almost reeling. She had constantly thought about Luke, about his past and his future, and about every impossible thing that prevented an attachment between them. She mentally tallied all the barriers that separated them: their past hurts and losses . . . their financial burdens . . . the mistakes each of them had made . . . the fears they both struggled with.

But then, with a heart lightened by wings of hope, she had leaped over each hurdle. Maybe God would heal the past, she had prayed as she lay alone in bed at night. Maybe he would ease financial worries and mend tattered spirits and wipe away all regret. Maybe he would calm fears and create newness out of lives that felt stale, lonely, and empty. It was possible. Darcy believed in the power of the Spirit to whom she had entrusted her life.

Still, every time she looked at Luke, reality came crashing in. Impossible. What had she been thinking? There could be nothing between them.

As he and Montgomery approached now, she turned away. She would find Kaye Zimmerman and show her how the fullness in her hair had held up all these hours. She would meet Kaye's husband, Nathan, and ask him about his sundries store on the corner of River Street and Main. But as she started in their direction, her focus fell on a man standing at the edge of the clearing.

"I thought I'd warn you," Luke said, his voice low as he moved to Darcy's side. "But I see you've already spotted him."

It was Will Damyon.

TEN

Will Damyon stood with his back to the crowd, but Darcy recognized the broad shoulders and sweat-stained jacket. He looked just like his son. The man was chatting with Pearlene Fox and her husband, Phil, who was the local barber and a city councilman. As if on cue, all three turned and stared at Darcy. Swallowing hard, she lifted her chin and stared back.

"What's he doing here?" she said to no one in particular.

"I noticed him earlier this afternoon at the bus station," Luke said. "I figured he might show up at the picnic."

"You shouldn't have come for this, Luke." She looked into his blue eyes. "You can't protect me from him. I'm going to have to handle the situation myself."

"I didn't come to the picnic to protect you. I came because Nick invited Montgomery." He paused, searching her face. "It's been a long time since I've had anything to do with the church. But watching you . . . your faith in God in spite of Will Damyon and the things people say and do to you . . . has made me do some thinking."

"My faith in God isn't *in spite* of Will Damyon and the rest of it. It's *because* of all that. It's because I need God's help to make it through each day. It's because I'm so grateful . . ." She paused, emotion welling up inside her. "I'm grateful to Christ for what he did for me."

"We're different that way. You're grateful because you believe God got you out of a mess. I'm angry because I believe he dropped Montgomery and me right into one."

"We're all in the middle of a mess, Luke." Darcy shrugged. "Mine's still going on. Outwardly, nothing has changed that much. It's inside that I've changed."

"I believe you." He gave her a half grin. "There's got to be a reason you're the way you are. Special."

Darcy studied the admiring twinkle in his eyes and tried to calm her heart. She couldn't let him keep saying these things. She couldn't keep wanting to hear them. He reached across the space between them and gave the ends of her hair a little tug.

"Looks good. Did Kaye Zimmerman do this?"

"A few hours ago. I don't know if I can get it to be this full tomorrow. You have to blow-dry it upside down."

He didn't respond, but his eyes trailed over her hair and down her neck. She felt herself flush. For years, she had pushed away her femininity, fearful of attracting the attention of the guards or the gangs of predatory women in prison. Now she felt herself blossoming, unfolding petal by petal like a spring tulip, leafing outward toward the sunshine of Luke's attention.

"Your cheeks are turning pink," he said with a wink.

"Well, if you'd stop staring at me . . ." She glanced away in time to see Pearlene Fox make a beeline for Pastor Paul, the kindhearted minister of their church. "Oh, Luke, he's told them. Will has told the Foxes about me. About what I did. I've got to get out of here."

"Stay." He took her hand. "Come sit with Montgomery and me. We're over there by the Chalmerses."

"No, Luke." She pulled away. "I want to go back to the house. Ruby made a huge mess in the kitchen, and I need to clean it up. I'll just—"

"Stay here, Darcy. Remember what you told me a few minutes ago? You said God is with you. You have faith in him. Show me your faith, Darcy. Show me the new woman."

Forcing down the lump of dismay in her throat, Darcy allowed Luke to walk beside her past Phil Fox, who was deep in conversation with Cleo Mueller, the mayor of Ambleside. The two men stopped speaking and watched the couple walk all the way to the red-plaid blanket spread near the edge of the pavilion. Darcy tried to smile at Ruby and the others. But as she sat down, she could see that Pearlene had moved onward to the Zimmermans' blanket.

"Here comes the rain," Ruby said. "I can feel it in my bones."

"I can hear it in my ears," Nick responded as a rumble of thunder shuddered across the park. "We better move under the roof."

"Let's take that spot," Montgomery said. "Hurry up, before Pastor Paul prays."

Darcy joined in as the two groups raced to carry their blankets and picnic baskets under the protection of the large open-sided shelter. They were spreading out their things when the first droplets began to fall. The pastor started to say something, but a sizzling jag of lightning shot out of the sky and silenced his words. After the accompanying thunder rolled by, he began to speak again.

"Ambleside Community Chapel welcomes everyone to our annual summer picnic," he called out to the crowd from behind a podium. "This year, I'm afraid we might need an ark."

The crowd chuckled, and Darcy tried to relax. She could see Will Damyon sitting with the Foxes near the front of the pavilion. How had he ingratiated himself so quickly? The townspeople hardly knew her, and now they must be thinking the worst things imaginable. And, of course, they were all true.

"Dear Lord," Pastor Paul said, bowing his head, "we are so grateful for this community. We thank you for our church, for your rich blessings upon us. And now, Father, we thank you for this opportunity to gather in fellowship and love. We thank you for this abundant food and for this time to talk and share and laugh. Above all, we pray that today and every day we may remember your great sacrificial gift to us in the death and resurrection of your Son, Jesus Christ. It is in his name we pray these things, amen."

"He didn't say *lead, guide, and direct,*" Nick whispered, his green eyes sparkling. "I'm sure he didn't say it."

"But he said lots of other stuff," Montgomery said as sheets of rain began to pour down on the pavilion. "You're supposed to listen to the pastor and pray along with him, Nick. You're not supposed to be listening for *lead, guide, and direct.*"

"I didn't hear him say it. Or *bless the gift and the giver.* He didn't say that either."

"Well, he wasn't collecting the offering!"

"Is that fried chicken?" Ruby asked, leaning across Darcy's paper plate to have a closer look at the contents of the Chalmers family's basket. "I am greatly fond of fried chicken. A leg is my dearest pleasure."

"Jo can make really good fried chicken," Montgomery said. "She's the best. And you should taste her baked beans."

Darcy tried to keep her focus on the meal as a local singing group got up to perform. The quartet's medley of songs was punctuated by the regular crackle of lightning and the drumroll of thunder, but no one seemed to mind. As rain poured, the crowd under the pavilion passed around plates filled with fried chicken and ham, bowls of green bean casserole topped with onions, and cartons of potato salad, macaroni salad, and three-bean salad—all toted in from the Nifty Cafe.

The youth group's puppet team followed the quartet. They put on a short performance that drew all the children to the front of the pavilion. And then the desserts started around—pecan pies, Jell-O studded with cherries and marshmallows, and towering chocolate cakes dripping with thick icing.

"Thanks, young folks," Pastor Paul said as the puppet team folded up their stage. "And now we'll hear from one of our favorite soloists, Thelma Huff. Thelma, come on up here and—"

"If I could interrupt for just a second." Will Damyon stepped up to the podium. "I'm a newcomer to this town, but I'd like to say what a fine time I've had at your picnic this afternoon."

Darcy held her breath, her arms and legs suddenly ice-cold. Will smiled as he shook hands with Pastor Paul. Then he faced the crowd again.

"People as nice as you folks deserve to know what kind of trouble you've got brewing in your little town. And by that, I'm referring to another newcomer who calls herself Jo Callaway."

As he pointed across the crowd, every head turned and every eye focused on Darcy. She stiffened, unable to breathe, unable to move.

"Her name's not Jo Callaway, though," Will said. "It's Darcy Damyon, and she was once married to my son."

"We're certainly glad you could join us," Pastor Paul put in. He attempted to ease Will away from the podium, but the older man stood his ground.

"And not only that, but she just got out of prison!" he shouted. "For murdering my son in cold blood!"

"Well, now then." Pastor Paul spread his arms toward the crowd as everyone began to speak at once. "I do think we ought to move on with our program—"

"She shot him right in the head! That's what she did. Shot him dead!"

Darcy squeezed her hands together, trembling in horror.

"And then she pranced right out of prison and right into

your little town!" Will raised a pointed finger at her. "Now she's doing it again, seducing you fine folks into thinking kindly toward her. She's even got herself a new man, a new lover. Look at him there with her, name of Easton!"

Willing her legs to move, Darcy leapt up off the blanket and raced across the crowded pavilion. She could hear people gasping in shock, children shouting questions, someone screaming. Mortified, she dashed into the rain and splashed across the parking lot.

"Wait!" Someone was calling behind her. She thought it might be Luke, but she didn't care. She couldn't stop, couldn't let anyone find her. She had to get away. Had to escape.

She ran through a stand of oak trees, pushing her way through the grasping branches. Where could she go? Who would hide her? Tears streaming down her cheeks, mingling with the rain, she bolted through the park gates.

"Jo! Stop!"

The words sounded distant now. But she glanced back over her shoulder and she could see them coming. A whole crowd of people ran behind her through the rain, chasing her. "Oh, God, help me!" she cried out as she ran down the sidewalk. *Where can I go? How can I get away from them?*

How many times had she run from her husband, fear breathing down her neck as he came after her? He would be carrying a stick or a baseball bat. Or his fists would be doubled up, ready for her. She could almost smell him again as she sprinted through the darkness, down the rain-swept street.

"Jo! Jo!"

She had to get away. Had to hide. She remembered the old toolshed near the Chalmers house. It had a single door, unlocked. Who would look for her there? Breathing hard, she ran through the gated entrance to the old mansion. If he found her . . . if he caught her . . . if he came at her again . . . hitting and beating and tormenting . . .

There it was! She ran toward the shed, yanked open the door, threw herself inside. But as she pulled the door shut behind her, she could hear him coming.

"Jo! Wait!"

She curled into a ball, covering her head with her arms the way she always did. Maybe he wouldn't hurt her this time. Maybe she could fend him off.

The door flew open. "Jo? What are you—"

"Stay back!" Her mouth dry with terror, she grabbed for a weapon. Her hands found a long-handled hoe; she held it out in front of her, warding him off. "Don't come near me!" she cried, springing catlike to her feet and brandishing the hoe. "Don't touch me!"

She tried to see him in the dim light from the streetlamp. Shapes crowded the doorway—dark, angry, hulking shapes. She jabbed the hoe outward into thin air, and the shapes fell back muttering.

"Get away, all of you!" she shouted. "I won't let you hurt me!"

"Darcy, we don't want to hurt you." A warm, gentle voice sounded in the midst of the shapes. "Darcy, put down the hoe. It's me, Luke."

"Look at her!" Will Damyon spat. "She's at it again. She's a killer."

"Put down the hoe," Luke said. "No one's going to touch you."

"She'll brain somebody if she gets half the chance!" Will hollered.

"Back off, buster!" The sound of scuffling followed, and then Luke spoke again. "Darcy, give me the hoe."

Breathing hard, she lowered her weapon.

"It's Pastor Paul here," another voice said. "Jo, why don't you come out of the shed?"

"I promise I won't let anyone come near you," Luke added.

"Are you okay, Jo?" Kaye Zimmerman's words sounded small and frightened. "Nobody's going to hurt you, honey."

Staring at the shapes, Darcy felt the terror begin to recede. She dropped the hoe into the stack of tools. Then she wrapped her wet arms around herself and began to cry.

"She didn't show up to church Sunday," Floyd said, licking Chee-tos dust off his fingers. "I know that for a fact. After that deal at the picnic, I was watchin' for her. Figured she might have somethin' to say to the congregation, you know?"

"Like what?" Gabe asked. He was seated on the floor in the kitchen of Chalmers Mansion. Luke and Floyd occupied the chairs at the old oak table. "Like, 'Here I am, the town's new celebrity. Come on up and have a closer look at a real live murderer, everybody.' Of course she didn't come, Floyd. Would you want the whole town staring at you?"

"Well, I never kilt nobody. I reckon the least she oughta do is stand up and explain herself."

"How do you even know what that ol' coot said at the picnic is true, huh? Does Jo seem like the type to murder her husband?"

"No, but the way she run off into the rain that night made her look mighty guilty. And then she didn't show up to church, and here it is Wednesday, and she ain't come to work a single day this week."

"If it was me that happened to," Gabe said. "I'd be hiding too."

"Has she called in sick, Luke?" Floyd asked. "Maybe she took a chill runnin' in the rain."

"She hasn't called."

Luke took a bite of his sandwich and thought over the

situation as he chewed. Pastor Paul had driven Darcy home the night of the picnic. Luke had thought about going to church the next morning, just to see if Darcy would appear. Unlike those who just wanted to gawk, he was concerned about her well-being.

But in the end, he had decided against going to church. He hadn't been inside the building since Ellie's funeral, and showing up just to check on Darcy didn't seem appropriate. But he couldn't deny how worried he felt about her. He had made it a point to track Will Damyon to the bus station, so he knew the man had boarded a Greyhound bound for Joplin. But what would stop him from coming back?

"I don't mean to pry or nothin', Luke," Floyd said, "but I been doin' some thinkin' on what that man said about you and Jo. Is there something goin' on twixt the two of you that me and Gabe oughta know about?"

"There's nothing going on between Jo and me," Luke said. "Mr. Damyon saw us together the day I took her to Jefferson City, and he made some wrong assumptions. Jo's my employee, and that's all there is to it."

"Well, I can't figure out why you don't check up on her," Floyd said. "If I didn't show up to work on the wirin' some mornin', wouldn't you check on me?"

"No, he'd be grateful maybe you wouldn't burn down the mansion that day," Gabe said. He was laughing at his joke when Floyd threw one of his Chee-tos at him.

"I figure Jo just needs some time to herself," Luke said.

But his heart told him that she probably needed a friend. Was his embarrassment over Will Damyon's accusation about their relationship keeping him from reaching out to help Darcy? He thought about the way he'd touched her hair and kissed her. Maybe Damyon had been right after all. Maybe he had fallen under Darcy's spell, and he just didn't want to admit how much she meant to him.

Again, Luke wondered if Damyon had really taken that

Greyhound all the way back to Joplin. He thought about the man's anger over his son's death, and he wondered about Darcy's ability to defend herself. How could Luke let his own pride step in the way of her need?

"Maybe I ought to check on her," he said, pushing back from the table.

❧

Pulling up in front of the main house, Luke spotted Ruby McCann hunched over a bed of tulips that had spent their blooms. She had on a pair of trousers that must have belonged to Wilmer. They were enormous, and she had tied them at her waist with the belt from a blue terry-cloth bath-robe. Her white hair stood up between rows of curlers. Hearing the pickup, she got to her feet and waved.

"Good afternoon, Mr. Easton!" she called. "It's a lovely day, isn't it? Perfect for a spot of gardening."

Luke stepped out of his truck and walked toward her. "Mrs. McCann, why aren't you at the library?"

"The library?" Ruby's forehead puckered. "But we're always closed on Saturdays."

"Today's Wednesday."

The pink tinge drained from her cheeks. "Are you quite sure, Luke?"

"Absolutely. Montgomery and the other kids will be com-ing over for the reading group after school. You're reading them *The Secret Garden.*"

"Reading group? Great ghosts." Ruby tossed her trowel to the ground. "I'd better leave at once."

"Wait." Luke caught her arm as she headed for the old DeSoto. "Aren't you going to change clothes? And what about the . . . ?"

He indicated the crown of pink curlers in her hair. Ruby scowled at him. "What on earth are you jabbering about, young man? I didn't hire you to stand around gawking at me all day. Those tulips are overcrowded, and they won't bloom again next year unless you separate the bulbs. I shall have to tell Wilmer about this insolence. He always says we don't need a gardener!"

"Gardener?" Luke tried to keep his cool, but his gnawing worry about Darcy had him a little on edge. "Look, I'm not your gardener, Ruby, and—"

"You people take advantage of us. Oh yes you do, and don't think we're unaware of it! I've counted my silver in the past days only to find three forks missing. Three forks! And the sugar bowl was half empty when I made my coffee this morning. So there! You think you can just rob us blind—"

"Rob you? Why in the world would I want—"

"Oh, and what about those forks?" she shrieked. "Three forks, my best silver!"

"I don't have your precious forks, Ruby!"

"Watch your attitude with me, young man. I'll fire you! I'll put you out of house and home."

"Oh, yeah? Well, let me tell you something—"

"What's going on here?" Darcy walked through the front door of the house and set her hands on her hips. "Luke, what are you doing?"

"The gardener has stolen my good silver!" Ruby shouted. "Three of my forks are missing, and I know very well that he took them!"

Darcy glanced at Luke. Aware of the ridiculous argument he'd been having with Ruby, he felt suddenly ashamed, and the steam of his rage escaped in a sigh. "Forget it," he said. "I'm going back to work."

"That's right!" Ruby cried. "Back to work, you ingrate! Put half the tulips in that bed beside the door, and have it done by nightfall."

"Ruby, this is Luke Easton, remember?" Darcy said, laying

her hand on the old woman's arm. "He's Montgomery's father. He's not your gardener."

Luke swung around and headed for his pickup. He knew he should be patient with Ruby, but he didn't have the energy. As he reached for the door, Darcy's fingers covered his hand.

"She doesn't mean it," Darcy said. "This has been a bad day for her. It started with the shaving cream, and it's just gone downhill."

"What shaving cream?"

"Oh, she found some of Wilmer's old shaving cream. It was in a tube, and she brushed her teeth with it." She stared down at the gravel driveway.

Luke studied her, aware that her new hairstyle had gone flat. She was wearing her old jeans and heavy boots. She reminded him of the old Darcy, the one he had met on the street the day she came to Ambleside on the bus. Worn out. Defensive. Almost defeated.

"The shaving cream must have tasted pretty bad." She scuffed the gravel with her heel. "She's been crying all morning. She couldn't understand anything about the library. Didn't even remember she'd ever worked there. I finally got her outside to work on the tulips."

"So you've been taking care of Ruby all this time? Is that why you haven't been to work?"

Darcy shrugged. "After what happened Saturday, I didn't think I'd be welcome on the job. Now that the whole town knows about me, I mean. It wouldn't exactly look good for your company to have me on crew."

"I'm the one who makes the decisions about my crew." He reached out and tilted her chin with the tip of his finger. "Are you all right, Darcy? Damyon didn't find you, did he?"

"I'll be fine. It's Ruby who needs help. Pastor Paul said she never contacted him about becoming her executor. I don't know if she even went to see the lawyer or the bank.

But something has to be done, Luke. It's getting to the point where she needs watching all the time."

He stuck his hands into his pockets and looked across the driveway at Ruby. She was sitting on the front steps crying. When she noticed him, she stood and tottered toward him. He realized she was wearing a pair of purple high heels under Wilmer's trousers.

"Look, I'll talk to Sawyer-the-lawyer this afternoon," Luke said. "But I can't go to the bank. I'll see if . . . maybe Zachary Chalmers will go for me."

"Luke, what's happened? Something's wrong."

He looked into her eyes and knew he couldn't hide the truth. Anyway, it wouldn't be long before the whole town got wind of his own personal failure. "I got a letter yesterday, and I can't stop thinking about it," he said. "The bank foreclosed on my mortgage."

Understanding dawned on Darcy's face. "But your father is the president of the bank! Can't he do something?"

Luke frowned as he recalled the phone call he had made today. The little boy inside Luke, the child who still longed for his father's approval, had wanted to believe the man would help him. Instead, Frank Easton had just resurrected the old argument between them.

"My father told me that Montgomery and I would be welcome to move back home," Luke said. "He reminded me that he could always find me a position with the bank. I would have medical insurance, a retirement account, paid vacation time, even dental benefits."

"But you're a carpenter," Darcy said. "You build homes."

"Yeah, but I have to be reasonable. I have to be able to provide for my daughter, and I—"

He cut himself off before he could mention any future between the two of them, knowing it was impossible. "But the more I've thought about my father's offer, I know that's not the answer," he said firmly. "I won't work at the bank.

I'll never be a banker. There's nothing my father can do to force me into that mold."

He tried to go on, but the emotion inside him welled up and threatened to overflow. What would he do if he lost his house? Where would he and Montgomery live? Images of the little bungalow with its shady front porch and expansive backyard flooded his thoughts. Montgomery could walk to Nick's house through a series of adjoining lawns. She caught her school bus right in front of the house. A short walk took her to the mansion to spend time with her father or to the Corner Market to buy gumballs or across the square to get an ice cream cone at the Tastee Hut. Living so close to the center of town meant the shopkeepers looked out for her. She was safe and loved and secure.

Composing himself, he continued. "I've got to find a place to live. I have thirty days, and then the house will be put up for auction. It's the only home Montgomery's ever known, and—"

"Here," Ruby said, tightening the bathrobe tie that held up her pants. "You and Montgomery will move in here. My guesthouse! It's the perfect home for you."

"But that's where *I'm* staying," Jo said, turning on the little woman. "You can't do that. This is my—"

"It is *my* property, and *I* shall say who lives in it." Ruby patted Luke on the back. "You and your daughter will move here this very evening."

ELEVEN

From the second-floor window of Ruby's house, Darcy watched as Luke and Montgomery moved the last of their possessions into the little guesthouse down the lane. Zachary and Elizabeth Chalmers had each carried in several cardboard boxes, Boompah Jungemeyer hobbled around supervising the process, and Nick scooted baskets of toys off the bed of Luke's pickup into Montgomery's arms. The children seemed delighted with the prospect of the Eastons living in the small magical house. Nick chattered nonstop. Montgomery skipped around and around in the yard, her red braids flying.

At least the Eastons had waited until the weekend, Darcy thought. That had given her time to move her own scant possessions out of the little house. She now was camped in one of Ruby's many spare bedrooms. Her clothes lay folded on a chair. Her new brush and styling gel sample sat on an empty dresser. The few cans of soup and tuna she had managed to stockpile were stacked in Ruby's pantry. Darcy felt about like she had the day she walked out of prison—homeless, jobless, friendless.

Lifting an old Bible she had found on a shelf in Ruby's parlor, Darcy flipped the pages back and forth in search of a verse her Prison Fellowship mentor had discussed in chapel one evening. The passage had spoken about God's plans, about how the heavenly Father wanted good for his children and not evil. Though she'd been looking for that verse for three days, Darcy hadn't been able to find it. Maybe she'd just dreamed it up.

Maybe everything, in fact, was just a silly dream. Her hope of paying off her debts. Her desire to work at a well-paying job. Her plan to finish her last two years of college. Her wish for a home of her own. Even her faith in a living, caring God.

She closed the Bible and held it tightly. She had trusted God with her life—but where was he now? Things couldn't be much worse. She had been evicted from the guesthouse. She hadn't had the courage to return to her job at Chalmers Mansion—and even if she had, it sounded as if Luke's business was going to be shut down. She hadn't set foot in town for fear of stares and murmured comments, now that Will Damyon had announced to all the world who she really was. It wasn't long until her next parole meeting, and she would have to confess to the officer that she'd accomplished nothing. What a joke to think that a man like Luke Easton could be interested in her. She was a complete failure in everything she'd tried, just as she had been before she went to prison. Maybe nothing had changed, not even her heart.

"Where is Wilmer?" Ruby asked, coming into the bedroom. "Have you seen him, my dear?"

Darcy drank down a deep breath. It took every ounce of patience she possessed to take care of Ruby. As it turned out, the elderly woman had visited the bank and the lawyer, as Luke had instructed her. But rather than making Pastor Paul her executor, she had named Luke to fill that role. Now he had the responsibility of finding a solution to her situation—on top of his own concerns.

"Wilmer isn't around today, Ruby," Darcy said. She had learned that trying to explain Mr. McCann's death always upset Ruby, who refused to believe it. "Here, let me fix your blouse."

As she realigned the mismatched buttons on the yellow silk blouse, Darcy noted that Ruby had clipped a pearl earring on one earlobe and a rhinestone on the other. And she had smeared blue eye shadow on her mouth instead of lipstick.

"What's that you're reading?" Ruby asked, taking the Bible from the windowsill where Darcy had set it. "Oh, my favorite! I know it back to front. Ask me anything. Anything at all!"

She closed her eyes and held out the Bible. Darcy sighed. "Okay, there's a verse that says God has good plans for us—"

"Jeremiah 29:11." Ruby opened her eyes and flipped through the Bible. In less than thirty seconds, she began reading. "'For I know the plans I have for you,' says the Lord. 'They are plans for good and not for disaster, to give you a future and a hope.' There, give me another one!"

Darcy stared at the older woman in amazement. How on earth had Ruby managed to dredge that up out of the confusion in her mind?

"Let me see that," Darcy said.

She took the Bible and read the verse for herself: *"Plans for good and not for disaster."* Could such a thing be true? Look at Ruby with her Alzheimer's, and Luke thrown out of his house, and herself without any prospects for a happy future. All around her, people were suffering. Even Will Damyon, who had tormented Darcy so much, had done it because he was still mourning the death of his son. How could God promise he had good plans for his people?

"Ask me another!" Ruby insisted.

"I don't know any others. I don't know the Bible very well."

"First Peter 1:4, then. It's one of my favorites." Ruby flipped through the pages. "'For God has reserved a priceless inheritance for his children. It is kept in heaven for you, pure and undefiled, beyond the reach of change and decay.' That is not at all the way I learned it when I was a child. It was *treasures* then. Treasures in heaven. But this is just as good. Better, in fact. There you are then; our inheritance is kept in heaven."

"In heaven?"

"Well, you didn't think we'd have them on earth, did you? Oh, this world is a dreadful place, full of suffering and pain. It is the kingdom of Satan, you know. But we who are Christians have God's presence ever within us to comfort and guide us."

Darcy blinked. Of course, that's what the Prison Fellowship leader had talked about. But somehow, she'd expected things to go a little bit better. She had thought that being a Christian meant she'd always feel at peace, that she'd have a crystal-clear sense of direction, that she'd understand what was happening to her.

"Oh yes, here's another favorite." Ruby traced her finger along the lines of a verse she'd found. "'Keep on praying. No matter what happens, always be thankful, for this is God's will for you who belong to Christ Jesus.' It's from the first letter to the Thessalonians, the fifth chapter. Now then, have you ever heard such beautiful words, my dear? Such words of joy?"

Darcy swallowed as she watched Luke and Montgomery in the yard below, saying their good-byes to Boompah and the Chalmers family. Her blessings—all the treasures she longed for—were waiting for her in heaven, she realized. Here on earth, she had work to do. Work that went beyond her own self-centered needs and desires. *Oh, God, forgive me! I'm so new at this. I hardly understand it at all.*

"Wilmer is dead, isn't he?" Ruby said suddenly, setting the old Bible back on the windowsill. "I remember it now. My mind feels . . . organized somehow. My husband passed away many years ago. I live alone, and I manage the public library, and I have Alzheimer's disease. Oh, dear me!"

She threw her arms around the younger woman and began to weep. Darcy held Ruby tightly, aware for the first time that clarity could also bring terrible pain. In some ways, it was worse for Ruby to know, to remember, than for her to live in the fog that had begun to take over her mind.

"I'm going to pray," Darcy said. "That's what the verse in the Bible tells us to do. Pray continually and give thanks no matter what happens."

"First Thessalonians 5:17," Ruby said with a sniffle.

Darcy smiled and hugged her closer. "Dear Father in heaven, things are not looking that great right now down here on earth. In fact, Ruby and I are having a little trouble remembering that you have good plans for us. So, we ask for your help and your guidance. And we thank you for . . ." Darcy tried to think what she could possibly be thankful for in the midst of all the chaos in her life. "We thank you for . . ."

"For this beautiful summer afternoon," Ruby put in. "For our lovely town of Ambleside."

"Yes. And for a roof over our heads. Food in the pantry. Clothes to wear."

"For your Son, Jesus Christ! For our salvation!"

"For the promise of heaven."

"For the promise of your presence in our hearts."

"Amen," Darcy said. "Amen, amen, amen."

"And amen!" Ruby drew back and wiped her eyes. "Goodness, look at that! Someone's staying in the guesthouse. Whoever can it be?"

"It's Luke and Montgomery Easton."

"Well, what are we waiting for? We must go and fix them some dinner."

❧

Luke hadn't seen Darcy since the afternoon when Ruby gave away the guesthouse. Darcy was probably angry with him, he reasoned. After all, the little cottage had been her refuge.

But how could he turn down the offer of a free house to live in? How could he refuse to move Montgomery into a home so near their old one, within walking distance of Nick's house and Chalmers Mansion, across the street from the school-bus stop, and a few paces from the town square? He couldn't. His daughter came first, and her response to the idea of moving showed him he'd made the right decision. In fact, he had begun to wonder if they ought to have moved out of the old house before this. Maybe the memories of her mother had weighed on Montgomery just as heavily as they weighed on Luke.

He dropped into one of the overstuffed chairs near the window and looked out at the McCann house. He missed Darcy. He knew the scene with Will Damyon had frightened and embarrassed her. But hadn't Luke made it clear that her past was unimportant to him? The past few days had taught him how very much she had come to mean to him. He missed her whistling as she hung wallpaper. He missed her tossing Chee-tos back and forth with Floyd at lunch. He missed her smile every morning and her wave good-bye every night. He even missed her baked beans, and he'd only eaten them once. Their one kiss had awakened him to possibilities he'd never considered. He knew now that he was far beyond thinking of her as just an employee or a friend. He loved her.

"Knock, knock!" The voice at the door drew his attention just as Darcy herself stepped into the living room, a heavy wicker basket over one arm. "Meals-on-wheels. Or maybe I should say, Eats-on-feets." Laughing, she set the basket down and greeted Montgomery with a hug. "Hey, Little-bit; how's it going? You like your new place?"

"It's like a fairy tale!" Montgomery threw her arms around Darcy's waist. "Oh, we've missed you, haven't we, Daddy? Why didn't you come help us move in? It took hours and hours, because we had to put most of our furniture into a storage shed. Nick thought we were all going to live here together, you and me and Daddy, and I sort of hoped so too. But then I realized you were going to live with Mrs. McCann. Did you know she doesn't work at the library anymore? It's closed all the time. We don't even have story hour. We won't get to finish reading *The Secret Garden* and find out if Colin ever gets out of bed."

"Who?"

"Colin. He thinks he's a hunchback, but he's not. Daddy, look who's here. It's Jo—I mean . . . Darcy," Montgomery finished uncertainly.

"Calm down, Monkey." Luke crossed the living room and laid his hand on his daughter's head. "Hey, Darcy. How've you been?"

She shrugged. "I brought you guys some supper. Ruby and I fried up a platter of chicken, and here's a bowl of my beans."

"Baked beans." He took the warm dish from the basket and cupped it in his hands. "Would you like to eat with us?"

"Eat with us!" Montgomery pleaded, bouncing up and down on her toes. "Please, please, please!"

"Thanks, but I'd better go keep an eye on Ruby."

"Is she having another bad day?" Luke asked.

"A good one, actually. It was the old Bible that did it, almost like a miracle."

"An old Bible?"

"Like the one Nick gave me a long time ago!" Montgomery exclaimed. "I found it when we were packing. It used to belong to Grace Chalmers before she died. It's a miracle Bible, too. I'll go get it!"

As she raced off down the hall, Darcy continued speaking. "Ruby and I were talking about some verses of Scripture, and she suddenly clicked into perfect clarity, just as if a light went on inside her brain. And there it was—Jeremiah 29:11, the verse I'd been looking for all week. About God's good plans for us."

Luke nodded, but he didn't think he'd ever heard that Scripture.

"Then Ruby quoted another one that reminded me about our blessings being in heaven, you know. I'd been hoping to find them here on earth, but now I realize my focus here isn't supposed to be on *me* at all. And that's why I'm feeling a lot better."

She brushed back her hair and started lifting dishes of food from the basket. Luke watched her, gratitude and amazement filling him. He knew Darcy had every reason to resent his presence in the guesthouse. The incident at the picnic had turned her life upside down. But she'd managed to keep loving mixed-up old Ruby—and she continued to trust God in spite of everything. No, he remembered. Darcy trusted God *because* of everything.

"Please stay," he said. "Stay for dinner, Darcy."

She looked up at him, her gray eyes searching. "Luke, do I still have my job? I know you're strapped for money, and now the bank pulled this foreclosure on you, and I realize I didn't show up for work last week—"

"The job is yours. We've missed you." He let out a breath. *"I've* missed you."

She glanced away. "Don't, Luke. I can't feel that way. I have to think about what I'm doing. I might be moving away from Ambleside, and I can't feel—"

"I told you how *I* was feeling. I missed you."

"I missed you, too," she whispered.

"Here it is!" Montgomery cried as she ran back into the kitchen and set a leather-bound Bible on the table. Luke didn't know if he'd ever seen the book before. "It's the family Bible," she said.

"Whose family?"

"Our family. Nick says this Bible helped turn him and his mom and Zachary into a family. And when my mommy died, he gave it to me, so I could get a new family one day, too."

"Monkey," Luke said, "the Bible is not some kind of a good-luck charm. It can't make families appear out of nowhere."

"Yes, it can!"

"No," he said, picking up the book, "it *can't*. We'll give this Bible to Darcy. We don't need it. We've already got one. Now, go wash your hands for supper."

Montgomery gave him a scornful glance and whirled around to head for the bathroom. Luke shrugged at Darcy. "I don't know what's gotten into her today. Must be the move."

Darcy smiled as she wrapped her arms around the old leather-bound book. "Little-bit's right about the Bible creating families, though. I mean, we're all in the family of God."

"Are you saying you're my sister?" Luke teased as he peeled the aluminum foil back from the platter of chicken. "Because if that's the case, I'm not crazy about the concept."

"There's a bond between us anyway." She paused for a moment. "I mean, there's a bond *if* you're in the family of Christ."

"You think I'm not?"

"I think you've turned your back on your heavenly Father. But he hasn't turned his back on you." She started for the door. "I'm finding out it's not easy being a Christian. But I wouldn't trade my place in God's family for anything."

Luke let her leave the house, watching her walk away and

wishing he had the words to make her stay. He knew it wasn't just Darcy he wanted. He longed to retouch the faith that gave her strength. Darcy was right. During the process of Ellie's long and painful death, he had slowly turned away from God. And why not? God had abandoned and betrayed him.

But Darcy had shown him a different way to walk the Christian path. She was learning that God didn't always clear obstacles out of the road. His children faced pain and suffering in this world. Yet Darcy put her faith in Christ's constant presence, in his guidance, in his love.

Luke walked across the room and picked up the old Bible that had belonged to his wife. He turned through the wrinkled pages, noticing the careful underlining of special verses. Would God even be willing to take Luke back into the family?

He flipped through Psalms, remembering David's terrible sin and God's patient forgiveness. His fingers brushed past the story of the prodigal son, the boy who had wandered away from his father but was welcomed back with open arms. And then he thought of Peter, the apostle who had denied Christ during the Savior's most difficult hours before his death on the cross.

"He hasn't turned his back on you," Darcy had said. God was waiting for him, arms outstretched in love. Luke's vision blurred as he lifted up a prayer of repentance for his months of anger at God, for his willful rejection of Christianity, for showing his daughter a weak and stumbling walk of faith. More than anything else in his difficult, almost overwhelming circumstances, Luke saw how much he needed the presence of his heavenly Father. He needed God's healing. He needed God's direction. He needed God's love.

"Did Darcy leave?" Montgomery asked, skipping back into the kitchen. "Did you let her go?"

"She needed to get back to check on Mrs. McCann."

"I think Darcy loves Mrs. McCann a whole lot, and I don't care what anybody says about her."

"About Mrs. McCann?"

"No, about Darcy. I heard that man say Darcy was in prison for shooting somebody and killing him. But I think it was just a lie. Darcy wouldn't ever do anything that terrible. She's the nicest person I ever met."

As Montgomery sat down at the table and picked up a chicken leg, Luke pulled out his chair. He'd have to explain the truth to Montgomery later, but for now he simply agreed with her final assessment. "Yes, she is the nicest person," he said. "And don't start eating that until we've said grace."

Approaching the chapel the following morning, Darcy realized she felt more nervous than she could ever remember. She gripped the old Bible as though it might scamper away, and twice she stumbled over broken concrete in the sidewalk. What would people think about her? What would they say to her? And why did she care so much?

"It sure is a pretty day," Ruby announced as Darcy helped her climb the steps of the small church. "And I ain't just a-whistlin' Dixie when I say it, neither."

Darcy stiffened at the unfamiliar drawl that emerged from the old woman's lips. What now? It seemed that sections of Ruby's brain were likely to open and shut at random, either pouring out their contents or clamming up tight, and nothing she said was predictable.

Nothing Ruby did was reliable either. This morning she had insisted on wearing a pair of Wilmer's huge, black wing-tip shoes to church. Nothing Darcy could say would sway her. And so they tromped down the aisle, the shoes clippity-clomping all the way to the front pew.

"How 'bout them apples, huh?" Ruby said, displaying her handbag for everyone in the pew behind her to see. It was

brown leather, one of her plainer accessories. "You ever
seen such a fine purse as this? I bought it over to Très Chic
on the square. It cost a pretty penny, you know. But then,
when Wilmer passed on, he left me mighty well-heeled, as
I reckon you're all aware of."

Obviously pleased with herself, Ruby sat down in the
pew and smoothed out her skirt. Darcy kept her focus on
the front of the chapel and prayed for grace. Maybe she
shouldn't have come to church this morning. Certainly Ruby
was having another of her off days, and there was no telling
what might happen.

"Morning, Darcy." The deep voice drew her attention as
Luke and Montgomery slipped into the pew beside her.

"What are you doing here?" The moment the words were
out, Darcy knew she shouldn't have spoken them. But after
their conversation last night, she certainly hadn't expected
Luke to make an appearance in the chapel.

"I mean, I didn't think you'd come," she added lamely.

"Here I am," he said. "Back in the family."

Luke was smiling more broadly than Darcy had ever
seen, and she breathed a prayer of astonished gratitude. As
the choir entered the chapel and took their places behind
the altar, she turned over his words. *"Back in the family."*
Did that mean Luke had recommitted his life to Christ? Had
he somehow come to an understanding of God's working
through Ellie's death, through the problems with the bank,
through everything that seemed so awful?

"Strike up the band!" Ruby called out loudly enough to
elicit a chorus of gasps. "How 'bout a little do-si-do?"

A child giggled behind them, and Darcy laid her hand on
the older woman's arm. "We're in church, Ruby," she whispered. "The choir is going to sing hymns."

"Hush up, afore I stomp the bejeebers outta you, girl!"
Ruby rose to her feet and spread her arms toward the choir.
Then she began to sing at the top of her lungs. "Do-si-do

and the little boy, doe! And boy in the bread pan playing in the dough! And the little boy doe by doe by doe—"

"Ruby!" Darcy reached up and grabbed her shoulder. "Oh, Ruby, please don't—"

"And little boy doe," Ruby sang, squirming away, "and oh, by golly and oh, by Joe!"

"And out we go," Luke finished, corralling the tiny woman under his arm and do-si-do-ing her right back down the aisle. Darcy hurried along behind them, feeling the gawking eyes of everyone in the church. She took Montgomery's hand, and they followed Luke and Ruby down the stairs to the pickup truck.

"Hold on a minute, Luke!" Zachary Chalmers called out from the doorway. Behind him, half the congregation began pushing outside onto the steps. Pastor Paul elbowed his way through the crowd and rushed to the pickup.

"Mrs. McCann," the pastor said, grasping the old woman's hand, "are you feeling all right today?"

"I'm just jim-dandy!" Ruby pinched him on the cheek. "Long time no see, cutie pie. How you been?"

"Well, I'm fine, Mrs. McCann, but—" He glanced at Darcy. "Luke, what is going on here?"

"Ruby has Alzheimer's disease, Pastor Paul," Luke said. "Didn't she tell you? She's known for some time now. Darcy's been taking care of her, but it's getting worse."

"Disease? What a load of hooey!" Ruby exclaimed. "I'm fit as a fiddle."

"Alzheimer's?" The pastor shook his head. "I had no idea. You didn't mention it the night of the picnic, Miss Callaway. When I went to your home to visit you—"

"I thought Ruby had already told you, Pastor Paul. She promised Luke she would talk with you, the bank, her lawyer, and several others. We're just learning that she didn't do half the things on the list Luke made for her."

"Oh, my. Listen, I want you both to understand that the

church is prepared to do whatever we can to help. Have you looked into nursing—"

"Everybody whirl!" Ruby cried, suddenly bursting into a series of square dance steps. Wilmer's big shoes flopped up and down on the sidewalk. "Wave the ocean, wave the shore; wave that pretty girl back once more!"

"Darcy and I can take care of Ruby for now," Luke said. "We're both living near her. We'll keep her safe. But, Pastor, we could use your help figuring out what to do in the long run."

"Of course. Mrs. McCann has been a member of our family for many years. We'll do all we can for her."

"Family," Luke repeated. He grinned at Darcy as he scooped Ruby off her feet and gave her a twirl. "Come on, pretty little miss. Let's get you back to the house so the congregation can get on with solemn worship." He winked at Pastor Paul.

"Wave the ocean, wave the sea," Ruby sang while Luke deposited her in the pickup's cab. "And wave that pretty girl back to me!"

Darcy and Montgomery ran hand in hand to the old DeSoto. "My daddy's the hero of the day!" the child exclaimed. "Did you see him? He saved Mrs. McCann."

"Yes, your father is quite a hero," Darcy said. As she drove past the church steps, an odd sense of pride filled her chest. Once again she was reminded of her image of Luke as a knight in shining armor. This man was special, of that Darcy was certain—bold and courageous and determined. Luke would fight Ruby's dragons for her, just as he had stepped to Darcy's side in the church to signal his willingness to champion her. There were other dragons to battle, too—a lost wife, a lost home, a struggling business, a controlling father. But Darcy felt a smile filter across her face. Somehow Luke was going to win those battles, she realized. He was in God's family . . . and God's army.

TWELVE

For nearly half an hour into her meeting with her parole officer, Darcy thought she had escaped Will Damyon. And then he knocked on the parole officer's door. He walked into the room, sat down, and laid a sheet of paper on the man's desk.

"I've made a list of the perpetrator's violations," he announced. "Take a close look."

Darcy's heart constricted as the officer picked up the paper. Earlier that day, she and Luke had brought Ruby to Jefferson City for another visit to the neurologist. The older woman's condition seemed to be worsening rapidly. The library board had placed her on medical leave, and she required almost constant care. Because Darcy's monthly parole meeting overlapped with Ruby's doctor appointment, Darcy was on her own today. Luke was planning to pick her up in fifteen minutes, but she wished he was by her side at this moment.

"Evicted from housing." The officer read aloud the first item on the list. "I already know about that situation, Mr. Damyon. Your daughter-in-law explained that someone else needed to use the guesthouse on the McCann property. Apparently, she has moved in with Mrs. McCann to help her with light housekeeping duties."

"Light housekeeping," Will said with a snort. "That's not what I hear from the townsfolk. They say she's been trying to get in good with the old lady so she can con her out of money. She shows up at the grocery store with Mrs.

McCann's purse and buys whatever she wants. She even wears her clothes."

Darcy could feel her cheeks grow hot. "Mrs. McCann sends me to the store to buy groceries for her. I take a list. I never buy anything for myself with Ruby's money. And she loaned me the clothes when she realized I didn't have anything to wear after I got out of prison."

"Yeah, right. You inform an old woman you're an ex-con, and she turns around and gives you her clothes and her purse? That's a likely story."

The parole officer leaned forward. "Does Mrs. McCann know about your prison record?"

Darcy shook her head. "I'm not sure. Probably not. But I swear I haven't taken advantage of her. I help her—"

"I'll need to speak with Mrs. McCann," the officer said. "Do you have a telephone number where I can reach her?"

"You won't get a thing out of the old lady," Damyon said. "She's crazy as a coot."

"She has Alzheimer's disease," Darcy shot back. "Ruby is my friend, and I would never do anything to harm her."

"We're supposed to believe that? You've weaseled your way into that town just like you weaseled your way into my son's life. And now you're doing all you can to use those good folks to your benefit. Taking advantage of a senile old woman . . . what a low-down thing to do."

He reached out and pointed a thick finger at the sheet of paper on the officer's desk. "But it don't stop with getting thrown out of her house. Take a look at the second thing on the list. She didn't show up at work for a whole week. Never set foot inside that mansion where she's supposed to be hanging wallpaper. I talked to one of the fellows that works for Easton Construction. He told me she didn't call in sick. Didn't call in at all, as a matter of fact. She just didn't show up."

"Is this true?" the officer asked Darcy.

She drew in a deep breath. "Yes, sir. But I went back to work this week. I've been there every morning right at eight. My employer understands the situation."

"The employer is her *boyfriend,*" Damyon said. "Of course he let her off the hook. But that's not the point. The point is, she violated her parole by not going to work. Send her back to prison, Officer. That's where she belongs!"

Darcy twisted her purse strap as she waited for the officer to respond. When he didn't say anything, she searched for a response. But what could she say in her defense? Will Damyon's words were true. She *had* violated her parole.

"And if you don't think that's bad enough," Damyon said, tapping the paper again, "take a look right here, Officer. I was an eyewitness to this one. And so were a whole bunch of other folks. There's no way she can bat her long lashes and get out of it."

"'On the night of June fifteen,'" the officer read, "'Darcy Damyon used a garden hoe as a weapon to threaten several of the citizens of Ambleside with physical assault. It took the pastor of the church to talk her into dropping the weapon before she could attack anyone.'" The officer glanced up at Darcy. "A hoe?"

"She was hiding out in a toolshed," Damyon said. "She grabbed that hoe and swung it—"

"I did not swing it!" She rounded on the man. "I never swung the hoe at anybody! I was holding it up to protect myself, because I thought . . . I thought—"

"Look at her! See what I've been trying to tell you, officer? She's violent!"

"Sir, Mr. Damyon showed up at the Ambleside church picnic. He told everyone about my past. He announced it for all the world to hear. I was so humiliated and fright- ened, and I—"

"They deserved to know! You're a convicted murderer!"

"That's who I *was*. It's not who I *am*. I'm trying to build a new life, and if you would just let me—"

"You're a killer, that's who you *are!* And I'm going to make sure you never forget it."

Darcy clapped her hands over her ears and shook her head. "I'll never forget what I did. Never. But I have to go forward."

"My son can't go forward. Why should you get the chance? Tell me that!"

"All right," the officer spoke up. "I'm going to look into these allegations. If it's true that you've violated the conditions of your parole, ma'am, then you'll have to face the consequences. I would recommend that you contact your attorney."

Darcy felt as though she had been punched in the stomach. She had just begun to pay off her huge debt to Mr. Abel. Now she would have to start all over again. But the thought of going back into that prison was more than she could stand.

"Meanwhile, I'll be making a trip to Ambleside," the officer said.

"I called the police about that hoe incident, but she was gone by the time they got there," Damyon said. "It's the townspeople you want to talk to. They'll tell you the truth about her."

Darcy looked down at the tightly twisted purse strap in her lap. She could just imagine what Pearlene Fox and her husband would have to say. Who would be willing to stand up in defense of a stranger, an outsider? The citizens of Ambleside wouldn't want to stick their necks out for a convicted felon. It was a quiet town; its residents were determined to retain its quaintness and peace. Trying to keep herself isolated, Darcy had formed no real friendships. The Chalmers family hardly knew her. Pastor Paul had visited with her in person only once. Even friendly Kaye

Zimmerman knew little about Darcy beyond the color of her hair.

Her two main supporters wouldn't stand up well in her defense. Ruby's mental condition would make her an unreliable witness. And Luke Easton had been painted as the "new boyfriend."

As the officer stood to escort her out of his office, Darcy lifted her chin in determination. "Sir," she said, "it's not easy moving into a new town and trying to fit in with the people there. It's especially hard when someone is determined to make you stumble every step of the way. But the bottom line is that I do have a place to live. I have a job, sir. And I never assaulted anyone. I'm trying my hardest to succeed."

"She hasn't assaulted anyone *yet*," Damyon chipped in. "Give her time, Officer. She'll show you what she's really made of. You'll see what's inside this woman. Don't be fooled by the blonde hair and the pretty words and all the churchgoing. Don't let her try to make you think she's changed. She's no different from what she ever was."

Darcy stood by the door, fighting the rush of anger and tears that swelled inside her. Maybe Will Damyon was right. She had been a fool to think that Christ could make her into a new person. She felt awful and filthy and evil again. She felt hopeless and empty. Where was God when she needed him? Why didn't he come to her rescue?

"Mrs. Damyon," the parole officer said. "In my office, I talk to a lot of people just like you. People trying to make a new start. People messing up and getting sent back to prison."

Darcy nodded. "Yes, sir."

"I don't want you to become one of them, and my job is to try to keep that from happening. What I'm hearing today is that you've already messed up, or you're on the verge of it. What I'm also seeing is that you've got a man making things harder for you than they ought to be. Now, I'll remind you that you can take out a restraining order against Mr. Damyon. You have the right to be free of harassment."

"Yeah, she took out a restraining order against my son right before she shot him," Will Damyon said. "He wasn't even armed when she gunned him down like a dog."

"Ma'am, would you like to file a restraining order?" the officer asked. "The court will give you ten days' immediate protection against Mr. Damyon. Then he and you will need to appear before a judge here in Jefferson City and clarify your positions. After that, a new order can be issued. Personally, I believe a certain amount of physical distance would benefit both of you."

Darcy thought about the offer, considering the implications of taking legal action against Will Damyon. The whole town would soon find out, of course. The Ambleside police force—both of them—would be watching him, but they'd also start watching Darcy a lot more closely. And what good would it do? Her husband had violated the restraining order more than once. What would keep his father from doing the same thing?

"Not right now," she managed.

"I want you to succeed," the officer said. "But I can't rescue you from your own mistakes."

Darcy nodded. As she thanked the man, she heard an echo of her cry to God just moments before. *Where was God when she needed him? Why didn't he come to her rescue?* But he had! This man had been put into Darcy's life for a reason. God had sent the parole officer to help her—and she had refused his assistance because she was determined to do everything on her own.

The officer turned to close the door, and she reached out to him. "Wait, sir. I've changed my mind. I want to take out a restraining order. Can you tell me what to do?"

"What?" Damyon bellowed. "You wouldn't dare!"

Darcy felt instantly in the presence of her husband again.

Heart hammering, she backed up against the wall of the corridor. Damyon bore down on her, his hard eyes glittering. He was so like Bill it was uncanny. "Don't think you can get away with this!"

"I have to do it." She forced herself to stand straight. Christ was inside her. She spoke with his power now, not her own. "My life is different now, and I won't let you force me backward."

Down the hall, the elevator doors opened and Luke and Ruby stepped into the corridor. Darcy glanced at the parole officer, who was calling for assistance on his cell phone. She squared her shoulders, strengthened by the presence of those God had brought to support her.

"I'm a new person, Will," she said. "I've asked you to forgive me for what I did. And I want to—"

"You think you can keep me from seeing that you get what you deserve, girl?" Damyon snarled. "Go ahead and put a restraining order on me. I'll get someone else to help me bring you down. Someone who hates you as much as I do. Maybe more."

Darcy stared at him, unable to think who he could be talking about.

"You don't know who I mean, huh? File that restraining order, and you'll find out."

He gave a derisive laugh and started down the hallway. He passed first Luke and Ruby, then the two security guards who had just stepped out of the elevator.

"Are you all right?" Luke asked Darcy as he laid a hand on her arm.

Darcy bit her lip and looked away as an awful realization dawned on her. She knew who Will would bring to Ambleside to assure her downfall. It was a man convicted three times for assault and battery, a man who earned his living as a bouncer at a Joplin bar.

It was Buck Damyon, her husband's brother.

⟋⟍

Darkness settled across the rolling green hills of Missouri
as Luke drove his pickup toward Ambleside. He had made
arrangements for Montgomery to spend the night with the
Chalmers family, and he felt grateful for the peace of mind
that brought. At least he didn't have to worry about his
daughter.

The rest of his life was a mess. The symptoms of Ruby's
disease had been at their worst during her appointment
with the neurologist, which led the doctor to insist that a
plan be made for her immediate care. After the appointment, Luke had arrived at the parole office just in time to
find Darcy's father-in-law threatening her again. Luke's
blood had boiled, and it had taken all Darcy's persuasion to
keep him from following Will out to the parking lot and settling the matter right there.

After Darcy had filed the ten-day restraining order against
Will Damyon, the three of them drove to different banks in
Jefferson City. While Darcy and Ruby waited in the pickup,
Luke spoke with a loan officer at each bank. The response
was the same. No loan money was available for a man in
Luke's current financial position.

"I declare," Ruby said. "A mess of flapjacks would taste
mighty good right now."

Luke could feel the rise and fall of Darcy's sigh beside
him. For some reason, Ruby had taken to lapsing into the
dialect of her early childhood in the Missouri backwoods.
Right in the middle of one of her elegant teas, she might
announce, "I ain't et anything this good in a month of Sun-
days." Luke tried to see some humor in it, but he knew
Ruby's mental confusion weighed heavily on Darcy.

The younger woman sat next to him in the pickup, and it
was all Luke could do to keep from slipping his arm around
her shoulders. He knew Darcy didn't want to let him too

close emotionally or physically. She was struggling with so many obstacles of her own. But he also knew his feelings for her were very strong.

"Flapjacks and blackstrap molasses," Ruby said. "Yum yum. Mama makes that for us young'uns of a Sunday mornin' right before church. Why, her flapjacks make me grin like a mule eatin' briars. I could eat me a stack of my mama's flapjacks right now."

"We just had supper, Ruby," Darcy said. "Don't you remember? We stopped at the McDonald's on Missouri Boulevard, and you ordered a double cheeseburger."

"I'm hungry," Ruby insisted. "I want some . . . some . . . what was it?"

"Flapjacks," Darcy said.

"What?" Ruby leaned across Darcy and touched Luke's arm. "What's she talking about?"

"Ruby, hush!" Luke said, suddenly fed up to his ears with the old woman's ramblings. "Just sit there like a good girl and be still!"

At his harsh response, he could sense the hurt that settled over both women. Well, what was he supposed to do? Jabber with them about double cheeseburgers and flapjacks? He had more important concerns than Ruby's appetite.

As the last of the sunlight filtered across the oak leaves and painted the highway a deep pink, he turned over the possibility of declaring bankruptcy. It was the last thing he wanted to do. Without Ellie's medical debts, he would have had no trouble keeping his construction company profitable. But now he wondered if he even had a choice.

For the first time in more than a year, Luke lifted up a prayer for God's guidance and help. He knew he couldn't do this on his own. Darcy had told him she relied on her faith in Christ because life often seemed overwhelming. Though his determination hadn't wavered, he had to admit he was in a pit that he couldn't climb out of by himself.

"Where am I?" Ruby asked. "I don't know where I am."

"This is Luke's pickup," Darcy said softly.

"Somebody tell me where I am!" Ruby's voice rose in panic.

"You're in Missouri. We're on our way to Ambleside. Luke is driving us home, Ruby."

"I can't see where I am!"

"You're in Luke's pickup."

"Ohhh-ohhh-ohh." Ruby began to moan, but when Darcy reached out to calm her, she screeched and slapped Darcy's hand away. "Stop it! Stop hurting me! You're hurting me!"

"Ouch!"

"Ouch, ouch, ouch!" Ruby repeated. "Oh, I don't know where I am. I'm lost. Where's Wilmer?"

"Ruby, this is Luke's pickup—"

"Darcy, just leave her alone," Luke said. "Ruby's had a long day. The doctor told me this was part of the disease. Agitation, confusion, frustration. He said she might be aggressive sometimes."

"She's crying again. She cries so much, Luke."

"Depression. He wants to try some medications on her. He gave me a prescription for some antidepressants."

"She's not depressed all the time, though. Sometimes she's very happy."

"I'm just telling you what the doctor said."

"Did you tell him how she wanders around at night? That she can't sleep?"

Luke glanced across at her, his frustration building. "How was I supposed to know she wanders at night?"

"I told you on the way to town today. I said Ruby doesn't sleep very well."

"I told him the other things. About how she puts stuff in the wrong places."

"But I wanted him to know about the wandering."

"I forgot that, okay?"

"Did you tell him she can't open things anymore? And she can't figure out the can opener or the telephone?"

Luke swung the pickup onto the turnoff toward Ambleside. "I told him what she did in church the other day," he said. "The square dancing. And how she talks like a hillbilly."

"Where am I?" Ruby called out.

"What about her accidents? Luke, I don't know what to do with her anymore. When I get home from work, I have to spend at least an hour cleaning her up and washing her. And the house is—"

"Ohh," Ruby moaned, "I'm lost."

"I told him everything I could think of," Luke said. "I told him what I thought seemed important."

"He needed to know about her sleeping and bathroom problems! And the wandering!"

"Okay, you can call his office tomorrow and tell them."

"How am I supposed to do that? I've got to be working every minute in case that parole officer shows up to check on me. And Will is going to go back to Joplin and get Buck, and they'll try to push me into doing something I shouldn't, and then I'll—"

"What? Who's Buck?"

"I'm lost!" Ruby cried loudly. "Somebody help me!"

"I'm helping you all I can!" Darcy shouted back. "I'm doing everything I can for you!"

"Who's Buck?" Luke repeated.

"Ouch, ouch, ouch!" Ruby screamed.

"Stop it, Ruby!" Darcy grabbed the old woman's flailing arms and tried to pin them in her lap. "Stop hitting me!"

"Ouch, ouch, ouch!"

"Stop it!"

"Stop it, both of you!" Luke pulled the pickup to a halt in front of Ruby's house. For a moment, he sat with his hands gripping the steering wheel as he tried to calm himself. The two women had fallen silent, one of them weeping softly.

"Home," Ruby whispered, craning to peer through the windshield at the old building. "This is my home."

Luke let out a deep breath and pulled Darcy into his arms. "I'm sorry," he said. "I'll call the neurologist tomorrow morning from work. We'll make a list of the things you want me to tell him."

"Have you ever been to my home?" Ruby asked.

"And don't forget you took out that restraining order against Will Damyon," Luke continued, stroking Darcy's hair. Her cheek pressed against his shoulder, and he could feel her tears soaking through his shirt. He wished he could do more, hold her closer, be the man she needed right now. "I'll talk to Mick and Ben at the police station. They're both good guys. I'll make sure they know who Damyon is, and I'll tell them to warn us at the first sight of him in town."

"I have a lovely, lovely home," Ruby said. "Would you care to join me for a cup of tea?"

"The neurologist told me he has several possibilities in mind for Ruby," Luke went on as Darcy clung to his shirt. "A lot depends on what she's able to afford, so I'll be checking on that. One option is home health care. And some of the retirement homes have special units for Alzheimer's patients. We could visit her anytime—"

"In the parlor. That's where I prefer to take my tea."

"Darcy?" He cupped the side of her face, wishing he could make her stop crying. "It's going to be all right. Remember what you told me? You said God has good plans for his people."

"Plans for good and not for evil," Ruby said. "To give you a future and a hope. Jeremiah 29:11."

"That's right, Ruby. Remind Darcy that God is with us right now. He's walking with us through this trouble."

"'Yea, though I walk through the valley of the shadow of death, I will fear no evil: for Thou art with me; thy rod and thy staff they comfort me. Thou preparest a table before me in the presence of mine enemies.'"

"There." Luke kissed Darcy's forehead. "Can you feel his presence? Darcy, I've walked through the valley of the shadow of death, and you're in the presence of your enemies. But he's here with us. I understand that now. He wants to comfort us."

"The Twenty-third Psalm my favorite, along with Psalm 116." Ruby cleared her throat. "'I love the Lord, because he hath heard my voice and my supplications. Because he hath inclined his ear unto me, therefore will I call upon him as long as I live. . . .'"

"Darcy," Luke whispered as Ruby continued to recite, "I'm here for you. If you need me, I'm here."

"'I found trouble and sorrow. Then called I upon the name of the Lord. O Lord, I beseech thee, deliver my soul. . . .'"

"Darcy?" He was beginning to worry. She hadn't moved, and he could tell she was still crying softly. "Are you all right?"

"'Our God is merciful. The Lord preserveth the simple: I was brought low, and he helped me. . . .'"

Darcy lifted her head and looked into Luke's eyes. "Nobody ever said that to me before," she managed.

"Said what?" he asked.

"I'm sorry." She swallowed a shuddering breath. "A few minutes ago, you got frustrated with Ruby and me, and then you said, 'I'm sorry.' I can't remember anyone ever saying that to me. I've never met . . . never known a man like you."

Luke felt a smile lift his spirits. "Is that what shook you up? A simple apology?"

"I've wanted that all my life. To forgive and be forgiven.

Kindness and tenderness. People I could care about, people I could love. And here in the middle of all this terrible . . . terrible stuff . . . here you are. I don't know what to do."

"'For thou hast delivered my soul from death, mine eyes from tears, and my feet from falling,'" Ruby intoned on the seat beside them. "'I will walk before the Lord in the land of the living.'"

"There," Luke said. "That's what you do. You 'walk before the Lord in the land of the living.'"

He felt a chuckle well up inside Darcy. She sniffled. "Okay," she said. "That's what I'll do."

He couldn't resist bending down and kissing her gently on the lips. Maybe he was giving her something she had longed for all her life. But he had the sense that she was giving him something of life itself. A new life of hope for the future. Of faith in God. And of love.

In his arms, Darcy leaned upward, slipping her hands around his shoulders as he kissed her again. Her lips were soft and warm and welcoming. He could feel the gentle pressure of her fingers along his neck. Heart hammering, he felt a rush of desire well up inside him. Darcy had become so much more than friend and companion. She was a woman—full and beautiful and desirable. And he was a man.

He pulled her closer, holding her tightly against him. Her mouth moved to his cheek as her hands slipped into his hair. The sensation sent trickles of fire down his spine.

"Flapjacks," Ruby said suddenly. "Flapjacks and black-strap molasses."

Darcy jerked upright at the sound of the older woman's voice. Pulling out of Luke's arms, she let out a shaky breath. "Oh no. I shouldn't have done that," she murmured.

"Oh yes you should," Ruby said. "You never tasted flap-jacks like my mama makes. Yum-yum."

Luke winked at Darcy and started to laugh. "Yum-yum is right."

Darcy cuffed his shoulder with her hand. "You rascal," she said. "Get out of this pickup right now, and help Ruby with her door. She doesn't remember how to open things."

"I certainly do," Ruby said, pulling the latch and throwing open the door. "I can do anything I put my mind to. Praise ye the Lord."

THIRTEEN

"This is what you call a lop-eared adapter," Luke said. "You use it to join a hose bib to a waterline."

"Well, I'll be jiggered." Floyd peered over Luke's shoulder in the tiny upstairs bathroom where the younger man was repairing a leaky sink. "A lop-eared adapter. Funny name for it, huh?"

"It's called lop-eared because it has two different sizes of connectors, see?"

"Yessir, but how come you call that faucet a hose bib?"

"That's its proper name. If you want to order a faucet over at the hardware store, you ask Bud Huff for a hose bib."

"Sakes alive. Who'd a thunk it?" Floyd chuckled. "You know, in some ways plumbin' ain't all that different from wirin'. You hook everything together, and then you turn it on. And you've either got water or current flowin' through."

Luke stuck his index finger into a can of flux and coated the copper pipe with the sticky material. "That's right, Floyd. And in plumbing you've got a valve to regulate your flow, while in wiring you've got a switch."

"You are one smart young feller," Floyd said. "You can fix plumbin' and floorin' and walls and ceilin's and just about anything a body could come up with that wants fixin'. I'll bet you could do wirin' if you put your mind to it."

Floyd watched as Luke fitted the pipe into the adapter and then turned on his soldering torch. When Luke squeezed his striker to spark a bright blue gas flame, the little electrician drew back.

"Now, there's something different twixt plumbin' and 'lectricity, sure as shootin'," Floyd said. "In wirin', we prefer not to see no sparks. If you got sparks, chances are you got trouble."

Luke held the torch near the adapter until the copper pipe began to glow green with the heat. Then he placed the tip of the solder coil against the joint and watched the open space fill with the silver-tin liquid. Ever since the last encounter with Will Damyon, Luke had been wondering how much Floyd was to blame for the problems Darcy was having with her former father-in-law. At the moment, Darcy was painting trim in the kitchen downstairs, and Luke knew she wouldn't hear their conversation.

"Speaking of trouble, Floyd," Luke began as he measured another length of copper pipe, "the other day, did a man by the name of Will Damyon drop by here and ask you some questions?"

"I don't know what the feller's name was, but he told me he was from the government, you know. He said he was checkin' up on Jo after she got out of prison for killin' her husband, and he wanted to know if she'd been comin' to work regular. So I told him we hadn't seen Jo for nigh onto a week, and we didn't none of us know what had become of her. I told him about the trouble over to the church picnic, and how I wasn't there or I'da got right up and told ever'body what a fine young lady Jo is. Maybe she done wrong in the past, though I can't hardly believe it of her. Not a nice girl like that, and real pretty, too. But whatever she done, it's over, and nowadays Jo is as good a human being as you'd ever want to meet. That's what I'da said at the picnic if I'da been there."

Luke shook his head as he coated the pipe with flux. "Floyd, that man who talked to you wasn't from the government. He was the fellow who came to the picnic and caused all the trouble for Jo."

"No-siree bobtail!"

"Yes, Floyd. And when you told him Jo hadn't shown up for work, he took the information right straight to her parole officer."

"Sure as shootin'? Well, that'll teach me to keep my mouth shut, won't it?"

Luke doubted it, but he didn't say anything as he soldered another length of pipe. Since they returned from Jefferson City, he had spent every moment of his spare time working on Ruby's situation. The neurologist had told him that Ruby had progressed beyond the initial stage of Alzheimer's disease, which involved mild forgetfulness, short-term memory loss, faulty judgment, and changes in personality. When Luke described how she wasn't always able to think clearly, and she sometimes forgot the names of familiar people and common things, the doctor said it appeared the disease had moved to a more severe level.

At this stage, Ruby was forgetting how to do simple tasks like washing her hands or shutting doors, and her ability to reason was limited. Although he couldn't predict how rapidly the illness would advance, the doctor said it seemed clear that Ruby already was becoming dependent on Darcy for her everyday care. And he told Luke that eventually she would become bedridden and likely to develop other illnesses and infections. Though Ruby could continue living in her home for the time being, the neurologist insisted that she would need care and monitoring around the clock.

Luke knew Darcy well enough by now to realize she would continue to watch over Ruby for as long as possible. But the doctor had made it clear that Ruby was going to need a medically trained caregiver. Luke hadn't talked to Darcy about the situation, because he realized her thoughts were taken up with her own predicament. She had mentioned she was thinking of moving to another town, and he knew she kept a close watch on her surroundings as though Will Damyon might appear out of nowhere to torment her.

"Want me to switch the water back on now, boss?" Floyd asked as Luke turned off his soldering torch. "I know right where the faucet is. I mean the *hose bib*. I'll turn your water on, and then we'll go have us some eats, what do you say? You won't believe what my wife put in my lunch sack today. Bugles is what they're called. They're shaped like tiny horns, and you eat 'em just the way you eat potato chips. Beats anything I ever seen."

"Bugles have been around for years, Floyd."

"No joke? Well, this batch is the first I ever et. Tasty little jobbers too." The older man strolled off. "I'll go turn on the water."

Luke began to pack away his tools. Had his life ever been so simple that lunch snacks were an occasion for excitement? He could hardly remember a time when he didn't have something weighing on him. Now he had the job of telling Ruby she was going to have to choose between the enormous cost of full-time medical care in her own house or the life-altering option of a nursing home. And how was someone in Ruby's condition supposed to make such a decision?

Down on his knees on the bathroom floor, it occurred to Luke that now was a perfect time to pray for guidance. He put one elbow on the toilet lid and closed his eyes. God hadn't kept death from Ellie or illness from Ruby or a stalker from haunting Darcy. But Luke had decided to trust that God could lead all of them through this valley of shadows, and he prayed for his heavenly Father's divine presence, his protection, his comfort, and his direction.

"He's here! He's here!" Floyd burst into the bathroom, slamming the door into Luke and knocking him off balance.

"That feller from the picnic is down in the kitchen with Jo, and he's got him a sidekick, and the two of 'em's talkin' mean as bears to her. You better call Mick and Ben pronto!"

Luke got to his feet and pushed past Floyd. "Follow me! My cell phone's in the foyer. You call the police."

"Boss, I don't know how to use them cell phones." Floyd was gasping for breath as he hurried down the stairs after Luke. "I don't know which button to push!"

"Get Gabe." Luke plunged down the long hallway toward the kitchen. "Tell him to do it."

"Gabe took the day off, boss! Don't you recall? Him and his girlfriend—"

Luke pushed open the kitchen door to find Darcy backed up against the cabinets. Will Damyon was grasping her shoulder roughly and shouting into her face. Behind him stood a taller, more muscular young man who had hold of Damyon by the shoulder. He was yelling, too, his face a bright red.

"Let her go!" Luke hollered. "Get your hands off her! She's got an order against you, Damyon."

At the sound of Luke's voice, both men turned. Darcy twisted loose from Damyon's grasp and fled across the kitchen floor toward an adjoining corridor.

"Darcy, wait!" Luke called, taking off after her.

"Come back here, girl! I ain't finished with you yet!"

Behind him, Luke could hear the other two men following him down the hall. He expected Darcy to head out the front door, but the instant she spotted Floyd in the foyer, she veered and headed up the curved staircase.

"Darcy, wait!" Luke grabbed the banister for support.

"Get her, Buck!" Will Damyon roared. "Don't let her get away!"

Darcy fled into the bathroom where Luke had been soldering and slammed the door behind her.

Luke pounded against it. "Darcy, open up! It's me." Luke

heard the key turn in the lock. "Darcy, I'm not going to let them hurt you."

"Move aside!" Damyon gave him a shove. "Bust the door down, Buck."

"You break this door, and I'll—"

"Bust it, Buck!"

"No!" Luke shouted.

As Will slammed shoulder-first against the door, Luke threw a body block into the older man's side. Both of them tumbled to the floor. Will came up swinging. Luke dodged a fist and felt the blow glance off his jaw. As Luke tried to fend off the attack, a hand clamped around his collar. It was Buck. He pulled Luke away from the older man and shoved him aside.

"Sit down, Dad!" the younger man bellowed. "You want to give yourself another heart attack?"

Luke pushed his way to the bathroom door, which was swinging open on one hinge. Dimly, he realized the newcomer was yet another member of the Damyon family. Was he, too, bent on revenge? No wonder Darcy was terrorized. As Buck bent over his father, Luke rushed into the tiny room. It was empty.

The window over the toilet had been raised. He stood on tiptoe to peer outside. Surely Darcy hadn't jumped from this height. If she had . . .

Luke climbed onto the toilet seat and leaned out the window. He spotted her below, climbing down from a drainpipe and landing on the lawn with a soft thud.

"Darcy!" he called.

Running toward the trees that edged the property, she never even looked back. As she headed for the forest, Luke noticed a dark figure waiting for her in the shadowy tangle of vines and undergrowth. To Luke's horror, the man grabbed Darcy's hand and drew her into the woods.

"I don't want to go into the forest," Montgomery said, squeezing her father's hand. "It's dark. It's scary in there. We might get lost."

"I'm afraid Darcy *did* get lost. That's why we have to find her." Luke studied the others in the search party who had gathered on the grounds behind the old Chalmers Mansion. When Darcy hadn't showed up to help Ruby make supper that evening, Luke's worry had turned to outright fear. Rather than trying to cook anything himself, he had loaded Ruby and Montgomery into the pickup and taken them to Tastee Hut for burgers and onion rings. That's where he told Gabe that Darcy was missing, and that's where the decision had been made to call out a search party.

He was a little amazed at how many townspeople had turned out to look for Darcy. It seemed she had touched more lives than just his. Gabe Zimmerman had brought his flashlight and his girlfriend. Zachary and Elizabeth Chalmers stood to one side on the mansion's lawn with their son, Nick. Each of the three carried flashlights. Nick carried a backpack filled with snacks and other small treasures that he had insisted on displaying for Montgomery one by one as they waited for the rest of the party to gather.

Pastor Paul had agreed to lead Ruby McCann into the forest. Once she learned that Darcy had been threatened, Ruby wouldn't hear of staying behind. She had pulled on a pair of her husband's trousers, secured them with the old bathrobe belt, and topped the outfit with one of Darcy's T-shirts. Her snow-white hair was protected by a flowered shower cap. Boompah Jungemeyer made the third member of that group. For the search party's refreshment, the elderly grocer had contributed a cardboard box filled with snack cakes that had gone past their expiration date.

Kaye Zimmerman and her husband, Nathan, were joined

by the mayor of Ambleside, Cleo Mueller. Cleo owned Redee-Quick Drugs, and he had supplied sodas and a large aerosol can of bug repellent. Kaye took it upon herself to go from person to person, spraying each one thoroughly whether they wanted her to or not. The chiggers, she informed the group, were especially bad this year.

"Everybody ready?" Luke called out, switching on his flashlight. The sun hadn't been down long, but trees and vines grew thickly in the forest that bordered the old mansion. "All right, each group has chosen a different area of the woods to search, and we're going to meet back here in two hours—no matter what. If you aren't back in two hours, we'll add you to the list of missing."

"And for your punishment," Boompah added, "you won't get any of my delicious snack cakes."

Luke smiled at the old man, whose kindness permeated everything he did. "Now, remember to stay away from the edge of the limestone bluff," he cautioned. "And don't anybody fall into the river. The current's too swift to swim in."

"Don't go near the train tracks either," Mayor Mueller called out. "There'll be a freight train coming through at seven-thirty, and the Amtrak follows it at eight. The best thing is just to steer clear of that whole area."

"But what if she's down there?" Kaye said. "What if she went down to the tracks on purpose? If she's really upset, she might just want to end it all."

"End it all?" Montgomery whispered, tugging on Luke's hand. "What does she mean, Daddy? Does she think Darcy might want a train to run over her?"

Luke studied his wide-eyed little daughter, her red braids hanging to her waist. There might have been a time when he tried to protect his child from the worst realities of the world. But Montgomery was too intelligent, and she had experienced too much already.

"That's what Kaye's worried about," he said. "But I don't

think Darcy would do something like that. She knows God is with her in all this trouble, and that will give her a lot of hope and courage."

As the parties began to move into the woods, Montgomery pulled her hand out of her father's grasp. "Daddy, I'm going to walk with Nick and his parents, okay?" she said. "Because I think you should look for Darcy by yourself . . . near the river and the tracks."

"Why's that, Monkey?"

"Because I think she was really scared of that bad man, and I think she went where other people would be too afraid to follow."

"You might be right about that, sweetheart."

"I want you to find her and bring her back to us, Daddy."

"I'll do my best."

"Okay." As she turned to join the Chalmers group, she called over her shoulder. "But be careful. I can't lose you, too."

Luke nodded. For the first few months after Ellie's death, the child had been afraid to let her father out of her sight. But she clearly had grown to love Darcy.

As he pushed through the tangle of undergrowth, Luke thought about his own feelings for Darcy. He knew he loved her, too. She was fun to be around, full of life, and always quick to tease or offer an opinion. He admired the way she went at her work, painting and hanging wallpaper with intense concentration. And she was good at it. More than once, Floyd had called him in to point out the clever way Darcy had wrapped a wallpaper border around a difficult corner, or the method she had used to paint the fretwork on a turret. But Luke's feelings had grown beyond admiration and affection. Far beyond those simple emotions to something deep and abiding.

Floyd had grown to love Darcy like a daughter, and Gabe treated her as a beloved older sister. In fact, Luke was a

little surprised that Floyd hadn't turned up to search for
Darcy this evening. But the elderly fellow had been com-
plaining about his arthritic feet lately. Maybe he was home
soaking them.

Luke stepped over a fallen log and shined his flashlight
down a small creek bed. Searching the damp ground for
fresh footprints, he saw only what appeared to be deer
tracks. Where could Darcy have gone? And who had led her
into the forest? It must have been someone she knew. She
wouldn't have gone willingly with a stranger.

But had she gone willingly? Or had the man dragged her
into the woods? Luke couldn't be certain of what he had
seen that afternoon. What if the man hidden in the trees
had been someone else that Will Damyon had brought
along? Someone from Darcy's past?

Fear twisted through Luke's stomach again, as it had ever
since he'd spotted Darcy climbing down the mansion's
drainpipe. All afternoon he had tried to assure himself she
was all right. Reason told him she was with someone she
knew, someone who would protect her. She was just resting. Just lying low until Will and Buck Damyon left the
area.

As Luke stepped out of the dense growth into a clearing
that adjoined the railroad tracks, concern prickled down his
spine. Surely Darcy wouldn't have gone anywhere really
dangerous. No way she would have been that desperate.
But what if she'd been injured accidentally? Thick with
brush and ivy, the edge of the bluff was hard to recognize.
Maybe she had fallen off, tumbling hundreds of feet down
to the river. The realization that she might be seriously hurt
ripped through his gut like a knife. He had lost Ellie. He
couldn't lose Darcy.

The moment the thought hit him, Luke stopped walking.
Did he love Darcy in the same way he had loved Ellie? Yes,
he loved Darcy. Luke couldn't deny it. But what he felt for

her was different somehow. This new love was more mature, based less on emotion and more on commitment, something he was determined to nurture and grow.

He and Ellie had been young, naive, driven by passion. Luke felt no doubt about his physical desire for Darcy. But she meant so much more to him than that. Darcy was a woman he had come to see as a whole person, a creature of pain and suffering and redemption and joy and faith.

"Darcy!" he called out for the hundredth time. "Darcy, it's Luke! Where are you?"

He could hear the breeze tousling the leaves on the oak trees overhead. The Missouri River gurgled along its banks nearby. Somewhere in the distance, a train whistle blew.

"Darcy!" He jogged down the tracks, aiming his flashlight down the wall of trees on one side and the riverbank on the other. "Darcy, where are you?"

The rails beneath his feet began to shiver. Gravel shifted and tumbled down the embankment. The whistle sounded again, long and low, as the train prepared to pass through the station at Ambleside. When the train's headlights rounded a bend and bore down on him, Luke leaped off the track and sprinted toward the river. *Father God, don't let Darcy be on that track!* he prayed. *Protect her!*

Luke slumped against the trunk of a large sycamore tree. Protect her? God hadn't protected Ellie, had he? Why was Luke such a fool as to believe God would look after Darcy? Why had he been such a fool to trust God at all?

"Darcy!" he cried out, his voice hoarse. The train rumbled past, and the tracks fell silent again. Luke sank to the ground and switched off his flashlight. For a moment he sat in the echoing stillness, staring upward into the black sky. He felt just as he had the night Ellie died, tangled and tormented and hopeless.

A year ago, his solution had been to reach for a bottle of beer . . . and then another. He had turned his back on a

God he thought had betrayed him, drowned himself in an alcoholic haze, and staggered through the ensuing months with no purpose other than survival. His focus had been on himself and his own pain. Even Montgomery, crying alone in her bed, could barely draw him from the slow waltz of agony.

And then Darcy had barged into his life with her own heavy load of suffering. But Darcy had shown Luke a different way to face the sorrow. She had pointed him back to Christ, led him into God's warm arms of love—arms that might not always protect from earthly pain, but an eternal embrace that would always welcome the heavy heart.

Was Luke's faith so weak that the moment he faced another trial, he ran from God again? Couldn't he trust the Father to fulfill his promises? As he searched the night sky, Luke felt his heart fill with those very promises, Scriptures he had memorized so long ago when he was a boy in Sunday school. *"I will never fail you. I will never forsake you. . . . Though they stumble, they will not fall, for the Lord holds them by the hand. . . . You can be sure that the more we suffer for Christ, the more God will shower us with his comfort through Christ. . . . Surely your goodness and unfailing love will pursue me all the days of my life. . . ."*

God had been pursuing him all his life, Luke realized. How long was he going to keep running away? When would he stop and rest in God's promises? He flipped on the flashlight and studied the narrow beam that fell on the leaves scattered around the base of the old sycamore tree. *Father, you know where Darcy is,* he prayed. *She's in your hands. I'm in your hands. Teach me how to rest in you.*

Getting to his feet, he walked down to the edge of the wide Missouri River. Moonlight glinted off the rushing water. Logs floated by, half submerged. An owl hooted overhead. Luke started along the bank. He had come down here several times to fish with Floyd after work. Usually, they just stood on the shore, drinking sodas and snacking on Chee-tos. But sometimes they went out in Floyd's boat. The old electrician had a little cabin just upriver—

Luke stopped, his heart constricting with realization. The dark figure in the forest this afternoon had been Floyd! He could see the old fellow now, small and gnarled, drawing Darcy into the shelter of the trees. Floyd had probably realized the predicament she was in and had offered to protect her. The fishing cabin!

Jogging along the bank, Luke splashed across a creek that had worked its way between the hills and down the valleys to join the mighty river. A half mile past the creek, he climbed over a barbed-wire fence. Then he skirted a marshy spot and crossed beneath an overhanging limestone bluff that took him back into the path of the train tracks. Finally he spotted the tiny shack built of corrugated tin and lit with a single bare bulb.

"Floyd!" he called. Luke ran up the rickety steps, but the minute he crossed onto the deck, a shrill alarm went off. Bells jangled overhead, floodlights flashed on, and Floyd burst through the front door, his rifle cocked and loaded for bear.

"Back off, you no-good rattlesnake!" the old man snarled. "This is private property, and you're trespassin' where you ain't wanted."

"Floyd!" Luke said. "Put down your rifle."

"Who's there? I can't see nothing with these dadburned floodlights a'shinin' in my eyes."

"It's me, Luke Easton."

"Boss? What you doin' down here to the river?"

"You're the one who has some explaining to do, Floyd. What's the meaning of this?"

The little electrician reached out and flipped a switch that shut off the bells and floodlights. "Pretty nifty burglar alarm system I set up here, don't you think?" he asked. "Kindy like

a booby trap, don't you know. I put it together this evenin'
out of a few things I had lyin' around the place."

"Where's Jo?" Luke said.

"Jo? I ain't—"

"I'm right here." She walked out onto the deck, her hands
shoved deeply into her pockets and her eyes hollow with
fear. "I guess I'll never be able to hide."

FOURTEEN

"Is he still out there looking for me?" Darcy shivered as she glanced toward the shadowy forest that surrounded Floyd's fishing cabin. She could almost picture Buck and Will Damyon creeping through the trees, their focus on the woman who stood on the deck. "Do you think anyone followed you, Luke?"

"Damyon and his son left the mansion hours ago. I don't know where they went."

"I shouldn't have run away."

"There's been a lot of that going on lately." Luke took a step toward her. "Darcy, are you all right?"

She nodded, feeling miserable. Luke crossed the deck and folded his arms around her. "Floyd, go fix us all some sodas and Chee-tos, why don't you? I need to talk to Darcy a minute."

"All I got is Bugles, boss. That's all I been eatin' lately, and the other day I brung a whole box of 'em—"

"Bugles will be fine, Floyd. We all like Bugles."

"Suit yourself." With a shrug, Floyd went back into the fishing cabin.

As Luke held Darcy, she silently thanked God for sending this man to comfort her. Though he was only human, right now Luke Easton seemed like a fortress against the trouble that surrounded her. Relief swept over her as she slipped her arms around his waist and rested her cheek against his shoulder. She could feel his heart beating, still pounding with the exertion of his trek through the woods to find her.

"Any idea how many people are out in this forest looking for you tonight?" he murmured softly.

She shook her head. "The police, I guess."

"Let's see, there's Zachary and Elizabeth, Nick and Montgomery, Gabe and his girlfriend, Kaye and Nathan Zimmerman, the mayor—"

"Mr. Mueller?"

"Cleo takes his job of protecting Ambleside's citizens pretty seriously." He brushed a strand of hair off her forehead. "And, of course, Pastor Paul came along. He's out there with Boompah Jungemeyer and Ruby—"

"Not Ruby!" Her breath caught, and she drew back. "Ruby shouldn't be in the forest at night. She'll get lost."

"She was worried *you'd* get lost. She insisted on joining the search party."

"Oh, Luke, I had no idea . . ."

"A lot of people care about you, Darcy. They're willing to risk their own safety to protect you. They love you."

Silent, grateful, amazed, she allowed him to hold her close. With one hand he tipped up her chin, forcing her to look into his eyes. Then he kissed her softly on the lips.

"*I* love you, Darcy," he said. "I don't know what to do about it. But I know it's true."

Deeply moved by his words and shaken by his tender kiss, Darcy found she couldn't bring herself to speak. Luke loved her. *Loved* her. She hadn't allowed herself to believe such a thing was possible. But she knew he meant it—and not in the flippant, meaningless way her husband had said the words, eager to lure her into his possession. As a young girl, she had ached for love, and she had wrongly believed she could earn it by catering to a man's every desire and whim—no matter how twisted.

Luke offered his love with no expectations. He asked for nothing in return. His statement was honest and vulnerable. And she believed him when he said it was true.

"Tonight when you didn't show up at Ruby's house," he said, "and when I couldn't find you anywhere, I began to realize how things would be without you. That's when I admitted to myself how deeply I love you. And that's when I recognized that I'd been running away from things too. Running from the possibility of love. Running from peace with my father. Running from God, mostly."

"I thought you had let him back into your life."

"I did, but I haven't gotten to trusting him completely."

"It's hard to do." She shook her head as she slipped out of his arms. "I've been running, too. Trying to find a place to hide."

She walked to the edge of Floyd's deck and sat down on the top step, overlooking the river. In the moonlight, her bare arms took on a pale silver glow as she bowed her head.

"I keep begging God to set me free," she said. "I feel like I'm still in prison. I run. I hide. But I can't ever get past these walls that hold me in. Ruby said freedom is something you find inside your heart. In my Christian faith, I feel free from the sins of my past. I really do, Luke. It's what's outside me that I can't escape."

"It's the consequences of that past sin." He sat down beside her and took her hand. Woven through hers, his fingers were warm and strong. "You're the one who said we have to leave the past behind. I remember a verse I memorized once. I can't think of the exact words, but it's something about running the race that's set before you, pressing forward toward the goal. It's kind of a sports thing."

"I didn't know the Bible talked about sports."

"I always liked that verse, because I used to be a hurdler on the track team in high school. And a pretty good one. But I found out that if I was always looking over my shoulder—always thinking of the guy behind me—I could never win. I would trip over the hurdles or lose my lane or get passed. It was only when I kept my eyes focused on that tape at the end of the race, when I pushed myself forward toward the goal ahead of me, that I could win."

"But I don't want to be in a race," she said. "I want to hide. Hide where no one can find me. Hide and never come out."

Luke stared out at the river so long that Darcy wondered if he had slipped away from her in his thoughts. Maybe her words had separated them. Maybe he was realizing how foolish he was to love someone like her. She couldn't relate to his story about the track team. After all, she hadn't even finished high school. Certainly she hadn't been on a sports team or done anything to distinguish herself. Her GED and two years of college credit had been earned inside the walls of a state penitentiary. Maybe Luke was realizing how little they had in common.

"Bugles!" Floyd announced, emerging through the screen door with an armful of three cans of Coke and a bowl of snacks. "Popped us some popcorn, too. None of that microwave stuff for me, no-siree. How I do it is I put them little kernels right into the pan with some oil, see. And then I close the lid on good and tight, and set her on the stove. Once she goes to poppin', why you got to keep your eye on her real close. The minute you hear them kernels slowin' down, you whisk her right off the burner, pour in some melted butter and sprinkle a good measure of salt over the whole kit 'n' caboodle. And there she be!"

Floyd presented the mixture of popcorn and Bugles with the flourish of a maitre d' at a five-star restaurant. Hunkering down onto the steps, he edged Luke over, jamming him up against Darcy. Then he handed out the sodas.

"Well," Floyd said, popping the tab on his can. "What you figurin' to do, Miss Jo? I'd welcome you to stay here in my cabin for as long as you like, but I reckon you know that mean ol' polecat is gonna find you someday."

"I know," she said. "I'll never be able to run fast enough or far enough to escape him."

"Darcy wants to hide," Luke said. "And I can't blame her."

"Puts me in mind of an old hymn my granny used to sing while she was doin' the Monday washin'." Floyd hummed for a moment, and then he began to sing.

He hideth my soul in the cleft of the rock
That shadows a dry, thirsty land.
He hideth my life in the depths of his love,
And covers me there with his hand,
And covers me there with his hand.

When no one spoke, Floyd took up a handful of snack mix. "As a boy, I wasn't rightly sure what a cleft was," he said. "Then I figured out it was somethin' kindy like a cave. I seen them caves in the bluff, places where the water carved a hole right through the limestone. That's what a cleft is, and that's where you're supposed to hide your soul."

Luke reached for the popcorn-and-Bugles mix. "Your soul can hide," he said. "Hide in the cleft of the rock and be covered with God's hand. But I think your body's got to step out and live."

"Take the bull by the horns, as they say." Floyd passed the bowl to Darcy. "Face the music. Take it on the chin. Fight the rattler and give him first bite. Be as gritty as eggs rolled in sand—"

"I think she's got the message, Floyd," Luke said.

"Yes," Darcy agreed, realizing what she had to do. "I've got the message."

Darcy settled Ruby into bed and tucked the sheet up around her chin. It had been a long night. After everyone had assembled on the mansion's lawn, congratulated Luke for finding Darcy, and eaten their fill of slightly stale snack cakes, Pastor Paul had addressed the group. He thanked all the people for committing themselves to the task of searching for their friend, for obeying Christ's command that Christians must be willing to lay down their lives for their sisters and brothers. Then he had turned to Darcy and assured her of the love and support that he and the church members wanted to offer her. After praying, he dismissed the group to return to their homes.

Later that night, as Darcy had helped Ruby into the bathtub, scrubbed away the mud, picked scores of tiny red seed ticks from her skin, and gently washed the bumps of poison ivy rash erupting on Ruby's arms—she recalled the words of love that had poured out of the people who had gathered to search for her.

"Please don't run away again," Montgomery had said. "We love you too much to lose you."

"If you fell off the bluff or drained in the river, we would be very sad." Nick had been almost in tears as he spoke. "Our hearts would crack."

"You're just too pretty and sweet to let anybody trouble you," Kaye Zimmerman had whispered in Darcy's ear. "You come on by the Kut-n-Kurl anytime you get to feeling low. We'll sit down with a couple of Dr. Peppers and have us a girl talk. Get it all right out in the open, how's that?"

"We don't allow troublemakers in our town," Cleo Mueller had intoned, giving Darcy's hand a firm shake. "I'm going to talk to Mick and Ben about those men who threatened you, young lady. I just won't permit that kind of thing—not to somebody who's been as fine a young citizen of Ambleside as you have been."

"They make me think of the Nazis," Boompah had said, giving Darcy a warm hug. "In the war, the Nazis never gave us a moment of peace. I know just how you feel."

Now Darcy smoothed a soft cotton blanket over Ruby's sheet and switched off the lamp nearby. The old woman reached out and caught Darcy's hand for a moment. She squeezed it softly. Then she closed her eyes and drifted off.

Wandering back across the hall to her own room, Darcy thought about her decision. Luke and Floyd had been right. She *could* hide forever—hide her soul in the cleft of the rock she knew as her heavenly Father. But her earthly body was going to have to face up to the consequences of the past. And that meant she needed to confront Will Damyon and try to find some way to make peace with him.

The only way Darcy could think of to start on that journey was to find her former father-in-law. She didn't want to do it. Will was mean enough and angry enough to hurt her badly. And Buck could kill her.

She sat down on the bed and looked out the window at the lights burning in the guesthouse below. Luke Easton had told her he loved her. The miracle of his words still reverberated through her like the sparkles that lingered after a burst of fireworks. The very idea of being loved flung open the doors of hope in Darcy's heart. Could there be a future for her and Luke? Might he want her as his wife one day? The thought of building a home and a family with Luke and Montgomery filled Darcy to the point of bursting. Was it possible? Did God really have such a magnificent gift in store for her?

She stared down at her old prison work boots. Her soul hid in the cleft of the rock. Her heart belonged to Luke Easton. But her muddy feet still walked in the mire of the past. How was she going to make her way through it? Would the Damyons ever forgive her?

With a sigh, she stood and pulled on a sweater Ruby had loaned her. Pale blue, the sweater had been knit of soft cashmere, and a pattern of tiny pearls formed delicate flowers around each buttonhole. Darcy smoothed down her

jeans and wiggled her toes inside her boots. *Okay,* she
lifted up to God, *help me be brave enough to fight the rattler
and let him have the first bite.*

After switching off her bedroom light, she tiptoed across
the hall and turned the key in Ruby's bedroom door. It
wouldn't do to have the dear woman suddenly decide to
wander around in her nightgown in the middle of the night.
Darcy crept down the long carpeted staircase and walked
along the hall past the portraits of all the McCann ancestors.
As she pushed open the front door and stepped outside, a
figure moved into the light.

"Where might you be going?"

A gasp of terror turned to a sigh of relief as she recognized the speaker. It was Luke Easton.

As they hurried down the sidewalk, Darcy argued vehe-
mently that Luke had to go home. He must leave her alone.

"Montgomery needs you!" she said.

"She's spending the night with Nick's family."

"But I don't want your help."

"Yes, you do."

"Luke, you could get hurt."

"So could you."

"If you get into trouble on my behalf, you could lose
everything."

"I know that."

"You shouldn't risk it, Luke. You can't afford to get
thrown in jail for even a night. And believe me, Will and
Buck can cause enough of a ruckus to get anybody thrown
in jail."

"Then why are you going looking for them?"

"Because I have to," she said. "I need to do this. Listen,
Luke, you've got to go home. If you lose your reputation in
this town, you won't get any more building contracts. The

bank is making it hard enough for you to keep your company going. You can't throw everything out the window just to try and protect me from those men."

"I'll do what I think is right." He marched along beside her, his chin jutting forward in determination. "I know what I'm risking. If I could stop you from doing this, I would. But I know you better than that by now."

"You don't know me at all. I've been working for you, what, a couple of months?"

"I knew the minute Floyd started in with his 'take the bull by the horns' business, you were going to head out and look for the Damyons tonight. I saw your bedroom light go off upstairs, and I knew you weren't heading to sleep like a good girl. So, I walked across the lawn to the front door, and bingo."

"Lucky guess."

"I thought you didn't believe in luck."

"Okay, maybe you do know me pretty well. That doesn't mean you should be out here with me."

"What am I supposed to do? Sit back and let them beat you to a pulp? Let them torment you until you strike back? They're either going to send you back to prison or kill you, Darcy. And I'm not about to let them get away with either one."

She walked in silence, realizing that what he said was true. The Damyons intended to destroy her, and her hope of preventing them was slim. But what choice did she have?

As she crossed Main Street and started around the town square, Darcy began looking for the two men. With no motel in Ambleside, either they had driven to another city to find a place to sleep, or they were camping out somewhere nearby. Knowing the Damyons, she doubted they would fork over the money for a motel.

She scanned the businesses that lined the square. The benches in front of the Redee-Quick drugstore were empty.

So were the white metal tables and chairs on the sidewalk outside the Nifty Cafe. No one had spread sleeping bags in the Victorian pavilion that anchored a corner of the square, and the sidewalk in front of Finders Keepers antiques shop was deserted.

"I'm going to walk down to Al's gas station," Darcy said. "He'll still be open. Maybe he's seen—"

"Darcy, can't I talk some sense into you?" Luke blocked her path and clamped his hands on her shoulders. "Floyd and I both saw Will Damyon threatening you in the kitchen today. He broke the bathroom door off its hinges trying to get to you. Darcy, the man clearly violated the restraining order you took out against him. He's the one who ought to be thrown in jail. Give me a chance to talk to Mick and Ben over at the police station and—"

"No, you can't do that, Luke."

"Why not? I'd testify against the Damyons. So would Floyd. We could get the father locked up. He'd have no choice but to go back to Joplin and leave you alone."

Darcy gave a derisive chuckle. "Oh, Luke, please. You saw the man. He's not going to go back to Joplin until he's finished with me."

"What if they're armed? We ought to at least let the police know what we're—"

"Luke!" Darcy caught his hand as the dim light shining through the basement windows of the old house registered. "They're in the mansion. The Damyons."

He swung around and studied the building on Walnut Street. "Then they're trespassing. They have no right to be in that house, and I'm going to call Mick and Ben."

For an instant, Darcy actually grasped at the hope that Luke held out in front of her. Maybe the police would really come and drive the Damyons out of town. Maybe the restraining order would keep Will Damyon away. Maybe a trespassing charge would assure that the men would never bother Darcy again.

But was that really the point? She knew the Damyons well enough to realize that their pursuit would never end. Will had been waiting six years for her to get out of prison. Almost the moment the Greyhound bus pulled away from Vandalia, he was on her trail.

"No," she said, laying her hand on Luke's arm. "Don't call the police yet. Give me a chance to try to talk to them. It's not just to try to stop them from following me. This is for me, Luke. I need to do this. If I can make them see . . . if they can accept my repentance . . . maybe they'll set me free."

Luke let out a deep breath. She knew he didn't want her to go. And she had to admit that she was taking a tremendous risk—maybe this was the stupidest thing she'd ever done. The chances of getting the Damyons to listen to her were minuscule. But she felt compelled to try. Luke didn't stop her as she walked past him and started down the sidewalk toward the mansion.

No doubt the two men had chosen the basement as a lair to lie in hiding until the following morning when she returned to work, Darcy realized. When she showed up, the assault would begin again. As she climbed the steps onto the porch, she prayed that this surprise appearance might throw them off guard, might give her a few moments to speak the words of peace she needed to say.

"They probably broke a window," Luke growled, inserting the skeleton key in the front door lock. "Another thing I'll need to fix."

"I don't know. These locks are pretty easy to pick." She stepped into the cool foyer. "Buck used to break into liquor stores. He even knocked over a few pharmacies. He's a pro."

"Great. Just great."

Darcy crept along the floor, hoping the floorboards wouldn't squeak. If the Damyons were prepared for an intruder, they might shoot first and look at their victims later. In the kitchen, she pushed open the door to the basement. From below, the sound of male voices drifted upward. The Damyons were arguing.

"They're mad at each other," she whispered over her shoulder.

"That's good. Maybe they'll leave us alone."

"No, that's bad. It means they've probably been drinking."

"Wonderful. This is getting better all the time."

Darcy grasped the iron railing and tiptoed down the steps. There was no hope of keeping the stairs from groaning, and when she moved out into the basement, she heard the men's voices fall silent.

Her heart slamming against her ribs, she hesitated, wanting to leave a path of escape. She might need to run. She looked up at the stairs, the only exit.

"Who's there?" Will Damyon called out.

Darcy drank down enough air to fill her lungs. "It's me," she answered.

"Darcy?"

"Yes, sir. I came to talk to you."

"Who'd you bring along? The police? Or maybe you're carrying that gun you used to shoot Bill."

"I'm not armed. Luke Easton is with me."

"Oh, your new boyfriend." Will Damyon stepped through the door of the old coal storage room. "You broke two of my ribs, buster. Fine way to treat a helpless old man."

"You were attacking a helpless young woman."

"Luke, please." Darcy put out a hand. "Could you wait upstairs for me? I need to talk to Will by myself."

"I don't think that's a good idea."

"Oh, get your hairy hide out of here!" Will snarled. "If the girl's got something to say, let her say it and be done."

"I'll stay right here," Luke said.

Buck emerged from the coal room. He was a tall, muscular man, his blue eyes intense in the glaring light of the bare bulb. He crossed his arms over his broad chest and stared at Darcy.

She took a step forward. "I came down here because I have something I need to say to you. To all the Damyons."

"Well, spit it out." Will walked toward her, his head held low. "Just looking at you is making me mad."

"I want to ask your forgiveness for what I did," she said, forcing her voice to stay calm. "I admit I shot and killed Bill. I know he wasn't armed. I won't make any excuses for myself. I did the wrong thing. I hurt your whole family. And I'm so . . . so very sorry."

For a moment, Will Damyon glared at her, saying nothing. Then he gave a loud snort. "What's this pretty little speech all about, girl? You think you can come to me and apologize and I'll let you off the hook? Is that it? You want me to leave you alone?"

"Of course she wants us to leave her alone," Buck said. "That's pretty obvious."

"I want to be left alone, but more than that I want to be forgiven." She hung her head. "I can't think of any other way for us all to go forward."

"I told you, there's not going to be any going forward for you, girl. You took away my son's future—so what makes you think you deserve one?"

"I don't deserve a future. I know that. I don't deserve anything. But I'm asking for your forgiveness."

"Forgiveness," he spat. "What is that? I'm supposed to say it was hunky-dory that you shot my son? I'm supposed to be happy as a clam that you got out of prison after a lousy six years?"

"What I did was wrong. I'm admitting that, and I don't expect you to say it wasn't. I just want you to forgive me."

"She wants you to let her go, Dad." Buck leaned one beefy shoulder against the door frame. "That's what she means. She wants you to go on and don't look back."

"Like it never happened? Don't you think I've tried to tell myself the same thing?" The old man's lip quivered. "Every time deer hunting season comes along, I think about my boy. How we used to go out into the woods and sit for hours, just listening to the birds. Just being together. How am I supposed to forget that? I remember how that little fellow used to come toddling across the porch and grab on to the seat of my britches until I'd pick him up. And how he bought that old Jeep he was fixing up. And the time he handed over his whole paycheck when I'd busted my arm in a fight and couldn't pay the doctor. That boy had a lot of goodness in him, and I won't ever forget him. The day you pulled that trigger, you blasted away part of my heart, girl."

Darcy fought the tears that filled her eyes. "I know you loved Bill, sir. I know you won't ever forget him."

"No, I won't! And don't think all this sorry talk will change my mind about you."

"I'm not asking you to say what I did was all right. And I'm not asking you to forget what happened." She brushed at her cheek. "I just want you to forgive me."

"Well, what in the name of Goshen is that supposed to mean?"

"It means you let go of it, Dad," Buck said. "You get on with your life, and you let her get on with hers."

"I'm not letting her get on with anything! She killed your brother. She doesn't deserve forgiveness—"

"I know I don't deserve it!" Darcy said, wringing her hands. "I don't deserve anything God has given me. But he forgave me anyway. He forgave all the wrong things I did—not just killing Bill, but choosing my own way again and again, thinking only of myself, following my own path.

I know I've been wrong. But God forgave me, and I'm asking you to do the same."

"I'm not God," Will said. "And all this forgiveness talk makes me sick! What did you do, girl, get jailhouse religion? Don't think I haven't seen that before—folks thinking they're at their wits' end and turning to God for help. Well, as far as I'm concerned, that's a bunch of hooey."

"It's not hooey. It's real." Darcy felt like that tiny flickering lamp her Prison Fellowship leader had talked about. Except that her little flame of faith seemed right on the verge of being snuffed out.

"Get out of here with your forgiveness bunkum," Will said. "I'm not dumb enough to fall for that. You just want me to leave you alone. Well, guess what, girlie? I'm not going to leave you alone—not now and not ever. It doesn't matter where you go, what town you move to, how far you try to run, or how deep you try to hide. I'm going to find you, and I'm going to make you pay!"

Darcy nodded as the tears she had been trying to quench spilled over. Luke slipped his arm around her shoulders and turned her toward the stairs.

FIFTEEN

By the time Luke took Darcy back to the McCann mansion and then returned to the police station, the Damyons had left Chalmers House. He filed a report anyway. He also told Mick, the officer on duty, about the incident in the kitchen.

At Mick's suggestion, they walked over to the old house on the corner, and Luke pointed out the bathroom door still hanging by one hinge. He explained how Darcy had climbed down the drainpipe, told about the search party, and discussed Floyd's part in the incident. When Luke and Mick went down into the basement, they found evidence of the Damyons' presence—several cigarette butts, an empty six-pack of beer cans, some candy bar wrappers. After making a report, Mick headed for the gas station to ask Al Huff if he'd sold anything to the Damyons. Luke drove back to the McCann estate and let himself inside with the key Ruby had given him. Though he didn't speak to Ruby or Darcy that night, he opted to sleep on the settee in Ruby's front parlor, just to make himself feel better.

For the next week, Luke felt like a haunted war veteran—constantly looking over his shoulder at the hint of a shadow in the doorway, racing up the stairs when Darcy accidentally dropped a ladder, leaping into the fray when Floyd and Gabe got into a shouting match over territorial rights to a bag of wood screws. At night, he dreamed that the Damyons were bothering Darcy, and he woke up in a cold sweat. The more he thought about Darcy's bold confrontation with them in the basement, the more he loved her. And the more he loved her, the more certain he became that he would lose her.

The cause of his concerns seemed to have vanished from the face of the earth. The Ambleside police had notified their counterparts in Jefferson City and Joplin. No one knew the whereabouts of the two men.

"Mick and Ben talked to Jo, didn't they?" Floyd asked Luke one afternoon as he and Luke were taking a soda break in the backyard. "Pearlene Fox told my wife that both them police boys went over to Ruby McCann's house and gave Jo a talkin' to."

"As though *she's* the criminal?"

Floyd took off his cap and scratched his head. "Well, now, boss, she *is* the criminal, ain't she?"

"Darcy's no criminal!"

"She killed her husband, didn't she?"

Luke took a swig of Coke to cool himself down. How strange that in the past weeks he had all but dismissed Darcy's past. It was so obvious how God had used the aftermath of that sin to shape her into the beautiful, whole-some woman she had become. And that woman was the only one Luke could see.

"The point is, Floyd," he said, "that Darcy is the one who's been assaulted here. The ten-day restraining order has expired, and I'm not sure if she'll make the effort to have it extended."

"How come? Don't she want 'em to lock that feller up and throw away the key?"

"She wants to be forgiven. That's all she'll say."

"What she's gonna get is killed." Floyd dug a toothpick out of his overalls pocket and began to work on the Chee-tos stuck between his teeth. "Forgiven, huh? Now, what's she talkin' about, do you suppose?"

"She believes if the Damyons will forgive her, she'll be set free."

"I guess that's somethin' to aim for, expecially if you been locked up in the hoosegow awhile."

"She feels like she's still in prison."

"Well, ain't we all? You'd think I was free as a bird, wouldn't you? I got me a good wife, a pension from the state government, a fine fishin' cabin. And now, I got this job a-workin' for you, boss. But the fact is, I'm a prisoner to my old age. Got these feet won't hardly walk no more, they ache so bad. What good's a fishin' cabin if you can't get yourself from the pickup to the deck?"

"I see what you mean, but it seems like Darcy's in a different kind of prison."

"Oh, it don't matter what it looks like. We all got some bars around us on this earth. Take Gabe and that crazy girl-friend of his. Gabe's plumb loco about her, and he can't turn to the left or the right without gettin' his feet tangled up. Love—now, there's a prison for you."

Luke thought about Floyd's words for a moment. The love he felt for Darcy didn't seem like a prison at all. It felt like freedom—like lightness and air and wonder. But he wasn't about to tell Floyd that.

"And you got your prison, too," the old man said. "Them bars is just a-squeezin' you so tight you can't hardly breathe."

"What are you talking about, Floyd? I know I struggled a lot after Ellie died, but I think I've moved on now. I'm focused in the right direction."

"I ain't talkin' about Ellie," Floyd said. "I'm talkin' about your pappy. Don't think I'm so dumb that I never took notice of how much you want your parents to be proud of you? You figure if you can just get this construction com-pany up and rollin' good, then maybe they'll finally accept you. All the work you're doin' is just buildin' the bars of your own prison."

Luke flattened his soda can with one hand. "I don't care

what my father thinks. As far as I'm concerned, he can just—"

"There you go. You can always tell what's got somebody locked up in prison by how flustrated they get over it. Mention that kooky girlfriend to Gabe, and you're liable to have a fight on your hands. Get me to goin' on about my rheumatiz, and I'll just about talk your ear off. And there you go blowin' your top over your pappy."

"I'm not blowing my top. I just don't care to—"

"You want to get out of that prison, you ought to do the same thing as Jo done. You ought to just set your pappy down and talk to him."

"It didn't do Darcy any good."

"No?" Floyd flipped his toothpick onto the ground. "I think you're wrong on that one, boss. The more I considerate on the matter, the more I think when Jo went down in that basement and done her apologizin', them prison bars just melted away. You bring up the subject of those Damyon fellows now, and I bet Jo won't hardly raise a hackle. You want to know why? It's because she's free now. Set free."

"So, you don't think it really matters if the Damyons forgive her. What matters is that she apologized."

"Maybe. I ain't no preacher or philosophizer or nothin'. I just know what I see with my own two eyes. She looks happier than I seen her look in a long time."

Luke and Floyd started back into the old mansion. Floyd might not be a philosopher, Luke knew, but he had a good head on his shoulders. Maybe Floyd was onto something. If Luke sat his father down and talked to him—instead of arguing and shouting—maybe the two of them could come to terms. Like the Damyons, Luke's father might not ever forgive his son for failing to live up to his expectations. But clearing the air between them might set Luke free.

As they reached the back porch, Luke could hear Gabe

and Darcy talking in the kitchen. Darcy glanced up when he walked in. "Luke, the bank called while you were out on break."

"What did they want?"

"Umm . . ." She let out a breath. "Maybe you'd better talk to them yourself."

"Go ahead and tell me what they said. We're all in this thing together anyway."

Her eyes softened as she spoke. "The bank has decided to call in your business loans."

Luke felt as though a knife had been jammed into his spine. He hurled the crushed soda can across the room. It smacked into the wall and dropped into the wastebasket.

"Good shot," Gabe said. "Maybe you can get a job with the NBA."

"Hush your mouth, Gabe," Floyd said.

"What are you going to do, boss?" Gabe asked. "Pack it up?"

"You could always talk to Zachary Chalmers, boss. He's rich. Maybe he could advance you some cash for this job."

"Or you could go to a bank in Jefferson City. They have money to loan out. I saw their ads on television."

"Anyhow, you don't have to pay my wages until this job's done," Floyd said. "I got my government pension and all."

"Well, I need my paycheck every week. And I know Jo needs hers." Gabe crossed his arms over his chest. "What are you going to do, boss?"

Luke studied Darcy for a moment. Her eyes were luminous as they focused on his face. Floyd had been right about her. She *did* look peaceful. Set free.

"What I'm going to do," Luke said, "is have company over for dinner tonight."

"Company, boss?" Floyd asked.

"I'm going to invite my parents." He turned to Darcy.

"How would you feel about making some of those prize-winning beans of yours?"

"I'm pretty good with fried chicken, too," she said.

❦

"My goodness, isn't this quaint?" Phyllis Easton stepped over the threshold and into the cottage guesthouse. "But I don't recognize this furniture, Luke. Where's that lovely rocking chair you made for Ellie when she was expecting Montgomery?"

Darcy dredged a chicken breast in a mixture of flour and spices and set it into the pan of hot oil. Though she had volunteered to prepare the dinner, she was apprehensive about meeting Luke's parents for the first time, especially in light of the feelings he had expressed to her. He'd said he loved her—so she knew she needed to make a good impression on his parents. But how could she? In the first place, she felt sure the Eastons had heard all the local gossip about her. And in the second place, she knew she didn't have the manners or education or social standing to make it through the evening without embarrassing herself. The state women's penitentiary at Vandalia wasn't exactly a school for etiquette. In fact, Darcy wasn't sure she remembered which side of the plates to put the knives, spoons, and forks on, so she had left that chore to Montgomery.

"Most of our furniture is in storage," Luke was saying.

"What about that beautiful bed you built as a wedding gift for Ellie?" Mrs. Easton asked. "Surely you didn't put that in storage. It'll be ruined!"

"It's packed away, Mom. It'll be all right."

"Oh, I miss Ellie so much." She hesitated. "I'm sorry, Luke. I don't mean to bring up painful memories. But I always thought you had the loveliest, sweetest wife in the whole world."

Darcy dug around in the utensil drawer in search of

tongs. She could almost feel Mrs. Easton's eyes boring into her. *You,* she seemed to be signaling, *were obviously the worst wife in the whole world.*

"I couldn't agree more," Mr. Easton spoke up. "Ellie was a gem. Smartest move you ever made, Luke."

Up until that moment, Frank Easton hadn't said a word to anyone. He had walked straight to one of the overstuffed, chintz-covered chairs beside the fireplace, pulled a news-paper from under his arm, unfolded it laboriously, and started reading the financial section.

"It's been rough without Ellie," Luke said. "But Montgom-ery and I are getting along all right these days. Aren't we, Monkey?"

"We're going to church again," the little girl said as she stirred the beans bubbling on the stove. "And we don't cry at night anymore."

"Cry at night?" Mrs. Easton's voice took on a quaver. "Oh, my."

She hurried across the room and sat down opposite her husband. The pair of them fell silent as Montgomery fin-ished setting the table and Luke checked the green beans. Darcy couldn't resist glancing at him, just to make sure he was all right.

He wasn't.

She could tell just by the strained look in his eyes that this was going to be a difficult occasion for him. The years of enmity between Luke and his father would make it hard to broach the subject that needed to be discussed. Though Luke hadn't told her what he planned, Darcy felt sure he was going to ask his father for a personal loan. And a job.

It would mean submitting to the older man's will, putting himself under Frank Easton's authority again. It would mean the death of Luke's dreams and the end of his freedom. But what choice did he have? At best, he could borrow enough money from his father to rent a small home where he and

Montgomery could live. Luke could go to work in his
father's bank. With a steady income and benefits, he could
slowly pay off his medical and business debts. Maybe one
day he could even own a home again.

It would all depend on this dinner. On that man in the
chair by the cold fireplace. And on God.

Darcy realized she shouldn't forget about God's power to
touch and change lives. As she loaded a platter with fried
chicken, she lifted up a prayer on Luke's behalf. She
begged the heavenly Father to give Luke courage to confront his earthly father. She asked for patience. For wisdom.
For grace.

"I hope it goes well," she said softly, touching Luke's arm.
"Come over later if you want to talk."

"You're not leaving, are you?" His eyes darkened. "I
thought you'd stay and eat with us. Montgomery set a place
for you."

"Oh, but—"

"I need you, Darcy."

"To stay for dinner? But I—"

"Please." He leaned over and kissed her cheek. "I could
use some backup."

Feeling about as nervous as she had when she'd
appeared before the parole board, Darcy sat down in a
chair at the round oak table. Mr. and Mrs. Easton took
places side by side, and then Luke offered the blessing. To
Darcy's relief, Montgomery started chattering the moment
the meal began. It seemed there had been another incident
between Nick Chalmers and his tormentor—the golden-
haired Heather—today.

"She's so mean to Nick," Montgomery said. "She won't let
him swing next to her, and she trips him on purpose."

"That's not polite," Mrs. Easton said.

"Every time she sees Nick, she says, 'Eee-yewww, you're
gross!' But he's not gross; he's just different. Heather thinks

everyone should be the same as her—pretty clothes and the teacher's pet. Nick is his own person. He's not the same as anybody, and that's why I like him. He's funny when he talks, and he's good at art, and he's kinder than any person I ever knew."

"I'm glad you're Nick's friend," Luke said.

"I think people ought to be just how they are—and nobody should be mean to them."

Darcy cleared her throat, venturing out onto thin ice. "I agree, Little-bit. Trying to force somebody to be just like you would be a cruel thing. God made each of us special, with different gifts and talents . . . like your father with his carpentry. Your dad's the best builder I've ever met. That's his gift to the world."

"And I like science, and I'm going to be an engineer, and so what if Heather says ladies can't be engineers. She's so dumb she thinks engineers run trains."

"Well, some of them do."

"But not the kind I'm going to be. I had to explain to Heather that my kind of engineer designs buildings and bridges and roads and airplanes and stuff like that. So, me and Nick are going to have our own company where he's the architect and I'm the engineer, and we're going to be rich and famous."

"That's great, Little-bit," Darcy said.

"I hate Heather."

"I know she makes you mad, but God tells us to love our enemies."

"I didn't realize you were so familiar with the Bible," Mrs. Easton said, fixing her cool blue gaze on Darcy.

Darcy dipped her head. "Oh, I'm not. I haven't been a Christian very long, and I don't know too much—"

"Darcy has been an example to a lot of people since she came to town," Luke spoke up. "To me, for one. And to the men on my crew."

"An example of *what,* may I ask?" Mrs. Easton said.

"Of Christ."

"I see."

Uncomfortable at becoming the focus of attention, Darcy glanced at Luke, but his eyes were on Montgomery. "I think my daughter has a good point about how we ought to treat people. We need to be kind. That's important, Monkey. And we need to accept each other's differences. But Darcy is right, too. We ought to love everyone, even if we don't always agree with them."

As Luke pushed back his plate, Darcy could feel the tension mounting. He was going to talk to his father now, and she wanted to be anywhere but at that table. Maybe she could take Montgomery for a walk. Or claim the need to check on Ruby. Or start clearing the dishes.

But before she could move, Luke began to address his parents. "I invited you to dinner tonight for an important reason," he said. "I have something I need to ask you."

Mr. Easton lifted his chin as a slow smile spread across his lips. "I thought you'd come around eventually, Son. Tell us what you need. I'm sure we can work something out."

"I need your forgiveness." Luke let out a breath. "I guess you know how all my life I've wanted to build things. Carpentry is kind of an art for me. It's the way I express myself. As a young man, I didn't care what you wanted for me. The more you steered me toward banking, the more I veered off in my own direction. I've come to realize that I didn't honor you. I didn't obey you. Most of all, I didn't respect you. I apologize for that, and I hope you can forgive me."

"Of course, Luke," Mrs. Easton said. "We love you, dear. You know that."

"Well, this is a relief." Mr. Easton folded his napkin and set it back on the table. "I was beginning to wonder if you'd ever come to your senses. I have a proposal for you, Son. I believe we might even avoid bankruptcy with this plan. There's a position opening in our trust department. It would be a good place for you to start, learn the ropes, and then—"

"I don't intend to work at the bank, Dad," Luke said.

"What?" his mother asked.

"But I thought you—"

"I was apologizing—not asking for a job. I'd like to make amends with you. Start over, if we can."

"Start over?" Mr. Easton pushed back from the table. "What does that mean? From what I know of your financial situation, you are at rock bottom, young man. The only way to start over is to accept a position at the bank. With a regular salary and good benefits, you'll be on your feet before long. We can assign a financial manager to organize the mess you've made of your business—"

"I haven't made a mess of my business." Luke was breathing fast, and Darcy could sense his struggle to stay calm. "I think you know exactly how my financial situation came about."

"Yes, if you'd been able to afford decent medical insurance, you wouldn't owe thousands of dollars for the unsuccessful attempt at saving your wife's—"

"Dad!" Luke shot a glance at Montgomery. "I did everything I could for Ellie—and I'd do it again. I don't consider the money we spent a waste. Until the bank started pressing me to repay my loans, my construction company had been growing and thriving. I'm not second-guessing the road I chose, and I'm not apologizing for doing the kind of work I believe God created me to do."

"God didn't create you; I did! You're my only son. I raised you, fed and clothed you, and you owe me!"

"Frank!" Mrs. Easton gaped at her husband. "Our son is trying to make peace."

"I don't want peace. I want a son I can be proud of—not

some impoverished construction worker living in a borrowed house."

Darcy squeezed her hands together under the table. Luke
had asked for backup, and she ached to defend him. But
angry confrontations took her straight to her past—to men
who would strike out with words and fists, to bloodied
noses and fractured jaws, to ambulance sirens wailing and
policemen hammering on doors. She flinched as Mr. Easton
hurled insults at his son and Mrs. Easton began to weep.
Instinct told her to crawl under the table.

"I've done everything I can to bring you to your senses,"
Mr. Easton shouted. "And all you can say is 'sorry.' What are
you sorry for? I'm the one who's sorry—sorry you were ever
born!"

"Oh, Frank!" Mrs. Easton blotted her nose on a napkin.
"Please, please don't—"

"I'm sorry I didn't honor and respect you," Luke said, the
veins in his temple standing out. "I apologize for the times
I offended you. I would like to have a relationship with
you—a relationship of mutual understanding. But if that's
not possible, I accept your decision."

"You're telling me you refuse to conform to my wishes?"

"If your wishes are that I quit doing the work God gave
me to do, yes. I'm a carpenter. I build things." He studied
his mother across the table. "But I'm also your son. I love
you, and I'd like to find a way for us to be at peace."

"This is ludicrous." Mr. Easton stood and started for the
door. "I came here expecting you to talk reason. I thought
you'd finally recognized your mistakes. Now I realize you're
never going to change."

"Grandpa, you want Daddy to change just the way
Heather wants Nick to change," Montgomery cried out. "It's
mean!"

"It's not mean. It's sensible." Mr. Easton studied his grand-
daughter. "Your father has been offered a choice. He has

chosen the selfish road. I trust that one day, when you're a rich and famous engineer, you'll understand exactly what I'm talking about."

"I understand now. Daddy wants to love you and be friends with you. But you won't do it because Daddy's different from you. He won't be the way you want him to be, so you're mean to him. It's just like Nick and Heather, and don't say it isn't!"

"Montgomery." Luke set his hand on his daughter's arm. "That's enough."

Mrs. Easton stood and took her husband's arm. "Luke, please reconsider your father's offer. It's the only way we're ever going to have peace."

Luke pulled Montgomery into his lap and wrapped his arms around her. "To tell you the truth, I'm feeling a lot of peace right now. I feel free."

"Free of what?"

"Free to go forward." He smiled at Darcy. "It's another one of the ways this woman has been an example for me."

"And a fine example she is." Mrs. Easton stared at Darcy. "A woman who murdered her husband in cold blood. An ex-convict. A thief. Yes, that's a very fine example, Luke."

Husband and wife turned away from the table and walked out the front door, letting the screen slam shut behind them. Darcy tried to think of something to say, something to make everything better. But what could possibly repair this hopeless situation? Luke had lost his family, he would be forced to close down his business, and she would have to move to another town to find work.

"Well, Grandma was wrong about one thing," Montgomery said. "Darcy's not a thief."

Luke chuckled as he gave his daughter's red braid a tug. "You're right, Monkey. She's not a thief."

SIXTEEN

A cool evening breeze sent the mosquitoes into hiding. Darcy shivered as she walked beside Luke and Montgomery. After washing and drying the dinner dishes, they had decided to stroll around the grounds of the McCann estate and then pay a brief visit to Ruby. When Luke slipped his arm around Darcy, she welcomed the warmth. Laying her head on his shoulder, she allowed the moment to sweep her away. Shouting parents, vengeful stalkers, and an uncertain future all faded into the peaceful whir of the cicadas and the gentle croak of bullfrogs.

"I like living in our new house," Montgomery said, her small fingers tightly woven through Darcy's. "There's a big yard to play in, and Nick lives just across the square. We have lots of pretty flowers and a pond and a driveway for my bike. And we have Darcy nearby."

"I like that part best," Luke said.

Darcy closed her eyes, listening to the deep tones of the man's voice, loving the way he spoke, cherishing each moment in his presence. She knew it couldn't last much longer. She shared the heaviness in his heart. Though his father would dispute it, Luke had chosen the higher road that night. He hadn't asked for money or a job. He had asked for forgiveness. For peace between them. For harmony. Though he hadn't received any of those, Luke's action had set him free.

Spiritually free. But physically, he was still burdened by the problems that both his father and circumstances had built around him. These would force him onto a path that would separate him from Darcy.

"Bud Huff has been asking me to work for him for years," Luke said. "He wants to expand the hardware store, and he'd like to have me on board. I've been thinking about taking the job."

Darcy pictured the thriving retail business on the corner of Walnut and River Streets. Though the Huff forefathers originally had been brought to Ambleside as slaves to the Chalmers family, they had gone far in the years since the Civil War. Al Huff owned the town's main gas station and the only repair garage. He also owned a good bit of the land that fronted River Street. Boompah Jungemeyer had managed to purchase from Al the property to build his corner grocery, but most of the businesses along that street rented space from Al.

Al's son, Bud, owned the town's only hardware and lumber store. Darcy had enjoyed shopping for her supplies there. Clean, well-lighted, and neatly organized, Bud's Hardware carried almost anything the home hobbyist or professional builder might need. Bud stocked top-quality paint, and his brushes were the exploded-tip kind that she had come to rely on. With Luke as an employee, the business would be assured of further growth.

"Bud wants me as the guy to take on the projects that people start and can't finish," Luke said. "Screened porches, decks, basement remodelings—those kinds of things. It would mean steady work and good pay. Plus, I'd be covered by Bud's insurance."

"Sounds great." Darcy stepped onto the porch that surrounded Ruby's house. "But what about your dreams, Luke? What about owning your own business? Building houses from the ground up? That's what you've always wanted to do. I hate to see you give it up."

Luke sat down on the porch swing as Montgomery went

into the house to find Ruby. Darcy leaned against one of the six white columns that edged the deep verandah. Though she longed to sit beside Luke, to snuggle up next to him and place a soft kiss on his clean-shaven jaw, she knew this was not the time. He was trying to tell her about his future, trying to prepare her for the impossibility of their love, and she forced herself to simply listen.

"I'm going to have to dissolve my company," Luke said, elbows on his knees as he stared at the porch floor. "I'll have to let you and the two men go. I'll probably have to declare bankruptcy. I don't see that I have any choice."

"Are you sure, Luke?"

"I could talk to Zachary about a personal loan. But I don't want to be indebted to a friend—and besides, he's already forking over a huge amount of money on the restoration of the mansion and the start-up of his architectural firm. Now he's going to have to find a new builder to finish the project." He stretched his legs. "No, I wouldn't feel right asking to borrow money from him."

"I know you want to do the right thing. And I'm sure you'll get back on your feet, over time."

"Lord willing." He straightened. "I have to do what's best for Montgomery. She comes first. That means I need a stable income and insurance. Working for Bud, I can have both—and I can continue to build."

"That's good, then."

"No," he said, rising from the swing and crossing the porch to where she stood. "It's not good. It's right, but it's not good. *Good* would be having *you* in my life. Darcy, I've told you how I feel about you. Nothing has changed. But I don't have anything to offer you. I don't have a home, a career, a bank account—anything that would give you what you need most. Stability. Security. Freedom."

"I'm free, Luke."

"Not the way I want you to be free. Not the way you deserve."

"I don't deserve anything."

"You're a wonderful woman, and you've had a hard life up to now. The last thing I would do is ask you to take on more hardship."

Darcy shook her head as she looked into his blue eyes. "Luke, I love you. There's no hardship in that."

With a deep groan, he pulled her into his embrace. Darcy wrapped her arms around him and held him close. How could he think she would turn away from him because he was going through a rough time? She had no fear of taking on Luke's burdens. But she would never—not in a million years—allow him to take on hers. Will Damyon had sworn to be a threat for the rest of Darcy's life, and she knew him well enough to believe he meant it. How could she saddle Luke and Montgomery with that constant fear and danger?

Equally impossible was the idea of expecting Montgomery to accept Darcy as a mother. Ellie Easton had been gone a little more than a year. Though Montgomery clearly liked Darcy, the child couldn't be expected to accept another woman in her mother's place. Especially a woman with Darcy's reputation. If Montgomery reacted to the slurs Nick endured, she would find herself backed against a wall by the taunts and jeers at her ex-convict stepmother. Darcy could never ask such a sacrifice of little Montgomery. She loved her too much.

"I'm thinking about moving to Springfield," Darcy said, her cheek against Luke's broad shoulder. "One of my brothers lives there. He has an apartment and works at a restaurant. When I got out of prison, he told me he might be able to help me find a job there. I came here instead because I thought I could hide from the Damyons, but that obviously didn't work. So I guess I'll go ahead and take my brother up on his offer. I might even be able to take some evening classes at the university."

"*Adios* Ambleside?"

She lifted her head. "I think it would be best. I had enough trouble finding the job with you, and I haven't heard of any other openings in Ambleside lately." Pulling out of his arms, she gave a shrug. "You know, I need to keep paying my lawyer. And the parole board expects me to stay employed. I don't have much choice but to move away. I've always liked Springfield, too. It's a beautiful city."

"Darcy, I don't want you to go."

"What alternatives do either of us have, Luke?"

"You could stay and take care of Ruby. I have her power of attorney. I could set up an account to pay you—"

"Luke, I'm not qualified to take care of Ruby. You know what the doctor said. She needs medical attention. It's only going to get worse for her, and I don't think I could—"

"Well, now! Isn't this a pretty sight?" The voice came from the end of the driveway, and Darcy recognized it immediately. "Two lovebirds, cooing and cuddling."

"It's Will Damyon," Darcy said under her breath. "Luke, he's been drinking. I want you to get Montgomery and Ruby to safety. You can go out the back door. Take them to the guesthouse and—"

"I'm not leaving you alone with that lunatic."

"Lovey-dovey, lovey-dovey! The killer and the carpenter." Will emerged into the light from the front porch. "The murderer and the handyman."

"I can handle this, Luke." Darcy clutched his shirt, trying to propel him to the front door. "Please go!"

"What's going on?" Montgomery stepped out onto the porch, her blue eyes widening. She was holding Ruby's hand. "Who's that man? Why can't he walk straight?"

"Who's here?" Ruby asked. "Well, what's everyone doing on the porch? Why don't we all—"

"Montgomery, get back inside!" Darcy darted for the child. "Ruby, go with Montgomery. Luke, please help me!"

"I got something for you, girlie girl," Will called out. "Recognize this?"

From his jacket pocket, Will pulled out a small handgun. Darcy felt a wave of panic. Was that the pistol that had belonged to Bill? The weapon Darcy had used to kill her husband?

"Will, what are you doing?" Abandoning Montgomery, Darcy flew back across the porch. "Luke, he's got a gun!"

"Put that thing away, Damyon."

"The police gave it back to us a couple years ago." Will neared the steps, waving the gun from side to side. "They'd been holding it, you know. Evidence."

"Hand me the gun," Luke said evenly, starting down the steps toward the older man.

"Step back, pretty boy!" Will aimed the barrel at Luke's chest.

Darcy screamed. "Luke!"

"Daddy!"

"Back off, back off!" Damyon swung the gun toward Darcy. "This is for her."

"Darcy, duck!" Luke lunged down the rest of the steps at Will as Darcy threw herself onto the porch. "Drop it, you fool!"

"Let go, let go!"

Her mouth open in a silent shriek, Darcy scrambled on her knees across the porch and pushed Ruby and Montgomery through the screen door. As she swung around, she heard the screech of brakes and the scatter of gravel as the beam of headlights crossed the yard. From the darkness beyond the porch light sounded a loud bang like a firecracker, followed instantaneously by a whizzing noise.

Montgomery wailed in terror and started back through

the door. Darcy caught her by the arm and yanked her to
the floor.

"Get off!" someone shouted. "Back away, now. Give me
that gun. Are you crazy?"

"I'm shot!"

"Who's bleeding? Move back!"

"Is my daddy dead?" Montgomery screamed.

Darcy gripped the child's skinny arms. "You can't go out
there, Little-bit!"

"I want my daddy!" She clung to Darcy and began sobbing. "I don't want my daddy to be dead!"

"Nobody's dead." At that moment, Luke bounded onto
the porch and knelt beside Darcy. Sweeping Montgomery
into his arms, he cradled his daughter. "I'm all right, Monkey. I'm fine."

"I thought that man shot you, Daddy!"

"No, honey. I'm all right. Come here, Darcy."

Luke reached for her, but she pushed him away. No, she
couldn't go to him. This was exactly what she had feared
for Luke and Montgomery. Weapons and blood and
drunken brawls. The nightmarish stuff of Darcy's own childhood. She wouldn't wish that on anyone, especially these
two precious people. Stumbling across the porch, she
peered into the darkness, searching for her tormentor.

"I'm taking you into the light now," a deep voice said. "I
can't see where you're hit."

"I'm dying, that's what! And I've lost the gun. I think her
boyfriend's got it."

Buck Damyon led his father into the circle of light that
surrounded the porch. Beyond them, Darcy could see the
outlines of their old pickup, the driver's door flung open
when Buck had leaped out to join the scuffle on the lawn.
Darcy stepped aside as the two men approached the porch.

"Everybody all right here?" Buck asked. He set his father
down on the porch swing and started examining him.

"I guess so," Darcy managed.

"Looks like you've dislocated your shoulder again, Dad. But I don't see any blood." The younger man took a pint bottle of whisky from inside his father's coat. "This didn't do you much good, did it? Don't you ever learn?"

"I was hit, boy! He shot me!"

"You probably busted a rib. Let me look. Where does it hurt?"

"Ow! Ow! Right there!"

"Stop hitting me, Dad. I'm trying to help you."

Rubbing his own shoulder, Luke walked up to the two men. "Listen, I want both of you off this property right now. We've had enough trouble from you tonight."

Buck straightened and held out his hand. "I don't think we've been introduced," he said. "I'm Buck. I'm the youngest of the Damyon boys."

Reluctantly, Luke shook the man's hand. "Luke Easton. I'm Darcy's boss."

"They call her Jo," Will spat from his place on the swing. "She never told them her real name was Darcy Damyon. Lied about who she was and what she did."

"You threatened her with a gun, Mr. Damyon," Luke said. "Save your whining for the police."

"I wish you wouldn't involve them," Buck said. He was a tall man with his father's blue eyes and massive shoulders. "I came up here to try and help my dad settle this thing. If you call the police, it's just going to get more complicated than ever."

"You intended to settle it by confronting Darcy? By threatening her life?"

"That's right!" Will barked. "Make her pay!"

"No, that's not right," Buck said. He turned to his father. "Dad, I've told you your way doesn't work. Doing things that way got Bill killed and landed Darcy in prison. And it landed me in jail more than once."

"Don't blame me for your troubles. I never—"

"Yes, you did. You taught us to settle our problems with drinking and fighting, and it doesn't work. Now let me look at those ribs."

"It's a bullet wound. That boyfriend of hers shot me!"

"Nobody shot you, Dad. You're not bleeding anywhere. Try to calm down, okay? You're going to be all right."

Darcy swallowed. She could hardly believe the gentle tone Buck was using. She'd seen him flatten a man with one blow. She'd seen him so drunk he couldn't stand up. She'd watched him bagging the prescription pills he'd stolen from a pharmacy he had robbed, and she knew he'd been involved in setting up a methamphetamine lab.

"Do you have any ice around here?" he asked, turning. His focus fell on Darcy, and he gave a sheepish grin. "Hey, Darcy. How've you been?"

"Buck, what's going on?"

"Just trying to keep tabs on Dad." He shrugged. "When he headed back up here with that gun, I decided I'd better come with him. See if I could talk some sense into him. It's not easy."

Darcy stared at him and tried to understand what he was saying. "What kind of sense?"

"I want him to go back to Joplin and settle down. Drop this crazy vengeance routine. It's going to get him killed."

"I'm wounded!" Will moaned. "Right here in my side. Burns like fire."

"I thought I had him corralled, but he got away from me." He glanced at his father. "Found yourself a liquor store, didn't you, Dad? Got all heated up again and came over here with your gun."

"Finish off what *she* started!" Will cried.

"Get yourself sent to prison. Or killed." He turned back to Darcy. "Look, I'm going to do my best to keep him in Joplin—"

"I ain't going nowhere till she's dead or back in prison."

"You're going home if I have to hog-tie you to get you there." Buck glanced over his shoulder. "I think he's popped a rib. Could anyone get me some ice and a . . ."

As his voice trailed off, Darcy turned and looked in the direction of his stare. The screen door was propped partially open. Wedging it was a crumpled form. A pale pink sweater. A cloud of white hair.

"Ruby!" Darcy screamed. She dashed across the porch and threw open the door. Ruby lay unmoving, her shoulder resting in a pool of bright red blood.

Seventeen

"Stand back, everyone!" Buck Damyon pushed his way past Darcy and knelt beside Ruby. "Somebody call an ambulance. Make sure both gates are open. I'm going to need towels. Move!"

Without questioning him, Darcy hurdled over Ruby's body and ran down the hall to the telephone. As she dialed, she could see Luke scoop Montgomery into his arms and sprint off to check the exit gate. In moments, she had notified the Ambleside police that Ruby McCann had been shot. They were dispatching an ambulance as she hung up and raced to the kitchen for towels.

The stray bullet must have gone through the screen door and hit Ruby, Darcy realized as she gathered up an armful of clean tea towels. *Oh, Father, please let her live!* she prayed. *Don't let Ruby die!*

"Towels," she said, setting the stack beside Buck.

He had pulled back Ruby's sweater and was working to stem the blood seeping from a wound in her chest.

"Is she alive?" Darcy asked. "Is she going to make it?"

"I've got a pulse, but she's not breathing well." He jerked up a towel and pressed it over the injury. "Do you have any medical history on this woman? Medications? Chronic illnesses?"

"She has Alzheimer's disease. She takes an antidepressant and something for high blood pressure and . . . some other things . . . I can't think . . . oh, Buck, is she going to live?"

"Gather up every medicine bottle you can find in the house. Put them all in a plastic bag. Go!"

Darcy leaped to obey. The bullet had been meant for her, she realized as she raced up the stairs to Ruby's bedroom. Will Damyon had wanted to kill her. And instead, he had shot Ruby! This was all Darcy's fault. If she hadn't come to Ambleside, none of this would have happened. Now Ruby was dying and Luke had risked his life and Montgomery was traumatized. Darcy had brought nothing but agony and confusion and hardship to everyone she'd met.

Sweeping Ruby's pill bottles into a plastic sack, she tried to squelch the tears. She should have just stepped in front of Will's gun and taken the bullet! He was right. She deserved the same fate she had dealt to her husband. At least Ruby wouldn't be lying on the porch bleeding to death. *Oh, Father, I'm so sorry! I don't know what to do . . . which way to turn. . . . Please spare Ruby's life!*

Running back down the stairs, she could hear sirens blaring as the local police car, an ambulance, and a fire truck roared up the drive to the old house. By the time Darcy got out to the front porch, it was crowded with paramedics. The emergency medical technicians slid a stretcher from the back of the ambulance and carried it across the lawn. Someone hooked up an IV. An oxygen mask covered Ruby's gray lips. Darcy stood at the edge of the crowd, tears rolling down her cheeks as the medics lifted the old woman onto the gurney and hustled her into the ambulance.

As quickly as they had come, the ambulance and fire truck pulled away from the front of the house. Flashing lights came on. Sirens began to wail. The vehicles roared through the open gates and vanished into the darkness.

"Boy howdy." The policeman on duty rubbed the back of his neck. "We haven't had a shooting in Ambleside since I don't know when."

"I don't think we've ever had one," Luke said, stepping

up onto the porch. "Mick, if it's okay with you, I'm going to take Darcy and Montgomery over to the clinic to wait while the doctors work on Ruby."

"I'm sorry, Luke," Mick said, "but you'll have to hold up a minute on that. I need to collect evidence and fill out a report on what happened here tonight."

"I got shot, that's what happened!" Will Damyon called from the porch swing. "Shot in the ribs!"

"Two victims?" Mick's eyes widened. "But I thought Mrs. McCann was the only—"

"He's not seriously injured." Buck Damyon crossed the porch toward the policeman. He opened his jacket and pulled out a small black wallet. "I'm a deputy with the Jasper County sheriff's department." As he displayed the wallet, Darcy realized it contained a badge. "Name's Damyon. I can give you a full report on this incident, Officer."

"You're a deputy?" Darcy asked, disbelief pouring through her veins. Her voice lifted an octave. "With the sheriff's department?"

"A couple of years. I work undercover mostly. Meth labs."

"But, I thought you used to . . . to . . ."

"I did." He gave a slight grin. "The last time I got busted, the judge gave me a choice between prison and the military. I spent three years in the army, finished some of my college, and worked as an MP. After that, I took a job with the sheriff's department and finished up my college at night. I've applied for a position with the highway patrol."

"But you broke into the Chalmers Mansion," Luke said. "What kind of deputy does that?"

"It was Dad who broke in. I spotted him down there roaming around, and I climbed through the window to try and talk some sense into him."

"I got a fire in my gut!" Will Damyon wailed from the porch swing. "Somebody call me an ambulance."

"That's my father," Buck told Mick. "He popped a rib, but

he'll be fine once I get some ice on him. He's the one who pulled the trigger. The shooting was accidental."

"Is that true?" Mick asked Darcy.

She nodded. Luke stepped to her side and put an arm around her shoulder. "It was an accident, Mick. Mr. Damyon was threatening Darcy, and I tackled him. The gun went off, and the stray bullet must have hit Ruby. The weapon's lying somewhere in those bushes by the side of the house."

"Was Deputy Damyon involved in the shooting?" Mick asked.

"No, he had just pulled up in his truck when the gun went off. He's the one who took care of Mrs. McCann after the shooting." Luke glanced at Darcy. "Officer Mick, if you'd let us go check on Ruby, we'd be happy to fill you in on all the details later."

"I guess that would be all right." Mick shook his head. "The Ambleside police department—that's me and one other guy—we usually handle things like teenagers shoplifting bubble gum from the Corner Market or spray-painting their names on the park fountain. To tell you the truth, Deputy, it's been a long time since I reviewed the procedures on this kind of thing."

"This is right up my alley." Buck clapped Mick on the shoulder. "I think you can safely let these people go check on Mrs. McCann, and then you can take their story down when they get back. It's going to take a while to work the crime scene anyway. You'll need to find that gun, for starters."

"What about the perpetrator?" Mick glanced at Will Damyon. "What should I do with him?"

"If you'll watch him for a minute, I'll go get some ice to cool him down. A cup of stiff black coffee might help, too."

Darcy wiped her fingertips across her cheek. "Buck, I don't know what to say. I thought you were . . ."

"I was," he said, giving her a smile. "Then I made some changes for the better, like you did. Go check on your friend. I'll keep an eye on things here."

"Come on, Darcy." Holding Montgomery in one arm, Luke led Darcy down the porch steps and across the driveway to his own pickup. "It's going to be all right now. You'll see."

But as she walked through the darkness, Darcy felt the weight of her many, many sins clamp around her neck like a millstone. It wasn't going to be all right. Not at all.

ॐ

Clutching the old family Bible that Luke had given her, Darcy slipped into the back pew of the chapel just as the service was ending the following morning. Unable to join in the hymns of worship and praise, she sat with her head bowed and poured out her heart to God. Ruby had lived through the night. Barely. Even now, she was being transported to the university hospital in Columbia for surgery and follow-up care. But things didn't look hopeful.

"Before we conclude our worship today," Pastor Paul was saying, "I'd like for us to say a special prayer lifting our sister Ruby McCann to the Lord. If you'll join me . . ."

As he led in supplication, Darcy again felt tears of despair, exhaustion, and hopelessness tumble down her cheeks. Luke and Montgomery were at the guesthouse resting after the long night of waiting for word on Ruby's condition. But Darcy hadn't been able to fall asleep this morning, so she had hurried back to the clinic just in time to see the ambulance loading Ruby for her trip to the larger hospital. The old woman hadn't opened her eyes, and when Darcy had called her name, she'd shown no sign of hearing.

"Amen," Pastor Paul said. "I noticed Jo Callaway slipping into the pew back there."

Darcy lifted her head, startled to hear her assumed name. "Yes, sir?"

"I was wondering if you might have an update on Mrs. McCann's situation for us."

"Okay." She blotted her cheeks with a tissue and stood. "I just came from the clinic."

"Would you be willing to step up here to the microphone and share what you've learned?"

"Yes, sir," she managed to whisper. The last thing she wanted to do was expose herself to all these people. They must feel such scorn for her. Such disdain. She made her way to the front of the chapel. Pastor Paul handed her the microphone.

"Ruby . . . um, Mrs. McCann is on her way to the university hospital in Columbia," she said, holding the old Bible like a protective shield. Her amplified voice sounded loud and hollow, echoing from the oak rafters. "The bullet went through her chest up near the right shoulder. It missed her heart, but . . . but her lung collapsed. She's going to have surgery. The doctors don't know how she'll do. She lost a lot of blood, and she's very weak."

"Thank you, Jo," Pastor Paul said quietly.

Darcy started to hand back the microphone. But as she did, she looked out across the faces of those who had gathered to worship and pray. Kaye Zimmerman, who had cut and styled Darcy's hair. Nathan Zimmerman, who had joined his wife in searching for Darcy one night in the woods. Boompah Jungemeyer, who always handed her a lollipop as she left the Corner Market. Floyd, who had offered her a refuge in his fishing shack. And the others . . . the many others who had been so kind despite their wariness . . . despite knowing what she had done.

"I, um . . ." She cleared her throat and spoke into the microphone again. "I'll be leaving pretty soon, moving to Springfield to stay with my brother. But I wanted to thank you all for taking me in. For making me feel welcome in Ambleside. Even though I tried to hide out here, tried my best not to make friends or get involved in anybody's business, you reached out to me. So many of you were kind and generous, and I want to thank you for that. I guess everyone knows by now that my real name is Darcy Damyon. I shot my husband and spent six years in prison. I had thought I could keep the truth from you, but it wouldn't stay hidden. And some of you have suffered because of me." She fought to swallow her tears.

"Ruby," she said, "took the bullet that was meant for me. And I'm very sorry . . . very, very sorry. I just want you to know that."

She handed the microphone back to the pastor and started down the aisle. Before he could speak, she hurried out the door and ran along the sidewalk toward Ruby's house. Fearful that someone might try to stop her, she raced down the alleyway beside the Tastee Hut and scrambled over the wall that surrounded the McCann estate. Then she wrapped her arms around the trunk of a gnarled old maple tree and wept.

Luke had been making his rounds, and as he knocked on the door of the apartment behind Finders Keepers antiques shop, he knew this would be his final stop of the evening.

"Hey, Luke!" Elizabeth Chalmers stepped out onto the back porch. Barefooted, she wore a pair of cutoff shorts and a tank top. Her pretty eyes sparkled with contentment. "This is a nice surprise. Hey there, Montgomery."

"Where's Nick?" the little girl asked. "Daddy and I have been going visiting, and Floyd gave me a whole bag of Chee-tos all for myself. Can I share some with Nick?"

"Sure. He's up in his room." As the child darted past and

headed for the stairs, Elizabeth tilted her head. "You've been visiting?"

"Taking care of some business," Luke said. "Is Zachary here? I'd like to talk to him for a moment."

"Sure. He's working on some sketches." She led the way inside the cool apartment filled with antiques and soft candles. "Did you hear the Foxes are going to build a new home? They bought a lot in the McCann subdivision, and they've asked Zachary to help them with their floor plan. After all the trouble we had with Phil last year, I was really surprised they came to him. But you never can tell with people."

As he followed Elizabeth through the living room to the study, Luke felt as though he had been hit in the stomach. So, the Foxes would be putting up the first house in the new subdivision. He wondered whom they had hired for their builder.

"Hey, Luke!" Zachary pushed back from his desk. "How's everything going? How's Ruby? Darcy spoke for a moment in church this morning and told us they transferred Ruby to Columbia. Any word?"

"Her surgery is scheduled for first thing tomorrow morning. Darcy went over there on the bus this afternoon. She's going to spend the night at the hospital."

"Darcy is a good woman."

"Yes." Luke nodded. "She is."

"Well, the mansion is looking great. I was over there yesterday evening. The plumbing is done, and every light I flipped on came to life without a flicker."

Luke settled into a chair across from Zachary. "That's Floyd's doing. He knows his wiring—in spite of the trouble he had with that chandelier in the study."

Zachary laughed. "I knew he'd get it right one of these days. And Darcy has done some wonderful things with the wallpaper. Elizabeth and I are both amazed. Did you see the stenciling she did in the kitchen?"

"She's good, all right. Couldn't ask for a better employee."

"She looked pretty shaken up at church. Is she all right? I mean, the shooting was a big shock to everyone in town. I had no idea that guy was stalking her."

"I think Darcy's coping. Mick's got Damyon over at the station drying out. He'll probably be doing some time. He violated a restraining order, and the assault charges aren't going to help."

"And they say his son's with the sheriff's department? A deputy?" Zachary shook his head. "You never know with people, do you?"

"Nope." He shifted on the chair, dreading this moment. Taking a deep breath, Luke began. "Listen, Zachary, I came over to talk to you about the mansion project."

"Do you have some bills for me? I know the bank has been giving you a hard time, and I—"

"I'm dissolving my company. I'll be declaring bankruptcy in the morning. Floyd and Gabe know. I talked to both of them a few minutes ago. Darcy knows too. She's moving to Springfield."

"Luke? Are you serious?"

"I don't have any choice about this, Zachary. Ellie's medical bills really stacked up, and the bank wasn't willing to cut me any slack. But that's all water under the bridge." He stood. "I'm sorry I won't be able to finish the mansion project. It was good work, and you treated me fairly. Thanks, Zachary."

As he held out his hand, his friend also rose. "Luke, this seems too drastic. Have you explored other options?"

Luke nodded. They shook hands, and Luke moved toward the door. "I can trust God to be with me through the hard times. That's what Darcy taught me. I've had a job offer from Bud Huff on the table for years, and it'll be a good way to take care of Montgomery. I'll keep my hand in the building trade. Maybe one day I'll be able to get back on my feet."

"Luke, we could work out a personal loan if that would help you. I do have—"

"Thanks, Zachary, but I don't want anything like that to come between us. Some difficult things have fallen across my path. I lost Ellie, and now my business is shutting down. But this time things are different. I'm not going to turn my back on God. I'm not going to hide in my pain. I've chosen to trust—and that's what I'm going to do. Have faith in Christ. Put my future in his hands. I'd appreciate your prayers, Zachary. You and Elizabeth have been good friends."

"You know we'll do whatever we can."

"I know that." Luke walked back into the living room. He called up the stairwell. "Montgomery! Time to go home."

"Can't I play for a while longer?" Montgomery and Nick bounded down the stairs, their mouths coated with a bright orange film. "We're playing restaurant, and we're serving Chee-tos."

"I couldn't have guessed." Luke glanced at Zachary and gave him a grin. "Looks like you've been tasting some of the cooking."

"Just the Chee-tos," Nick said. "Not the beans. Magunnery made them out of green clay. It is not good to eat the clay."

Montgomery skipped across the room and took her father's hand. "Are you sure we can't stay? Please, Daddy?"

"No, Monkey. I want to go call the hospital and check on Ruby."

"Why do you call your daughter Monkey?" Nick asked as they all walked out onto the front porch. "Don't you know her name is Magunnery?"

"It's just a nickname," Luke said.

"No, Nick is *my* name. *Her* name is Magunnery." Nick

waved as Luke and his daughter started down the sidewalk. "Ma-gun-ner-y. It's not so hard if you practice a lot. Keep trying, Mr. Easton. You can do it!"

"Thanks, Nick."

Montgomery giggled as she and her father crossed the street toward the town square. "He's so funny. I just love Nick."

"And I just love you," Luke said, clutching her sticky orange fingers and thanking God for the moment.

Eighteen

Darcy leaned against the windowsill and gazed down at the small guesthouse in the distance. What a fairy-tale beginning she had experienced here in Ambleside, she thought as she clutched a paper bag with her few possessions bundled inside—her T-shirts, several pairs of socks and underwear, her jeans, and the old family Bible that Luke had given her. She had moved to town with nothing to call her own. God had sent a fairy godmother in the form of Ruby McCann, a precious woman who had offered Darcy a gingerbread cottage and a lifetime's worth of love and acceptance. And then God had provided a handsome prince—a courageous hero named Luke, who had swept Darcy out of her solitude and into his heart.

How could things have turned out so badly? She bowed her head, ashamed that her faith in Christ wasn't stronger. Things were not bad, she had to admit. For one thing, Ruby's surgery had gone well. In her mind's eye, Darcy could see the woman as she had been that morning, still frail and fragile as she lay in her hospital bed. Darcy had reached out and taken Ruby's hand, weeping with remorse for the suffering she had caused.

"Why are you crying, dear?" Ruby had whispered.

Darcy had looked up, surprised at these first words from her friend's mouth since the night of the shooting. "I'm so sorry, Ruby. You were hurt because of me."

"Hurt because of you?" Ruby frowned. "Rubbish."

"But this horrible wound is my fault. Will Damyon came

to your house looking for me. The bullet that hit you was meant for me."

"My dear girl, those things are all in the past. Forgotten!" She waved her thin hand in the air. Then she laid her fingers on Darcy's arm and gave a gentle squeeze. "But you . . . you are my angel sent from heaven."

Darcy had been unable to meet Ruby's eyes. "You're the one who saved me. You gave me a home, clothes to wear, friendship—"

"And you showed me the love of Christ." The old woman smiled. "Because of you, Jo, I find myself looking forward to the moment when finally I shall behold him face-to-face."

Even now, Darcy could see the beatific expression on Ruby's face, as though she were ready to meet her future. Ready . . . and even eager. But the doctors predicted that Ruby McCann still had a few years left on this earth. She would be moving home in a couple of weeks, and a full-time nurse had been hired to take care of her during recovery.

Darcy had to remind herself that even though she would miss Ruby, her friend would be in good hands. Not only that, but Will Damyon had been transferred to the jail in Jefferson City, where he would await trial. Darcy knew he was not going to be able to threaten her for a long time to come.

Luke's situation seemed brighter, too. He was to start his job at Bud's Hardware the following morning. He and Montgomery had a warm, cozy house to live in and the financial security they'd been needing.

Even Buck had stepped onto a path that promised hope and a good future. After spending a few days with the Ambleside police, he had asked to be reassigned to central Missouri while he waited for his training with the highway patrol to begin. Methamphetamine labs, it seemed, were becoming a real problem, and Buck was going to assist an investigating task force. He would be moving to the area within the month.

Darcy, of course, was leaving. She let out a deep breath and turned away from the window. Her brother had agreed to let her move into his apartment in Springfield, and he had lined up a job for her. She would be washing dishes at the restaurant where he worked. Once she had saved enough money, she would try to find her own apartment. Maybe she could even go back to college one day. She still had two years to go before completing a degree, and she was thinking of majoring in interior design.

Oh, but her heart ached as she walked down the long wood staircase for the last time. She would miss Ruby so much. Who would make sure her buttons were lined up straight? Who would take the stray curlers out of her hair? Who would know to check the pantry for the milk and to look in the refrigerator for her panty hose? Darcy realized others could be trained, but she felt she somehow understood Ruby's true spirit. Even when the old woman lashed out in unreasonable anger, Darcy felt a sense of patience and empathy. Ruby had been trapped by a horrible disease . . . imprisoned . . .

No, Darcy thought when she left the house and looked around at the grounds one final time. Ruby was not in prison. Ruby would insist that she was free—free because of her bondage to Christ. And in the same way, Darcy knew that she herself was truly free. Though her heart felt heavy and her feet seemed to drag, she heard the echo of Ruby reading the Scripture from Jeremiah: "'For I know the plans I have for you,' says the Lord. 'They are plans for good and not for disaster, to give you a future and a hope.'"

"A future and a hope," Darcy whispered to herself. But, oh, how she ached for that future to include Luke! The thought of seeing the man she loved for the last time . . . his thick brown hair and bright blue eyes . . . his warm smile . . . his forgiving spirit . . . his protective arms . . . his gentle touch . . .

"Oh, Father!" she prayed out loud as she hurried down the sidewalk toward Chalmers Mansion. *I can't say good-bye to him without crying. I just know I can't. Please, Lord, don't let him be there. Let me grab my paintbrushes and my seam roller, and let me get to the bus station without seeing him.*

Ducking her head, she hurried past Kaye's Kut-n-Kurl. If she could choose the perfect man for her, it would be Luke Easton. He loved her in spite of her past. He loved her for who she had become—and for who she might be someday in the future. He was kind and good and gentle. He was perfect. Well, not perfect, but wonderful! He loved his daughter. He worked so hard. He was talented, and his employees respected him.

"Oh, dear God!" she whispered again, her stomach twisting into a knot. *I need help, okay? I'm not going to be able to leave this town without your help. You brought me here, and now I need you to boot me out. Please, just force my feet onto that bus—*

In the distance, Darcy noticed a couple of people standing on the porch of Chalmers House, and her heart sank. She wouldn't be able to get away without chitchat. And that was the last thing she needed.

"Darcy!" A shout from the porch startled her. Luke waved, a broad grin lighting his face. "You've got to see this! Come here!"

For an instant, Darcy thought of making a fast break for the bus station. How could she bear to say good-bye to Luke in front of these folks who had gathered at the mansion? And who were all these people? What on earth were they doing?

As the scene came into focus, Darcy's heart stumbled. There stood Mayor Cleo Mueller. Phil and Pearlene Fox hovered next to him, each of them holding a plate piled with fresh fruit and cupcakes. Kaye Zimmerman emerged from the front doorway. She had gone blonde! She was laughing about something with Elizabeth Chalmers, who carried a cup full of some red drink. Then Boompah Jungemeyer stepped outside, and so did Pastor Paul. Luke kept waving wildly from the porch, until finally Darcy found herself climbing the steps of the old mansion where she had spent so many happy hours.

"You won't believe this!" Luke said, taking her by the arm and leading her to one side of the porch. "You'll never guess what happened. These people . . . these friends . . ."

His voice faltered. Darcy glanced around, startled to realize that almost everyone from the Ambleside business community had gathered here at Chalmers House. Many of the church members were there, too. A long folding table had been set up on the porch, and it was swaybacked under a load of pies, cakes, fruit salads, steaming casseroles, and donuts. A huge punch bowl swirled with a red beverage punctuated with dollops of floating ice cream.

"What . . ." Darcy tried to speak. "Luke, what's going on?"

"They all came over while I was packing my tools," he said. "Pastor Paul set it up. And Zachary, too. These people started dropping by. They brought food . . . and more. They brought contracts, Darcy."

"Contracts?"

"Hey, Darcy!" Elizabeth Chalmers waved from across the crowd. "Welcome to the celebration!"

"There's Miss Jo," Floyd said, catching her attention. "Ain't this a howdy-do for ya?"

The snaggletoothed old man was working his way across the porch when Luke took Darcy's arm and turned her to face him. "Every single one of these people came with a gift," he said. "Phil and Pearlene brought me an offer to build their new house. Cleo Mueller got approval from the city council to go after a bid on rehabbing the courthouse.

Sawyer-the-lawyer is retiring, and he wants me to build him
a home on the outskirts of town. And other people came
with money. Viola and her husband from Dandy Donuts
. . . Ez and Alma from the Nifty Cafe . . . and the
Zimmermans . . . and Boompah brought part of his savings.
. . ." He paused, almost unable to speak. "He took money
out of the bank account he started right after the war."

"Oh, Luke." Darcy squeezed his hands as the truth of the
moment sank in. "They love you so much."

"Bud Huff fired me," he said with a laugh. "He's not
going to let me work for him because he's determined not
to let Easton Construction go under. In fact, he handed me
seven remodeling contracts. And it's money in advance.
This whole town . . . they've all pledged to support my
company. They won't let me declare bankruptcy, Darcy.
They're not going to let it happen."

"Luke, this is wonderful!"

"They started a fund to help pay off Ellie's medical bills.
It has seven thousand dollars in it already, and it's all anon-
ymous. I don't even know who—"

"It's God," she said. "*God* has done this for you, Luke.
You were faithful to him, and he's blessed you for it."

"And the strange thing is—I was going to stay faithful
through the bankruptcy. Through the whole thing. I came
to the point where it didn't matter to me what God did with
me. And then—out of the blue—he did this! I never
expected this kind of support. This kind of love."

"Luke, come here a minute!" Zachary Chalmers took his
arm. "We've got a few more people who want to talk to
you. Jenny from over at the Tastee Hut came by to offer her
baby-sitting services. She says she'll watch Montgomery for
you whenever you need her."

As Luke was led away, Darcy leaned back against the
porch railing and drank down a deep breath. So this was
the amazing God she worshiped! She knew he didn't

always deliver happy endings, but she trusted his promise
to be with his people through all things. And now she
understood how faithful Christians showed God's love
through their deeds.

Now she could go away knowing that Luke would be all
right. He and Montgomery would be able to rest in the
security that their God and his people had provided.
Slipping along the edge of the crowd, Darcy made her way
through a side door and into the study. The chandelier was
brightly lit, all fifty bulbs blazing away. A smile crossed her
lips as she headed for the kitchen.

"A future and a hope," she whispered to herself all the
way down the long hall. "A future and a hope."

She reached the kitchen and flipped on the light. In one
corner, her tool bucket sat just as she had left it the Friday
before, its canvas apron pockets filled with wallpaper
razors, paint rollers, tape measures, and a small level. But
the only tools she owned were two brushes she had bought
at Bud's Hardware, and the hard seam roller that helped her
give a professional finish to each length of wallpaper.

Crouching beside the bucket, she opened her paper bag.
Carefully, she set the two brushes down on top of her
jeans. Then she settled the seam roller beside them.

"What's going on?"

At the accusing tone, she swung around, her heart slamming hard against her ribs. "They're mine. I bought them
with my own—oh . . ."

Luke, his hands hooked in his pockets, stood gazing
down at her. He shook his head. "Darcy, what are you
doing?"

"I bought these. I was going to take them with me."

"Take them where?"

"To Springfield. I have to catch the bus at one-thirty, and
I just . . ." She stood, rolling the paper bag. "Luke, I didn't

mean to see you again. I was hoping to get through this without . . . I don't want to say good-bye."

"Then don't."

"I thought you might try to hire me back." She attempted a smile. "I mean, you are pretty lousy with paint and wallpaper. But my brother is expecting me this evening, and I—"

"Darcy." In two strides, Luke caught her up in his arms. "Darcy, I'm not asking you to stay and work for me. I'm asking you to be my wife. I love you. I can't imagine life without you. Please say yes."

As his lips covered hers, Darcy felt a thousand sparks shower down her skin. She tried to breathe, but her thoughts swirled like a Tilt-A-Whirl at the fair. His wife? Had Luke really asked her to marry him? Did he mean it?

"Darcy, please," Luke said as he pulled away. Lifting his hands to the sides of her face, he cradled her head. "I've wanted to ask you for a long time now, but I knew I had nothing to offer you."

"I don't need anything, Luke."

"I couldn't ask you to come into the tangled life I was living. But now, because of those good people outside . . ." He kissed her again. "Say yes, Darcy."

"What about *my* tangled life? Luke, I could never cause you and Montgomery any more pain than you've already suffered. The other kids would tease her if they knew about my past. And I can't guarantee that I'll ever be completely free of danger from Will Damyon."

"Montgomery's crazy about you, and she's been pestering me to propose. You know her well enough to realize how tough she is. She doesn't care what people say. She'll be proud to call you her mother."

Darcy's eyes filled with tears. "But what about the danger?"

"Will's going to be out of action for a long time. And with

Buck moving to Ambleside, the old man won't have a
chance to get near you. Darcy, I weighed all these things a
long time ago. What matters is us. Our love. Please say
you'll be my wife."

All doubts about her past, all fears for her future vanished
as she looked into his blue eyes. "Yes," she whispered.

With a sigh of relief, he drew her into his arms again and
held her close.

As she slipped her arms around him and nestled close
against his chest, she felt her heart soar on wings of freedom. With Christ as their foundation, Darcy knew she and
Luke could look forward together to God's promise of good
plans to bring them a future and a hope.

"Hey, you two better get out here fast!" Floyd called from
the kitchen door. "You won't believe what they brung
now."

"What?" Luke asked, his fingers tightening around Darcy's
hand. "What's happened, Floyd?"

"Chex Mix!" He held out his hands in amazement. "It's
got cereal an' nuts an' pretzels an' all kinds of stuff mixed
together with some kind of a flavorin' that's just downright
dandy. It beats anything I ever did taste in all my life."

Luke led Darcy toward the hall. "Will wonders never
cease?"

Floyd chuckled. "I reckon not."

A Note from the Author

Dear Friend,

Although I've never been locked inside a real prison, I sometimes find myself trapped behind bars of my own making. Unforgiveness, jealousy, fear, anger, hurt, and many other things can keep me immobile—and almost useless to God. I don't know why I have trouble remembering that by becoming a bond servant of Jesus Christ, I am free. If you're feeling trapped, remember the One who longs to wrap you in his arms of love. He's waiting!

As I wrote this book in my new office—a large, airy space carved out of our attic—I found myself thanking God again and again for *you!* Thank you for your letters of support and encouragement. Thank you for your faithfulness. And thank you, most of all, for your prayers.

You've followed the lives of Elizabeth and Zachary Chalmers in *Finders Keepers,* and you've watched the unfolding love between Darcy Damyon and Luke Easton in *Hide and Seek.* I can hardly wait to write my next HeartQuest book. In the meantime, enjoy my Christmas novella, "Behold the Lamb," in the anthology *A Victorian Christmas Keepsake* (available Fall 2001). Also watch for my first hardcover women's fiction novel coming soon!

Happy reading—
Catherine Palmer

About the Author

Catherine Palmer lives in Missouri with her husband, Tim, and sons, Geoffrey and Andrei. She is a graduate of Southwest Baptist University and has a master's degree in English from Baylor University. Her first book was published in 1988. Since then she has published more than twenty-five books and has won numerous awards for her writing, including Most Exotic Historical Romance Novel from *Romantic Times* magazine. Total sales of her novels number more than one million copies.

Her first suspense novel, *A Dangerous Silence,* has just been released by Tyndale House Publishers. Her HeartQuest books include the series A Town Called Hope *(Prairie Rose, Prairie Fire,* and *Prairie Storm); Finders Keepers*; and novellas in the anthologies *Prairie Christmas, A Victorian Christmas Cottage, A Victorian Christmas Quilt, A Victorian Christmas Tea,* and *With This Ring.*

Her original HeartQuest series, *The Treasure of Timbuktu* and *The Treasure of Zanzibar,* have recently been rereleased as the Treasures of the Heart series. The first two books are now titled *A Kiss of Adventure* and *A Whisper of*

Danger. Also look for the never-before-published third book in the series, *A Touch of Betrayal.*

Catherine welcomes letters written to her in care of Tyndale House Author Relations, P.O. Box 80, Wheaton, IL 60189-0080.

Visit www.HeartQuest.com for lots of info on
HeartQuest books and authors and more!

www.HeartQuest.com

*Register online today to receive a **free gift!***

Current HeartQuest Releases

- *Magnolia*, Ginny Aiken
- *Lark*, Ginny Aiken
- *Camellia*, Ginny Aiken
- *A Bouquet of Love*, Ginny Aiken, Ranee McCollum, Jeri Odell, and Debra White Smith
- *Dream Vacation*, Ginny Aiken, Jeri Odell, and Elizabeth White
- *Reunited*, Judy Baer, Jeri Odell, Jan Duffy, and Peggy Stoks
- *Sweet Delights*, Terri Blackstock, Ranee McCollum, and Elizabeth White
- *Awakening Mercy*, Angela Benson
- *Abiding Hope*, Angela Benson
- *Faith*, Lori Copeland
- *Hope*, Lori Copeland
- *June*, Lori Copeland
- *Glory*, Lori Copeland
- *With This Ring*, Lori Copeland, Dianna Crawford, Ginny Aiken, and Catherine Palmer
- *Freedom's Promise*, Dianna Crawford
- *Freedom's Hope*, Dianna Crawford
- *Freedom's Belle*, Dianna Crawford
- *Prairie Rose*, Catherine Palmer

- *Prairie Fire*, Catherine Palmer
- *Prairie Storm*, Catherine Palmer
- *Prairie Christmas*, Catherine Palmer, Elizabeth White, and Peggy Stoks
- *Finders Keepers*, Catherine Palmer
- *Hide and Seek*, Catherine Palmer
- *A Kiss of Adventure*, Catherine Palmer (original title: *The Treasure of Timbuktu*)
- *A Whisper of Danger*, Catherine Palmer (original title: *The Treasure of Zanzibar*)
- *A Touch of Betrayal*, Catherine Palmer
- *A Victorian Christmas Cottage*, Catherine Palmer, Debra White Smith, Jeri Odell, and Peggy Stoks
- *A Victorian Christmas Quilt*, Catherine Palmer, Debra White Smith, Ginny Aiken, and Peggy Stoks
- *A Victorian Christmas Tea*, Catherine Palmer, Dianna Crawford, Peggy Stoks, and Katherine Chute
- *Olivia's Touch*, Peggy Stoks
- *Romy's Walk*, Peggy Stoks

Coming Soon (Fall 2001)

- *A Victorian Christmas Keepsake*, Catherine Palmer, Kristin Billerbeck, Ginny Aiken

HeartQuest Books by Catherine Palmer

Finders Keepers—Blue-eyed, fiery-tempered Elizabeth Hayes hopes to move her growing antiques business into Chalmers House, the Victorian mansion next to her small shop. But Zachary Chalmers, heir to the mansion, has very different plans for the site. And Elizabeth's seven-year-old son, adopted from Romania two years earlier, has plans of his own: He thinks it's time for his mother to marry—and the tall, handsome man talking to her at the estate sale is the perfect candidate. In this first book of a new contemporary romance series, each must learn that God's plans are not our plans and his ways are not our ways.

A Town Called Hope series
Prairie Rose—Kansas held their future, but only faith could mend their past. Hope and love blossom on the untamed prairie as a young woman, searching for a place to call home, happens upon a Kansas homestead during the 1860s.

Prairie Fire—Will a burning secret extinguish the spark of love between Jack and Caitrin? The town of Hope discovers the importance of forgiveness, overcoming prejudice, and the dangers of keeping unhealthy family secrets.

Prairie Storm—Can one tiny baby calm the brewing storm between Lily's past and Elijah's future? Evangelist Elijah Book's zeal becomes sidetracked as the fate of an innocent child rests with a woman Eli must trust in spite of himself. United in their concern for the baby, Eli and Lily are forced to set aside their differences and learn to trust God's plan to see them through the storms of life.

Treasures of the Heart series
A Touch of Betrayal—Alexandra Prescott, looking for inspiration for the line of exotic fabrics she is designing, fully expects her trip to Kenya to be an adventure. But an attempt on her life wasn't quite what she had in mind! Anthropologist Grant Thornton wonders what he has gotten himself into when this beautiful stranger suddenly invades his world. Although they seem to have nothing in common, he is drawn to her—and to her unnerving faith in God. And when the hired killer strikes again, Grant finds that there is far more to Alexandra than meets the eye.

The long-awaited conclusion to *The Treasure of Timbuktu* and *The Treasure of Zanzibar*, a contemporary romance adventure series.

A Kiss of Adventure (original title: *The Treasure of Timbuktu*)—Abducted by a treasure hunter, Tillie Thornton becomes a pawn in a dangerous game. Desperate and on the run from a fierce nomadic tribe looking to kidnap her, Tillie finds herself in an uneasy partnership with a daring adventurer.

A Whisper of Danger (original title: *The Treasure of Zanzibar*)—An ancient house filled with secrets . . . a sunken treasure . . . an unknown enemy . . . a lost love. They all await Jessica Thornton on Zanzibar. Jessica returns to Africa with her son to claim her inheritance on the island of Zanzibar. Upon her arrival, she is reunited with her estranged husband.

HEART QUEST

Other Great Tyndale House Fiction

- *Jenny's Story*, Judy Baer
- *Libby's Story*, Judy Baer

- *Out of the Shadows*, Sigmund Brouwer

- *Ashes and Lace*, B. J. Hoff
- *Cloth of Heaven*, B. J. Hoff

- *The Price*, Jim and Terri Kraus
- *The Treasure*, Jim and Terri Kraus
- *The Promise*, Jim and Terri Kraus

- *Winter Passing*, Cindy McCormick Martinusen

- *Rift in Time*, Michael Phillips
- *Hidden in Time*, Michael Phillips

- *Unveiled*, Francine Rivers

- *Unashamed*, Francine Rivers
- *Unshaken*, Francine Rivers
- *A Voice in the Wind*, Francine Rivers
- *An Echo in the Darkness*, Francine Rivers
- *As Sure As the Dawn*, Francine Rivers
- *The Last Sin Eater*, Francine Rivers
- *Leota's Garden*, Francine Rivers
- *The Scarlet Thread*, Francine Rivers
- *The Atonement Child*, Francine Rivers

- *The Promise Remains*, Travis Thrasher